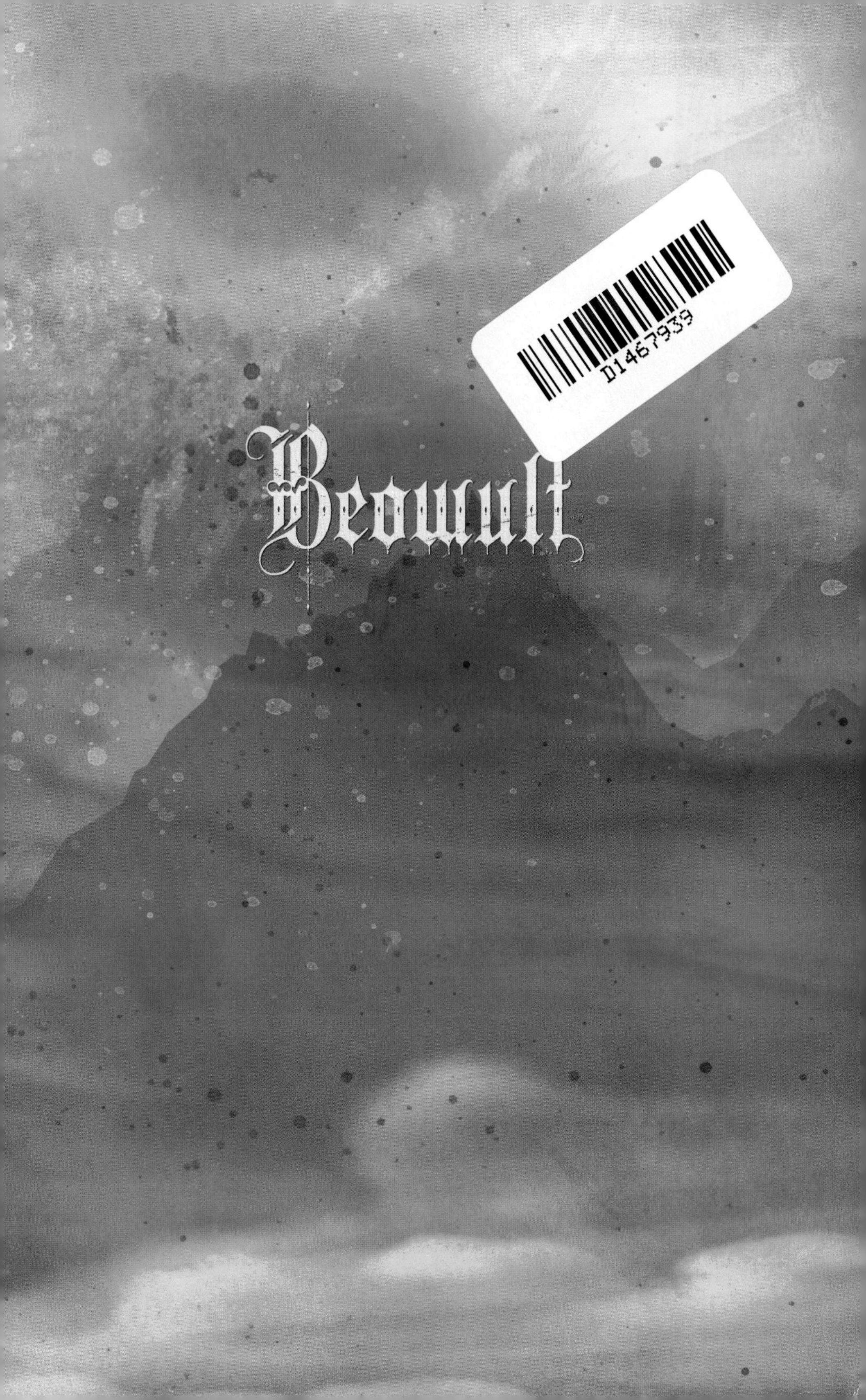
Beowulf

Harper Trophy® is a registered trademark of HarperCollins Publishers.

Beowulf
Text copyright © 2007 by Stefan Petrucha
Illustrations copyright © 2007 by Kody Chamberlain

Library of Congress Cataloging-in-Publication Data
Petrucha, Stefan.
      Beowulf / by Stefan Petrucha ; illustrated by Kody Chamberlain. — 1st Harper Trophy ed.
                      p. cm.
      ISBN 978-0-06-134390-2 (pbk. bdg.)
      1. Graphic novels. I. Chamberlain, Kody. II. Beowulf. III. Title.
PN6727.P4685B46 2007   2007003923
741.5'973—dc22   CIP
❖   AC
First Edition

Beowulf

story by   artwork by

STEFAN PETRUCHA ✦ KODY CHAMBERLAIN

Scott A. Keating · Kel Nuttall · Andrew Thibodeaux

colors   letters   production

HarperTrophy®

An Imprint of HarperCollinsPublishers

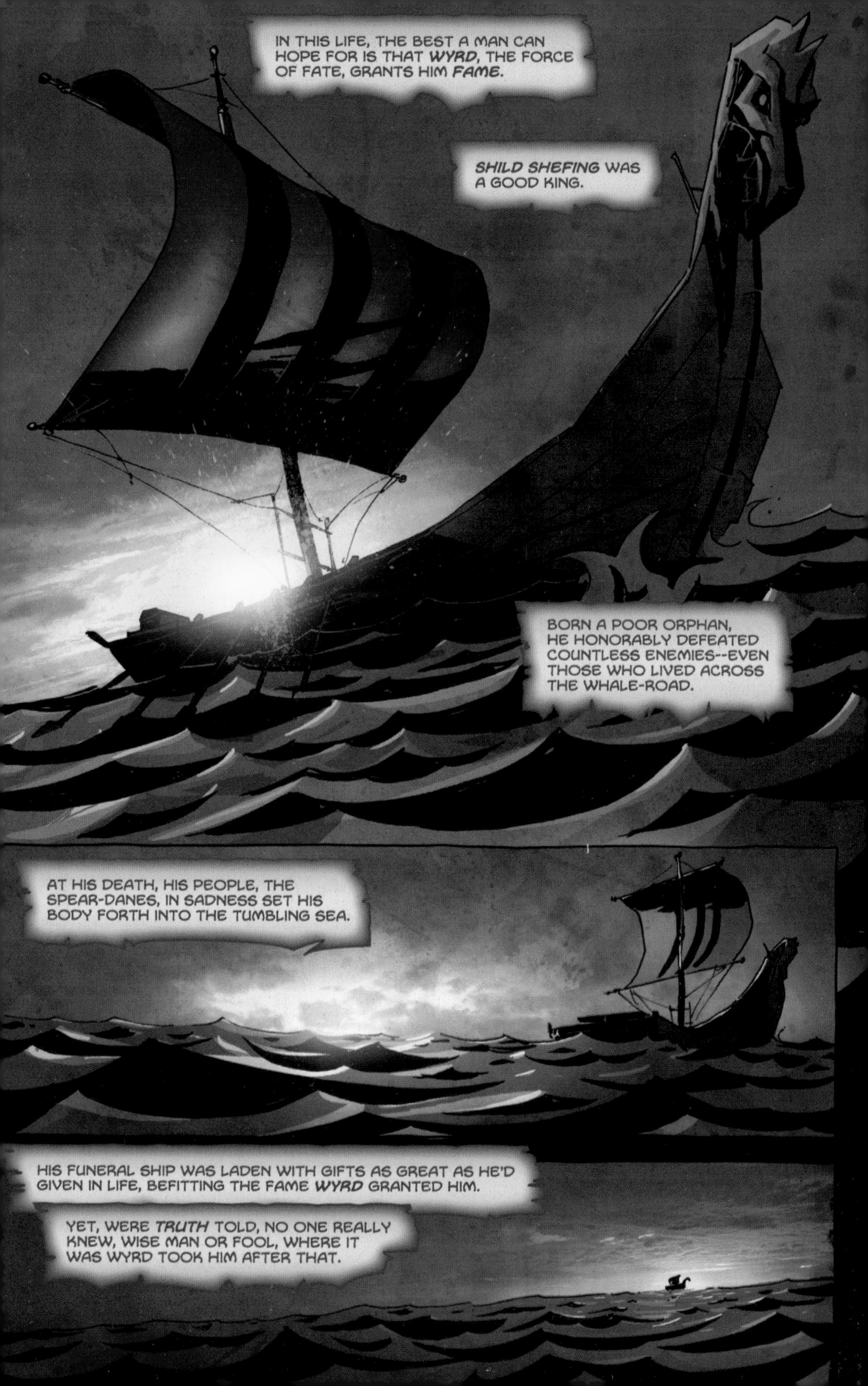
IN THIS LIFE, THE BEST A MAN CAN HOPE FOR IS THAT WYRD, THE FORCE OF FATE, GRANTS HIM FAME.
SHILD SHEFING WAS A GOOD KING.
BORN A POOR ORPHAN, HE HONORABLY DEFEATED COUNTLESS ENEMIES--EVEN THOSE WHO LIVED ACROSS THE WHALE-ROAD.
AT HIS DEATH, HIS PEOPLE, THE SPEAR-DANES, IN SADNESS SET HIS BODY FORTH INTO THE TUMBLING SEA.
HIS FUNERAL SHIP WAS LADEN WITH GIFTS AS GREAT AS HE'D GIVEN IN LIFE, BEFITTING THE FAME WYRD GRANTED HIM.
YET, WERE TRUTH TOLD, NO ONE REALLY KNEW, WISE MAN OR FOOL, WHERE IT WAS WYRD TOOK HIM AFTER THAT.

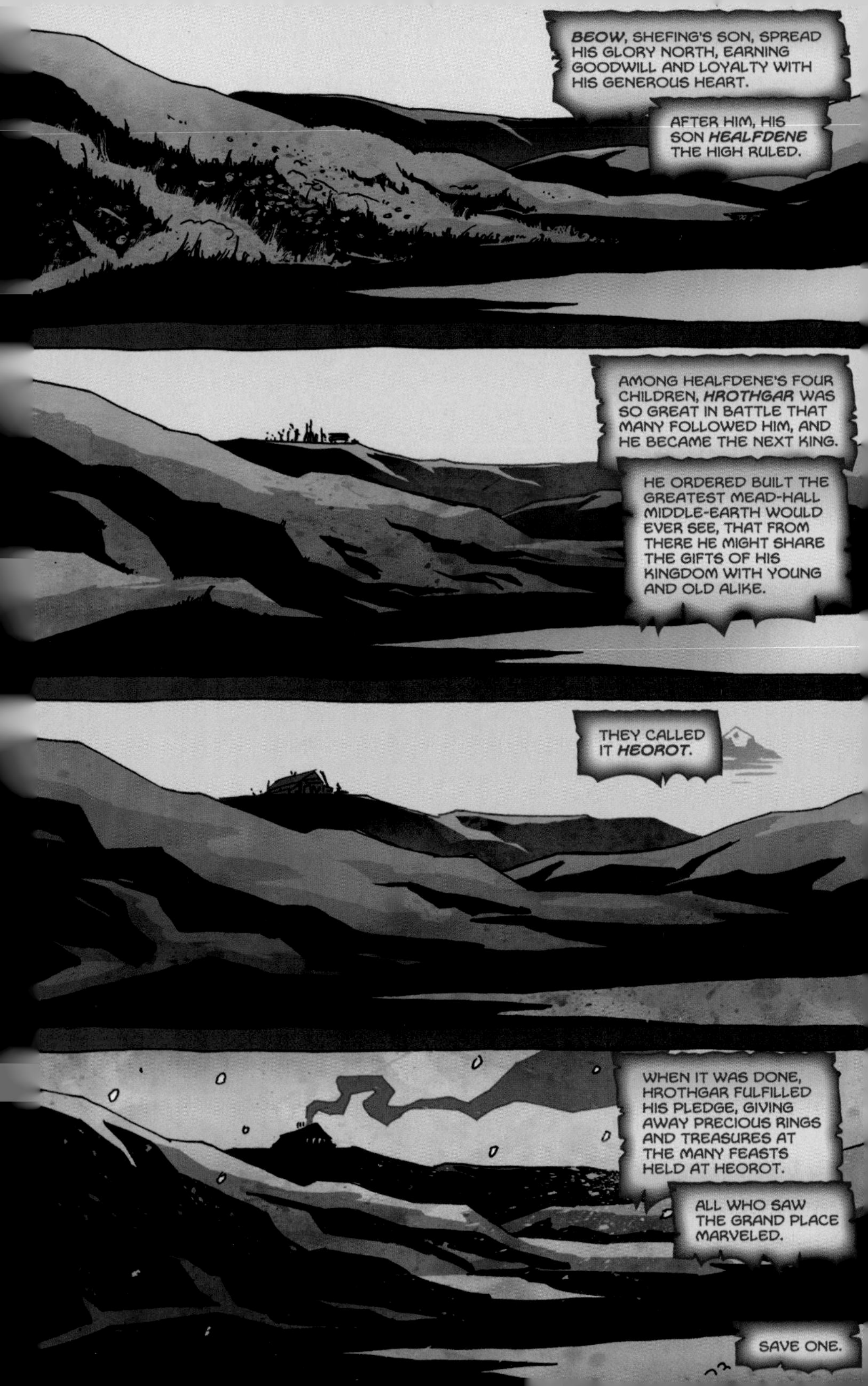
BEOW, SHEFING'S SON, SPREAD HIS GLORY NORTH, EARNING GOODWILL AND LOYALTY WITH HIS GENEROUS HEART.
AFTER HIM, HIS SON HEALFDENE THE HIGH RULED.
AMONG HEALFDENE'S FOUR CHILDREN, HROTHGAR WAS SO GREAT IN BATTLE THAT MANY FOLLOWED HIM, AND HE BECAME THE NEXT KING.
HE ORDERED BUILT THE GREATEST MEAD-HALL MIDDLE-EARTH WOULD EVER SEE, THAT FROM THERE HE MIGHT SHARE THE GIFTS OF HIS KINGDOM WITH YOUNG AND OLD ALIKE.
THEY CALLED IT HEOROT.
WHEN IT WAS DONE, HROTHGAR FULFILLED HIS PLEDGE, GIVING AWAY PRECIOUS RINGS AND TREASURES AT THE MANY FEASTS HELD AT HEOROT.
ALL WHO SAW THE GRAND PLACE MARVELED.
SAVE ONE.

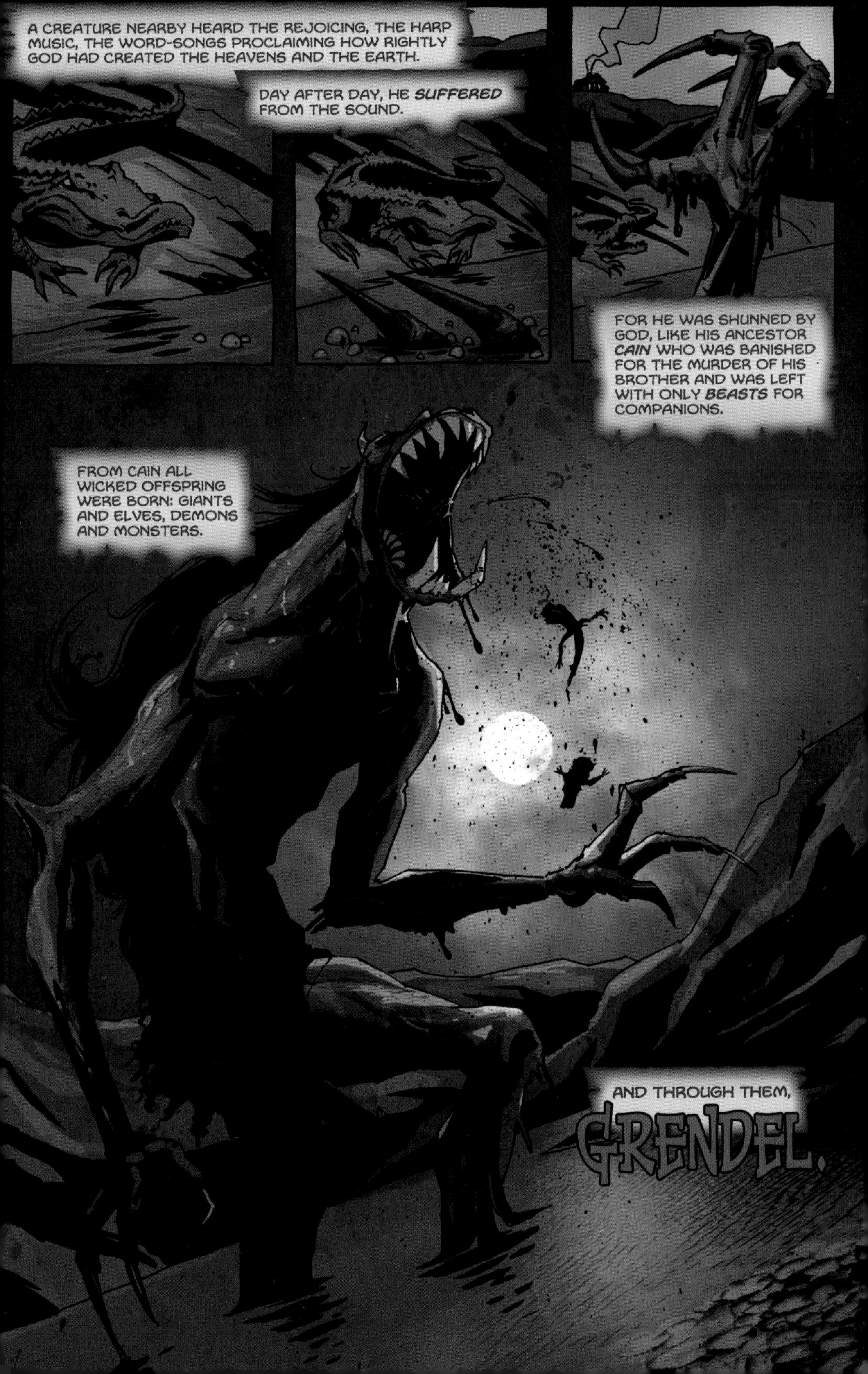
A CREATURE NEARBY HEARD THE REJOICING, THE HARP MUSIC, THE WORD-SONGS PROCLAIMING HOW RIGHTLY GOD HAD CREATED THE HEAVENS AND THE EARTH.
DAY AFTER DAY, HE SUFFERED FROM THE SOUND.
FOR HE WAS SHUNNED BY GOD, LIKE HIS ANCESTOR CAIN WHO WAS BANISHED FOR THE MURDER OF HIS BROTHER AND WAS LEFT WITH ONLY BEASTS FOR COMPANIONS.
FROM CAIN ALL WICKED OFFSPRING WERE BORN: GIANTS AND ELVES, DEMONS AND MONSTERS.
AND THROUGH THEM,
GRENDEL.

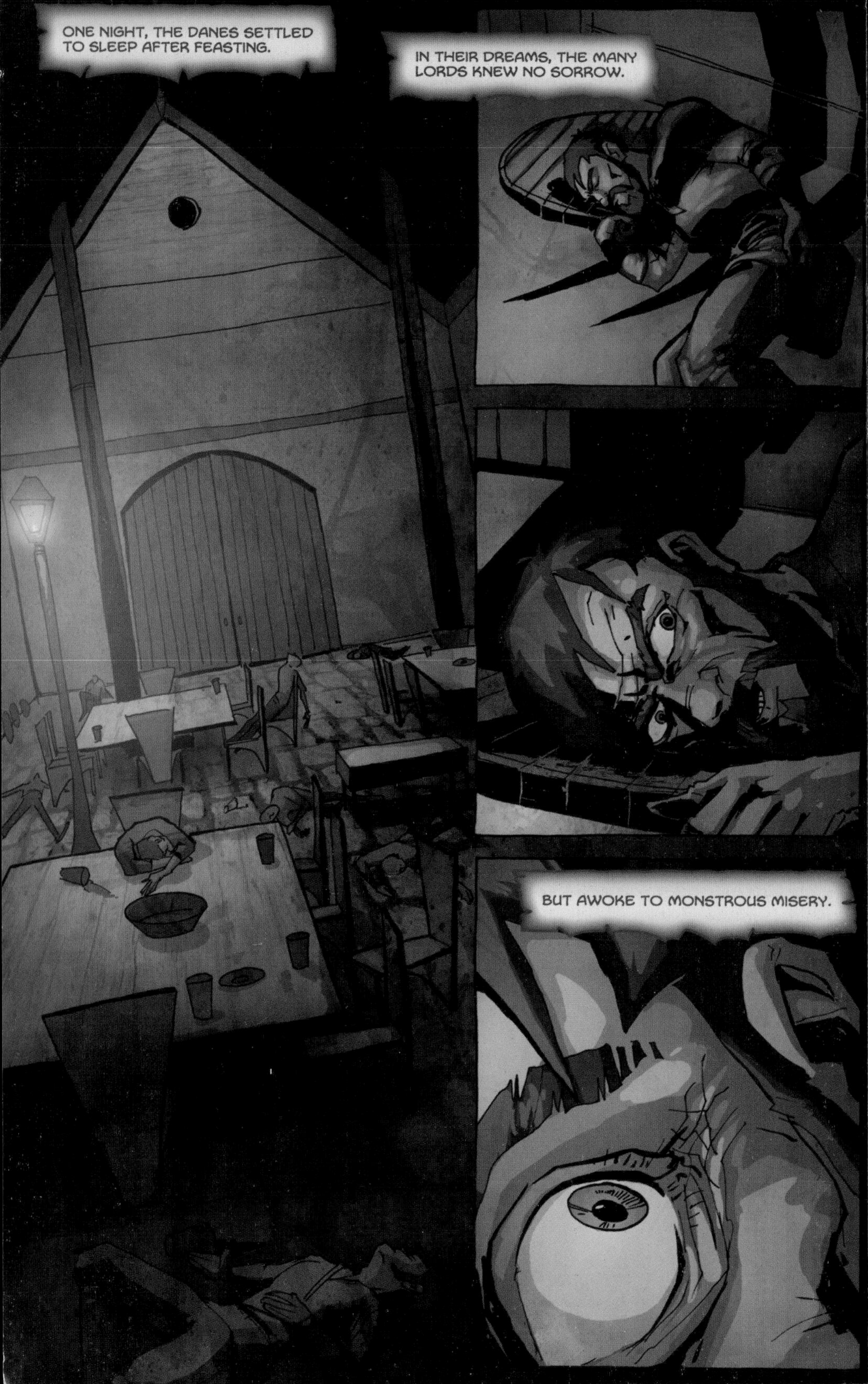
ONE NIGHT, THE DANES SETTLED TO SLEEP AFTER FEASTING.
IN THEIR DREAMS, THE MANY LORDS KNEW NO SORROW.
BUT AWOKE TO MONSTROUS MISERY.

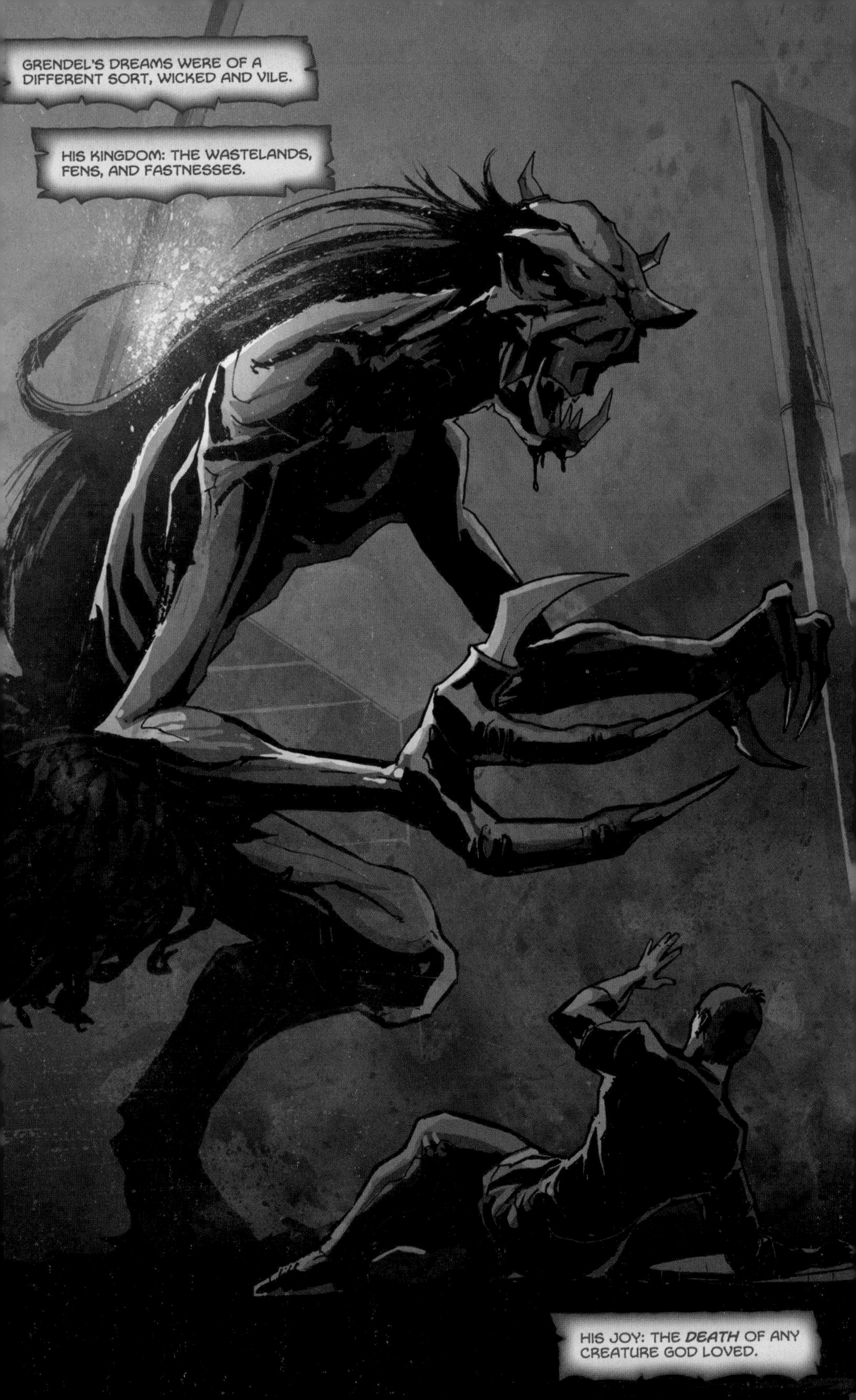
GRENDEL'S DREAMS WERE OF A DIFFERENT SORT, WICKED AND VILE.
HIS KINGDOM: THE WASTELANDS, FENS, AND FASTNESSES.
HIS JOY: THE *DEATH* OF ANY CREATURE GOD LOVED.

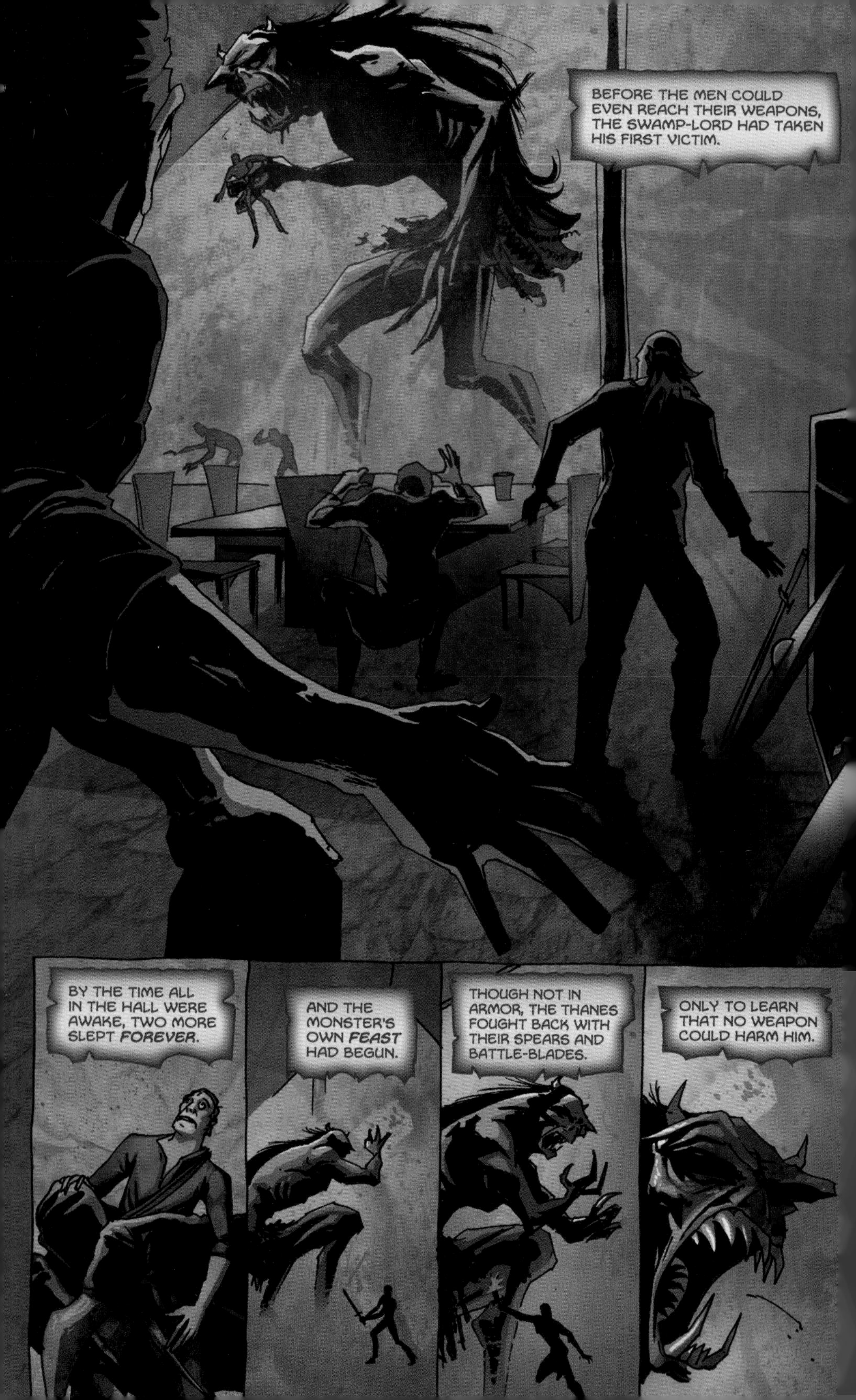
BEFORE THE MEN COULD EVEN REACH THEIR WEAPONS, THE SWAMP-LORD HAD TAKEN HIS FIRST VICTIM.
BY THE TIME ALL IN THE HALL WERE AWAKE, TWO MORE SLEPT *FOREVER*.
AND THE MONSTER'S OWN *FEAST* HAD BEGUN.
THOUGH NOT IN ARMOR, THE THANES FOUGHT BACK WITH THEIR SPEARS AND BATTLE-BLADES.
ONLY TO LEARN THAT NO WEAPON COULD HARM HIM.

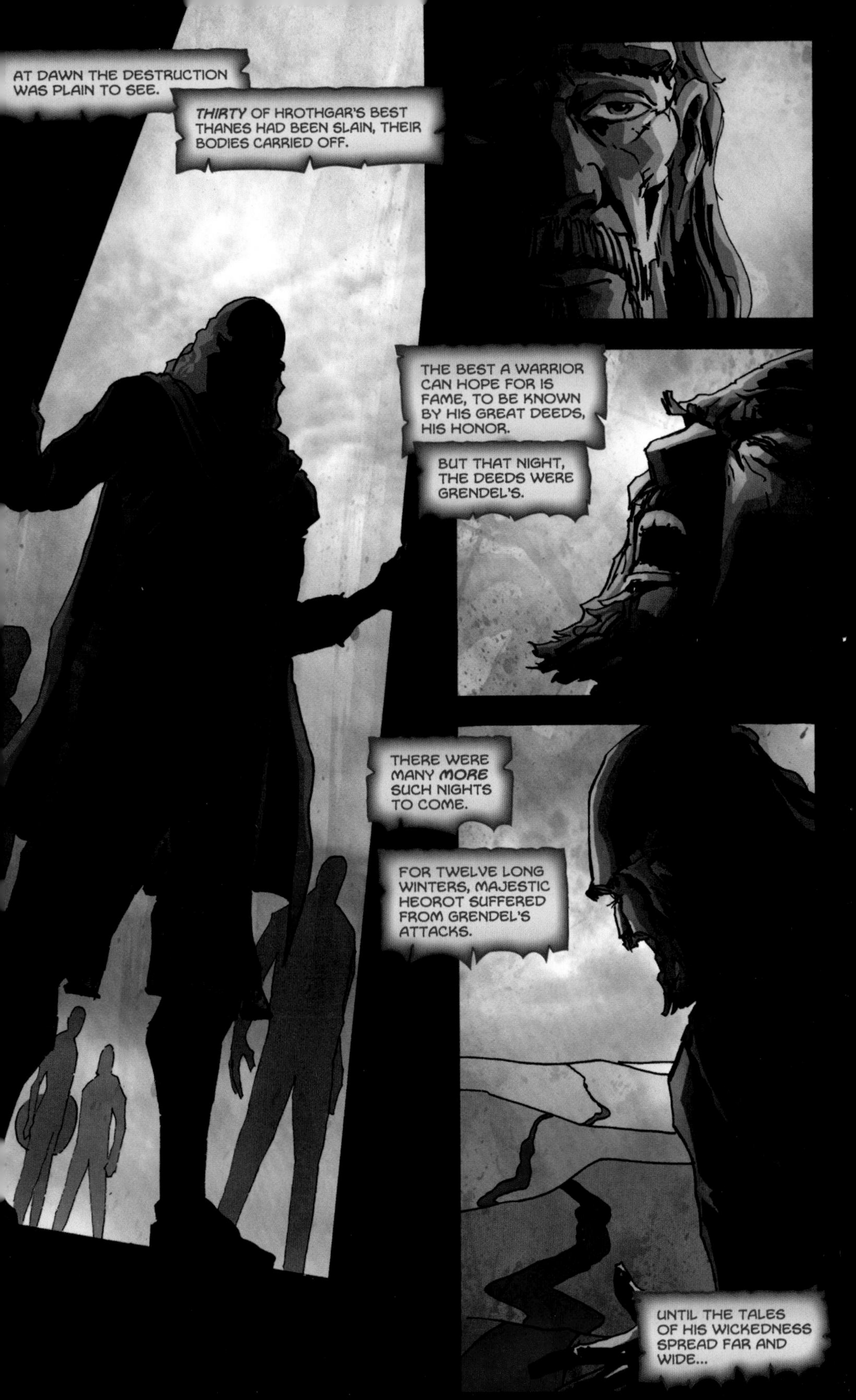
AT DAWN THE DESTRUCTION WAS PLAIN TO SEE.
THIRTY OF HROTHGAR'S BEST THANES HAD BEEN SLAIN, THEIR BODIES CARRIED OFF.
THE BEST A WARRIOR CAN HOPE FOR IS FAME, TO BE KNOWN BY HIS GREAT DEEDS, HIS HONOR.
BUT THAT NIGHT, THE DEEDS WERE GRENDEL'S.
THERE WERE MANY ***MORE*** SUCH NIGHTS TO COME.
FOR TWELVE LONG WINTERS, MAJESTIC HEOROT SUFFERED FROM GRENDEL'S ATTACKS.
UNTIL THE TALES OF HIS WICKEDNESS SPREAD FAR AND WIDE...

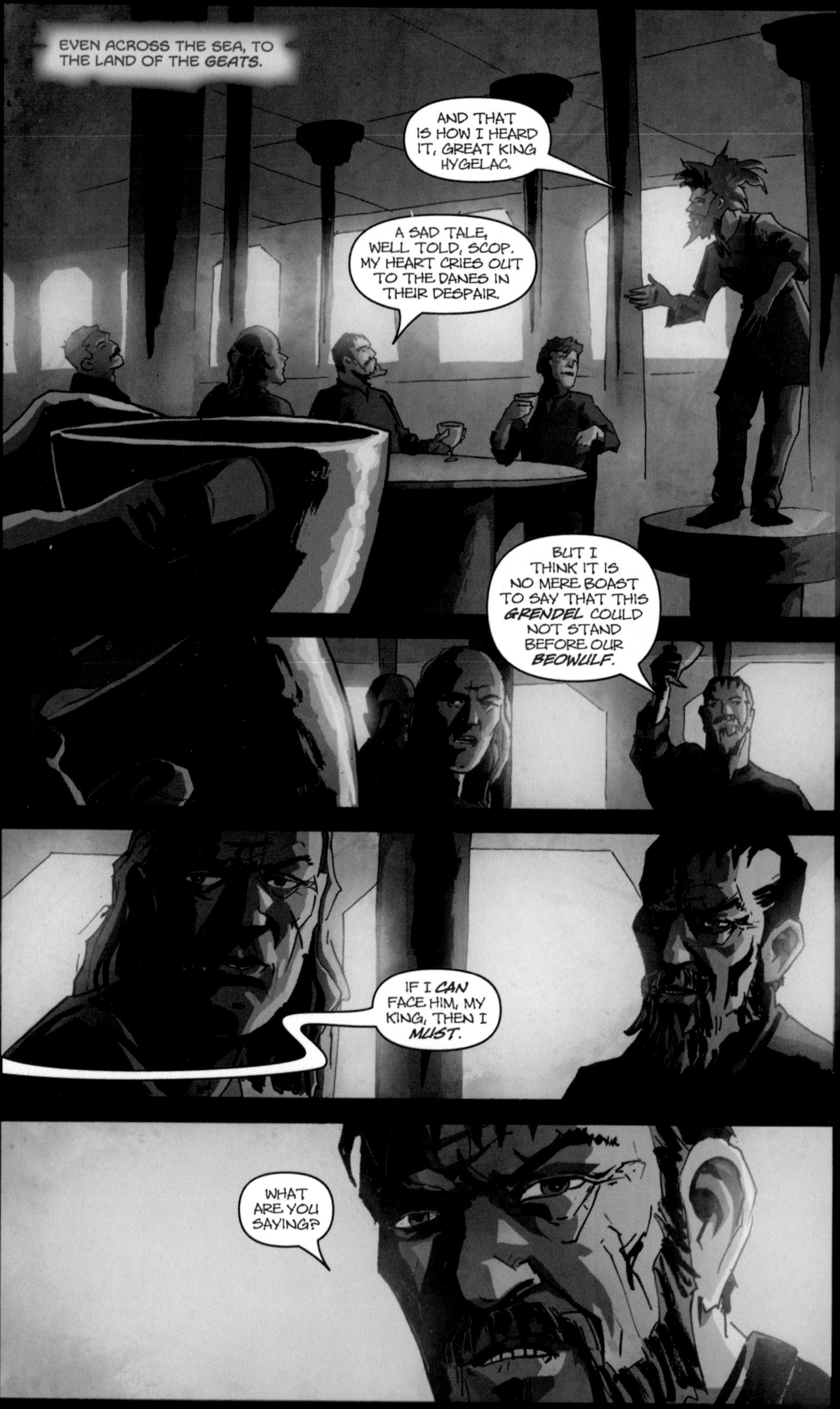
EVEN ACROSS THE SEA, TO THE LAND OF THE GEATS.
AND THAT IS HOW I HEARD IT, GREAT KING HYGELAC.
A SAD TALE, WELL TOLD, SCOP. MY HEART CRIES OUT TO THE DANES IN THEIR DESPAIR.
BUT I THINK IT IS NO MERE BOAST TO SAY THAT THIS GRENDEL COULD NOT STAND BEFORE OUR BEOWULF.
IF I CAN FACE HIM, MY KING, THEN I MUST.
WHAT ARE YOU SAYING?

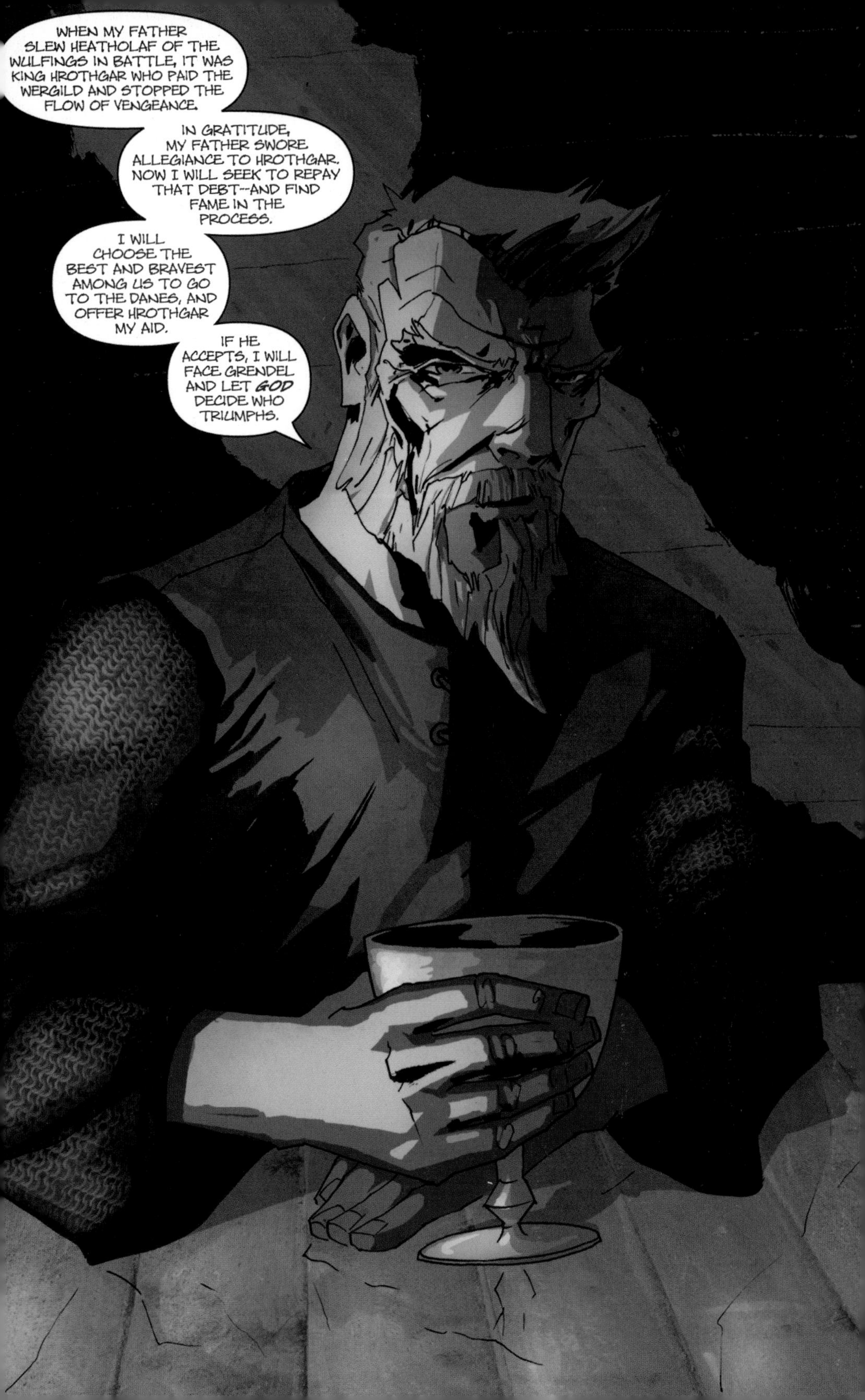
WHEN MY FATHER SLEW HEATHOLAF OF THE WULFINGS IN BATTLE, IT WAS KING HROTHGAR WHO PAID THE WERGILD AND STOPPED THE FLOW OF VENGEANCE.
IN GRATITUDE, MY FATHER SWORE ALLEGIANCE TO HROTHGAR. NOW I WILL SEEK TO REPAY THAT DEBT--AND FIND FAME IN THE PROCESS.
I WILL CHOOSE THE BEST AND BRAVEST AMONG US TO GO TO THE DANES, AND OFFER HROTHGAR MY AID.
IF HE ACCEPTS, I WILL FACE GRENDEL AND LET *GOD* DECIDE WHO TRIUMPHS.

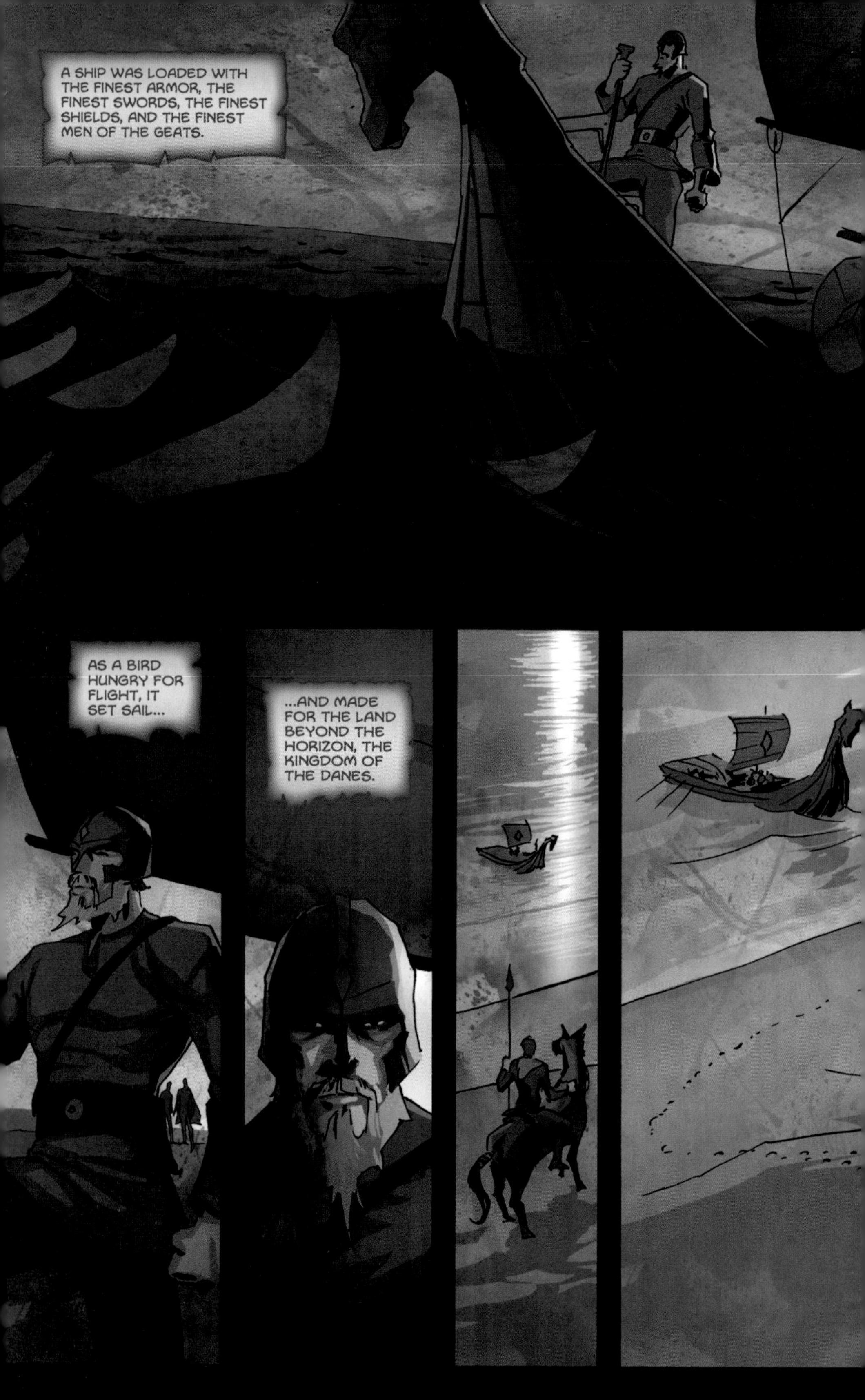
A SHIP WAS LOADED WITH THE FINEST ARMOR, THE FINEST SWORDS, THE FINEST SHIELDS, AND THE FINEST MEN OF THE GEATS.
AS A BIRD HUNGRY FOR FLIGHT, IT SET SAIL...
...AND MADE FOR THE LAND BEYOND THE HORIZON, THE KINGDOM OF THE DANES.

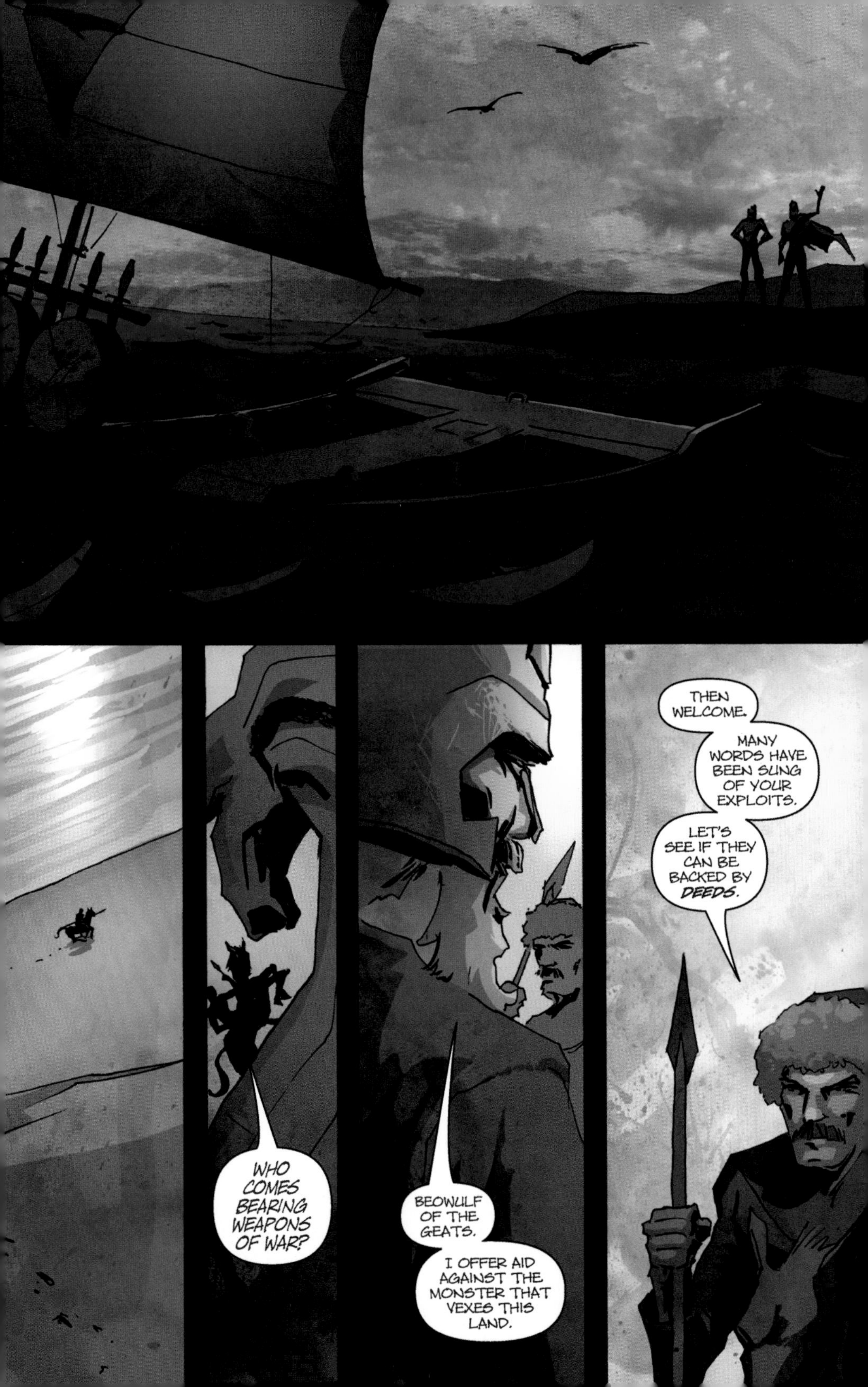
WHO COMES BEARING WEAPONS OF WAR?
BEOWULF OF THE GEATS.
I OFFER AID AGAINST THE MONSTER THAT VEXES THIS LAND.
THEN WELCOME.
MANY WORDS HAVE BEEN SUNG OF YOUR EXPLOITS.
LET'S SEE IF THEY CAN BE BACKED BY DEEDS.

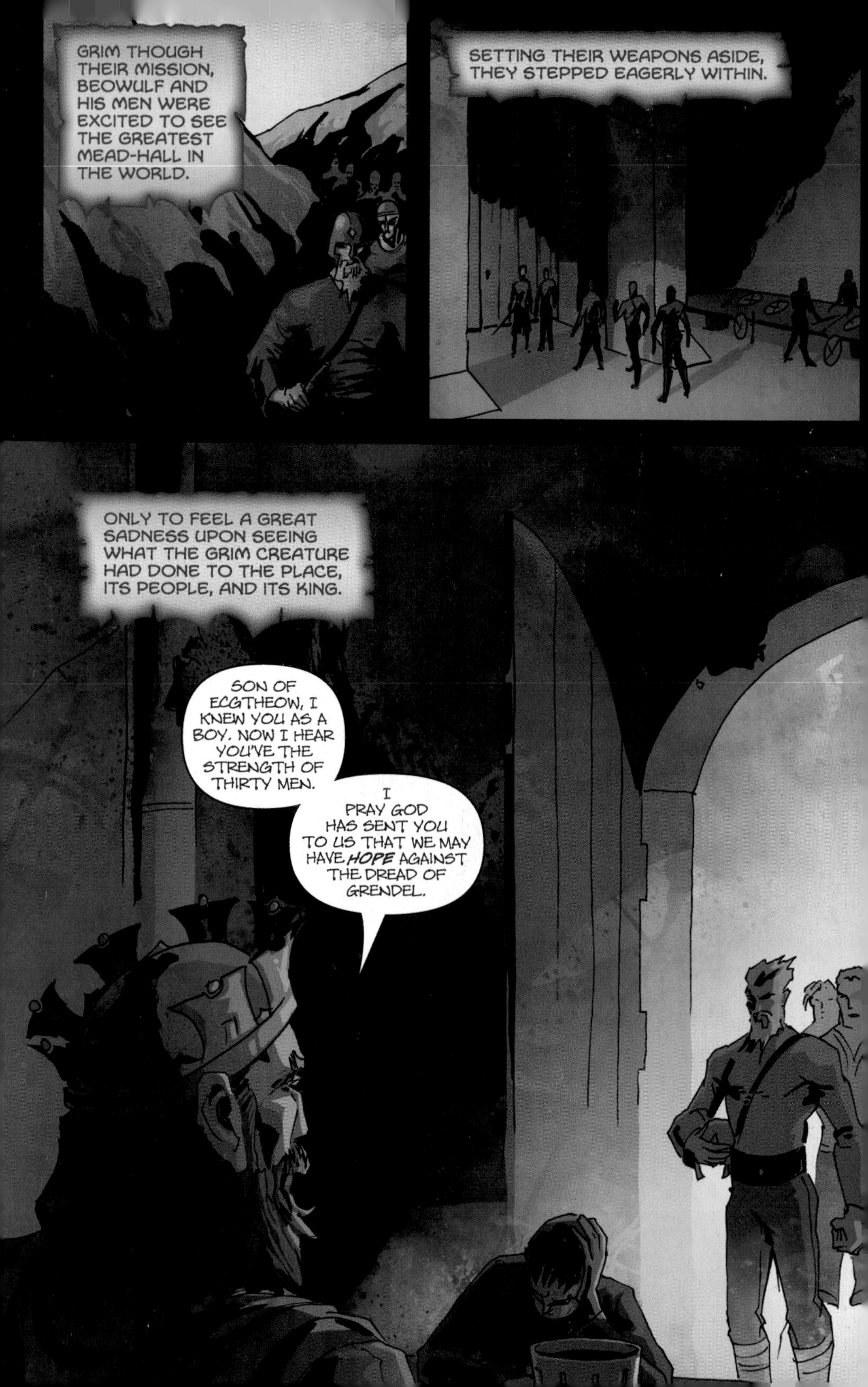
GRIM THOUGH THEIR MISSION, BEOWULF AND HIS MEN WERE EXCITED TO SEE THE GREATEST MEAD-HALL IN THE WORLD.
SETTING THEIR WEAPONS ASIDE, THEY STEPPED EAGERLY WITHIN.
ONLY TO FEEL A GREAT SADNESS UPON SEEING WHAT THE GRIM CREATURE HAD DONE TO THE PLACE, ITS PEOPLE, AND ITS KING.
SON OF ECGTHEOW, I KNEW YOU AS A BOY. NOW I HEAR YOU'VE THE STRENGTH OF THIRTY MEN.
I PRAY GOD HAS SENT YOU TO US THAT WE MAY HAVE *HOPE* AGAINST THE DREAD OF GRENDEL.

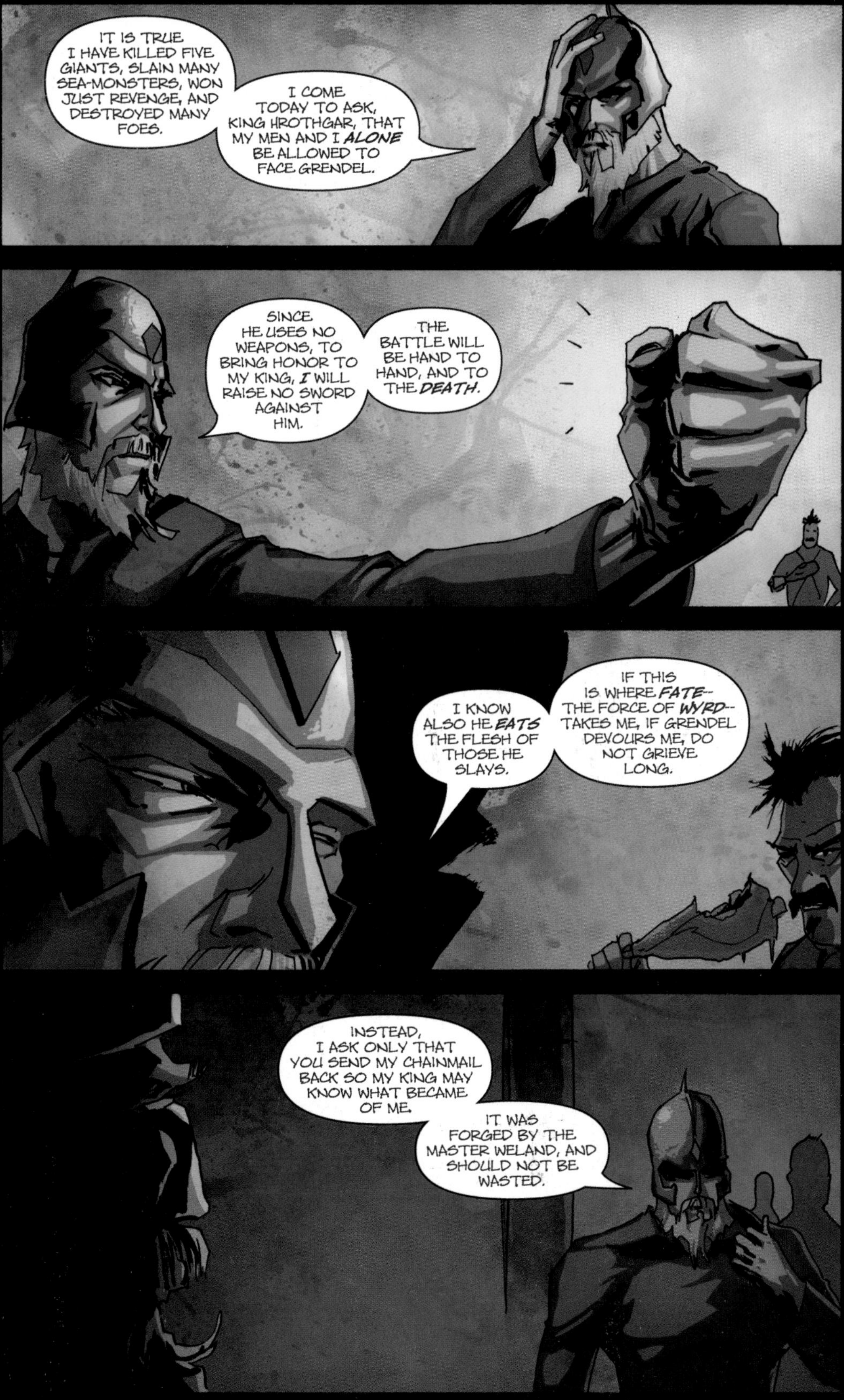
IT IS TRUE I HAVE KILLED FIVE GIANTS, SLAIN MANY SEA-MONSTERS, WON JUST REVENGE, AND DESTROYED MANY FOES.
I COME TODAY TO ASK, KING HROTHGAR, THAT MY MEN AND I *ALONE* BE ALLOWED TO FACE GRENDEL.
SINCE HE USES NO WEAPONS, TO BRING HONOR TO MY KING, *I* WILL RAISE NO SWORD AGAINST HIM.
THE BATTLE WILL BE HAND TO HAND, AND TO THE *DEATH*.
I KNOW ALSO HE *EATS* THE FLESH OF THOSE HE SLAYS.
IF THIS IS WHERE *FATE*-- THE FORCE OF *WYRD*-- TAKES ME, IF GRENDEL DEVOURS ME, DO NOT GRIEVE LONG.
INSTEAD, I ASK ONLY THAT YOU SEND MY CHAINMAIL BACK SO MY KING MAY KNOW WHAT BECAME OF ME.
IT WAS FORGED BY THE MASTER WELAND, AND SHOULD NOT BE WASTED.

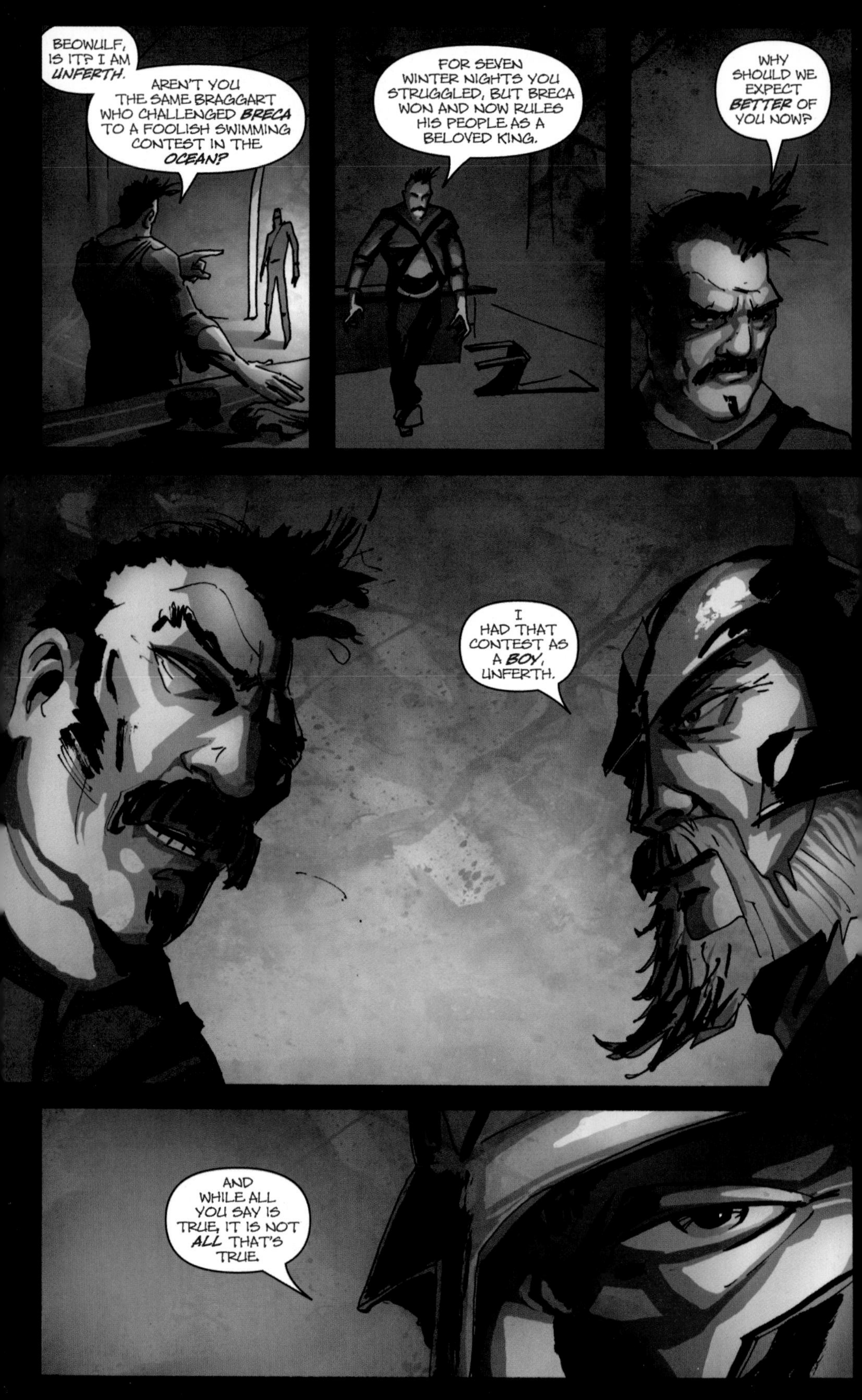
BEOWULF, IS IT? I AM UNFERTH.
AREN'T YOU THE SAME BRAGGART WHO CHALLENGED BRECA TO A FOOLISH SWIMMING CONTEST IN THE OCEAN?
FOR SEVEN WINTER NIGHTS YOU STRUGGLED, BUT BRECA WON AND NOW RULES HIS PEOPLE AS A BELOVED KING.
WHY SHOULD WE EXPECT BETTER OF YOU NOW?
I HAD THAT CONTEST AS A BOY, UNFERTH.
AND WHILE ALL YOU SAY IS TRUE, IT IS NOT ALL THAT'S TRUE.

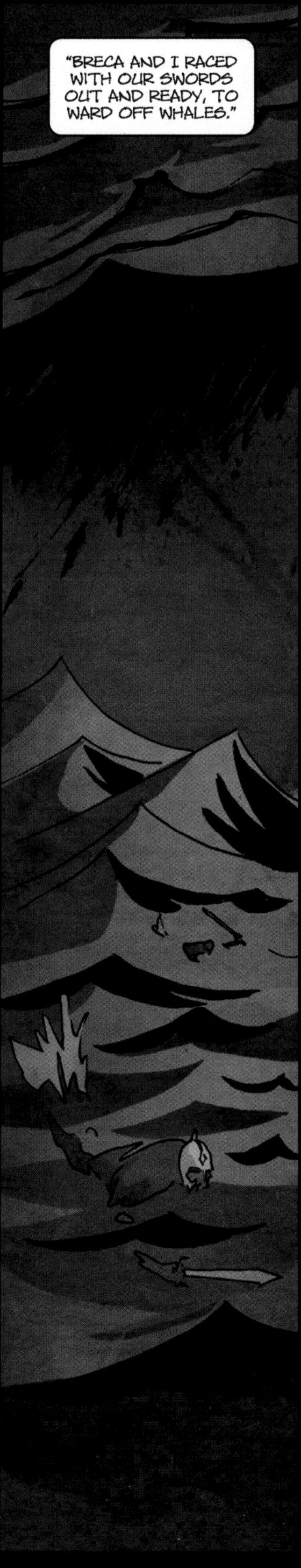
"BRECA AND I RACED WITH OUR SWORDS OUT AND READY, TO WARD OFF WHALES."

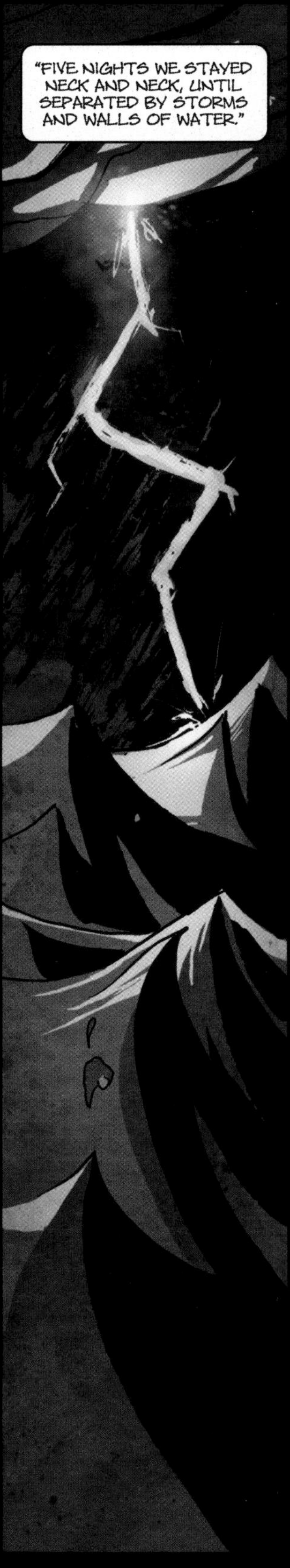
"FIVE NIGHTS WE STAYED NECK AND NECK, UNTIL SEPARATED BY STORMS AND WALLS OF WATER."

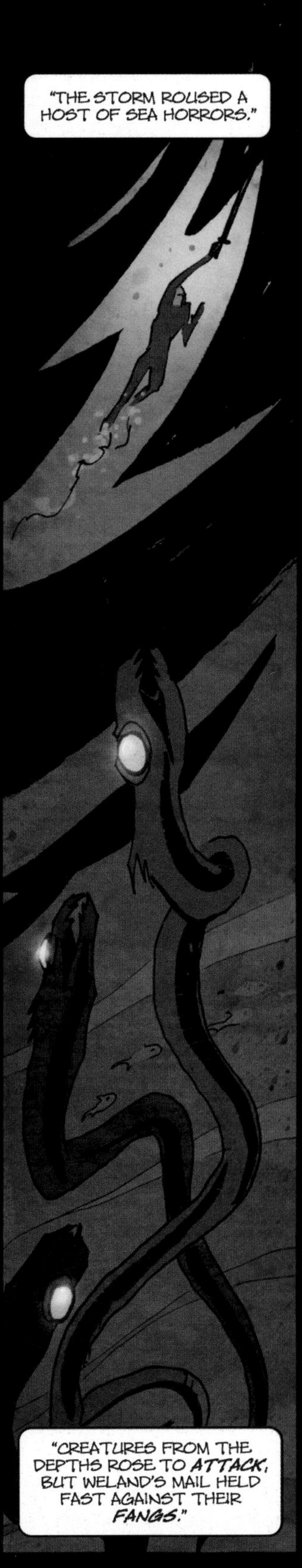
"THE STORM ROUSED A HOST OF SEA HORRORS."
"CREATURES FROM THE DEPTHS ROSE TO *ATTACK*, BUT WELAND'S MAIL HELD FAST AGAINST THEIR *FANGS*."

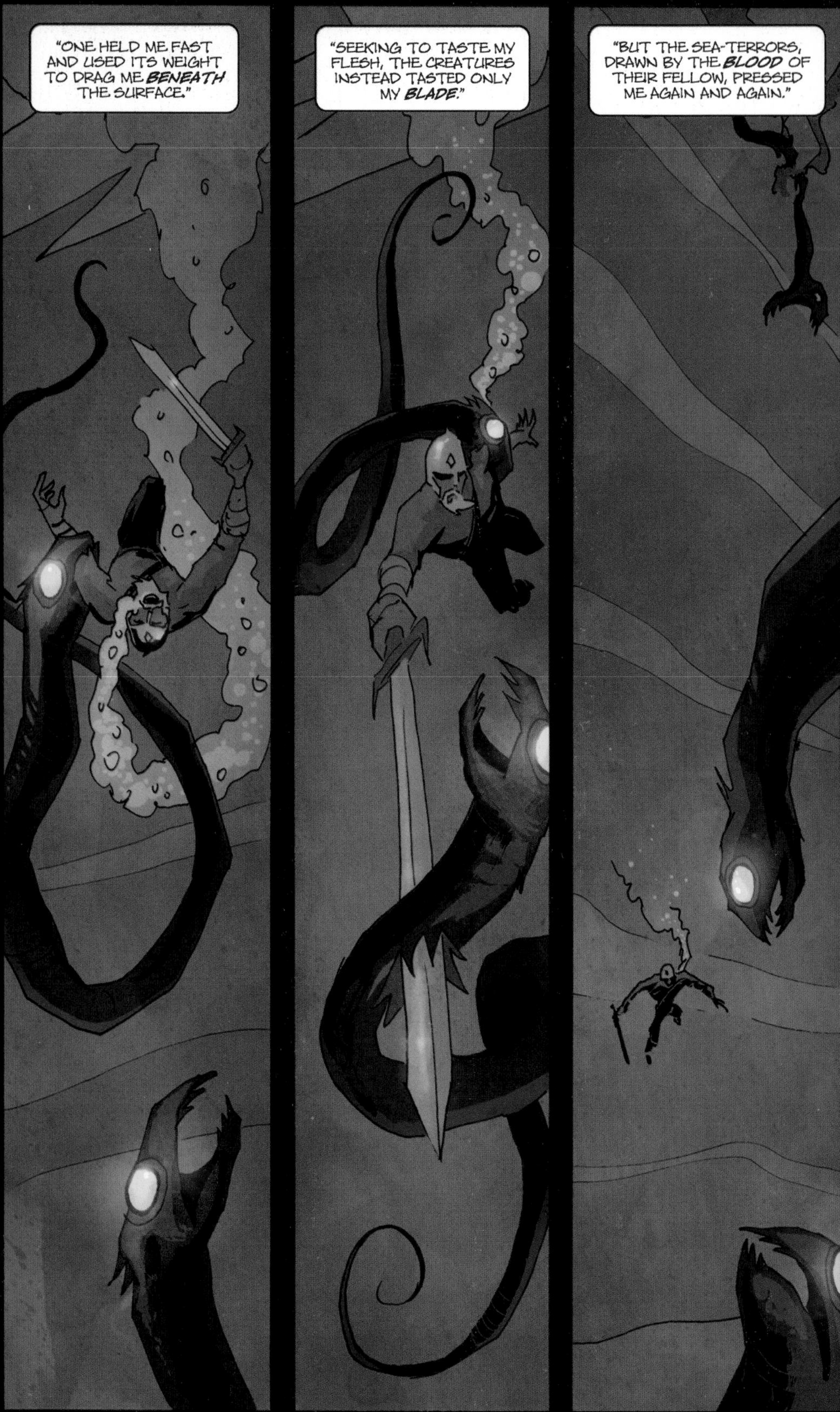
"ONE HELD ME FAST AND USED ITS WEIGHT TO DRAG ME BENEATH THE SURFACE."
"SEEKING TO TASTE MY FLESH, THE CREATURES INSTEAD TASTED ONLY MY BLADE."
"BUT THE SEA-TERRORS, DRAWN BY THE BLOOD OF THEIR FELLOW, PRESSED ME AGAIN AND AGAIN."

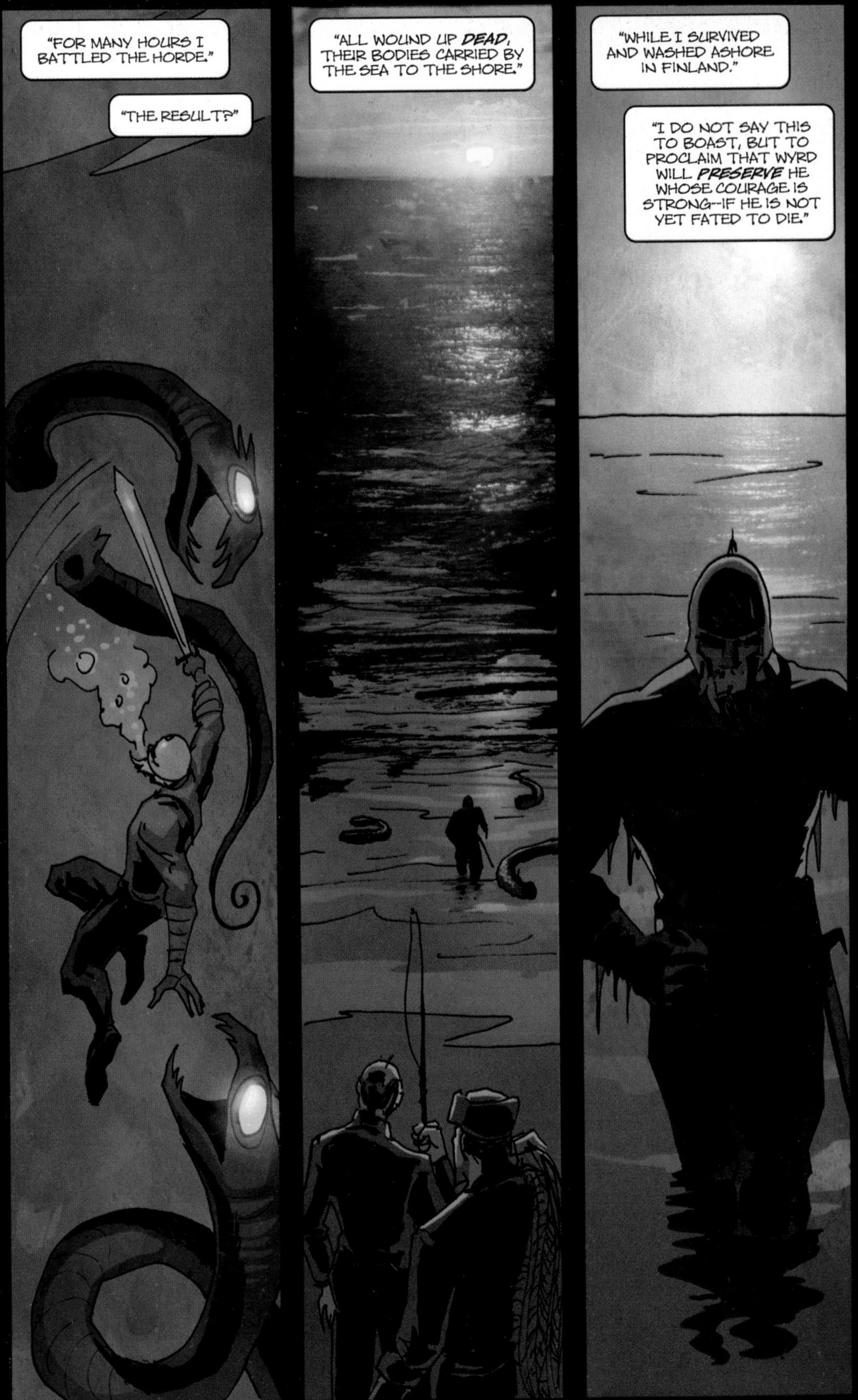
"FOR MANY HOURS I BATTLED THE HORDE."
"THE RESULT?"
"ALL WOUND UP DEAD, THEIR BODIES CARRIED BY THE SEA TO THE SHORE."
"WHILE I SURVIVED AND WASHED ASHORE IN FINLAND."
"I DO NOT SAY THIS TO BOAST, BUT TO PROCLAIM THAT WYRD WILL PRESERVE HE WHOSE COURAGE IS STRONG--IF HE IS NOT YET FATED TO DIE."

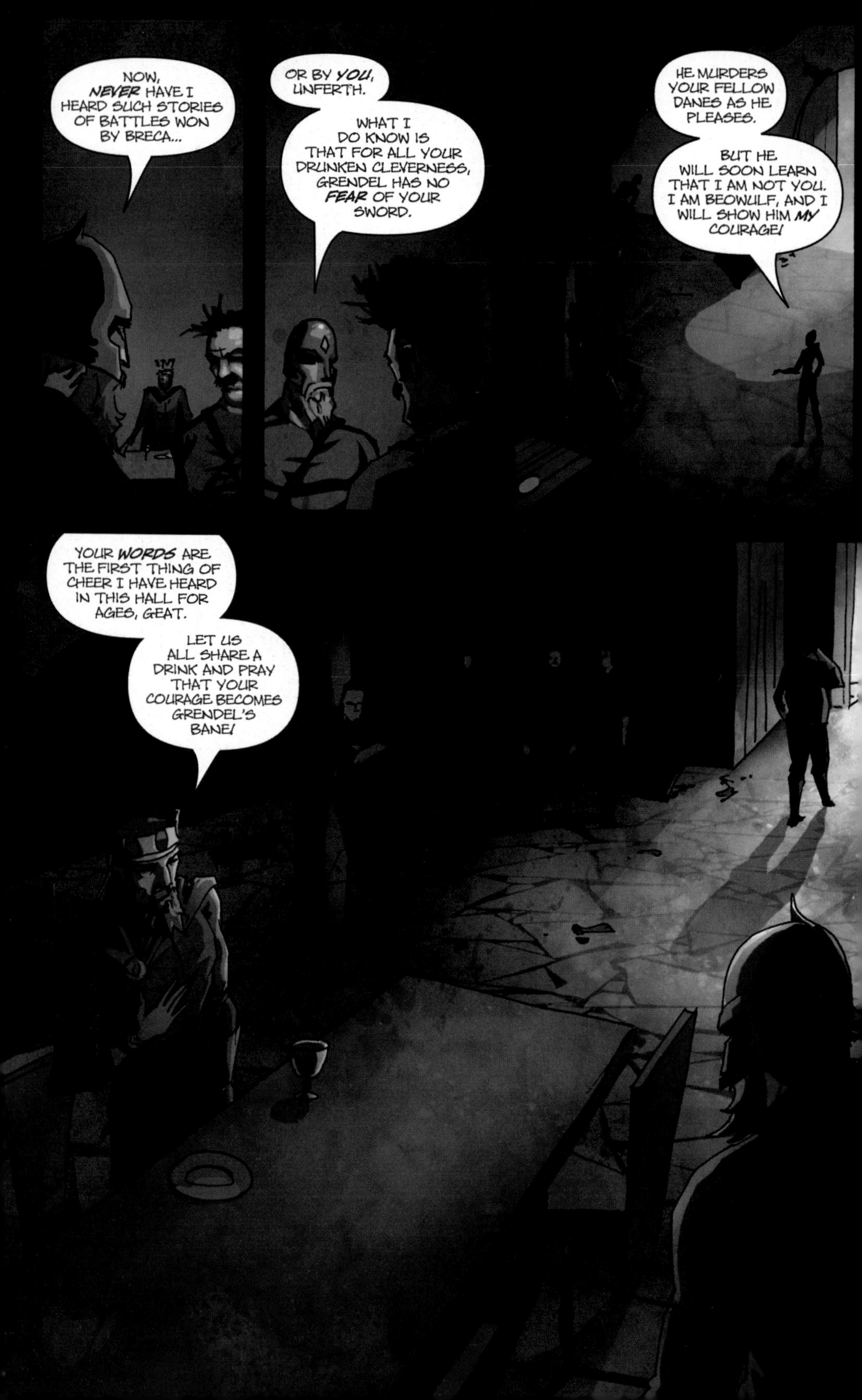
NOW, NEVER HAVE I HEARD SUCH STORIES OF BATTLES WON BY BRECA...
OR BY YOU, UNFERTH.
WHAT I DO KNOW IS THAT FOR ALL YOUR DRUNKEN CLEVERNESS, GRENDEL HAS NO FEAR OF YOUR SWORD.
HE MURDERS YOUR FELLOW DANES AS HE PLEASES.
BUT HE WILL SOON LEARN THAT I AM NOT YOU. I AM BEOWULF, AND I WILL SHOW HIM MY COURAGE!
YOUR WORDS ARE THE FIRST THING OF CHEER I HAVE HEARD IN THIS HALL FOR AGES, GEAT.
LET US ALL SHARE A DRINK AND PRAY THAT YOUR COURAGE BECOMES GRENDEL'S BANE!

MY KING AND HUSBAND, LET *ME* BE THE ONE WHO SERVES THE DRINK TO THIS BRAVE MAN AND HIS COMPANIONS.

IT IS MOST *FITTING* YOU DO SO, QUEEN WEALHTHEOW.

TO THE BEST OF FRIENDS, WHO COME IN OUR GREATEST NEED.

TO THE BEST OF FRIENDS,

I WILL DO AS I HAVE PROMISED FOR YOUR PEOPLE.

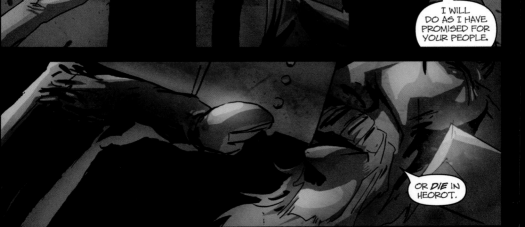

OR *DIE* IN HEOROT.

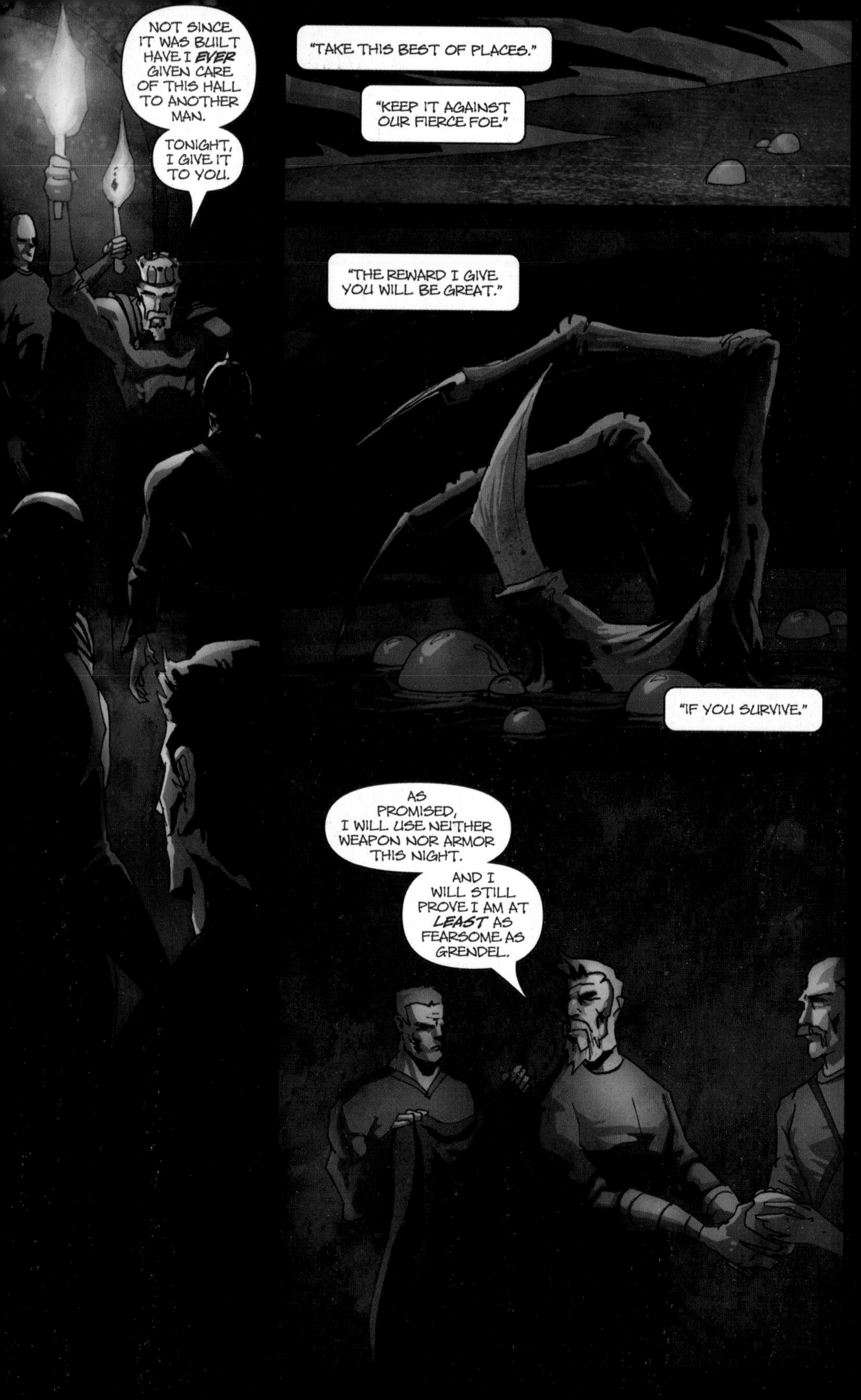
NOT SINCE IT WAS BUILT HAVE I *EVER* GIVEN CARE OF THIS HALL TO ANOTHER MAN.
TONIGHT, I GIVE IT TO YOU.
"TAKE THIS BEST OF PLACES."
"KEEP IT AGAINST OUR FIERCE FOE."
"THE REWARD I GIVE YOU WILL BE GREAT."
"IF YOU SURVIVE."
AS PROMISED, I WILL USE NEITHER WEAPON NOR ARMOR THIS NIGHT.
AND I WILL STILL PROVE I AM AT *LEAST* AS FEARSOME AS GRENDEL.

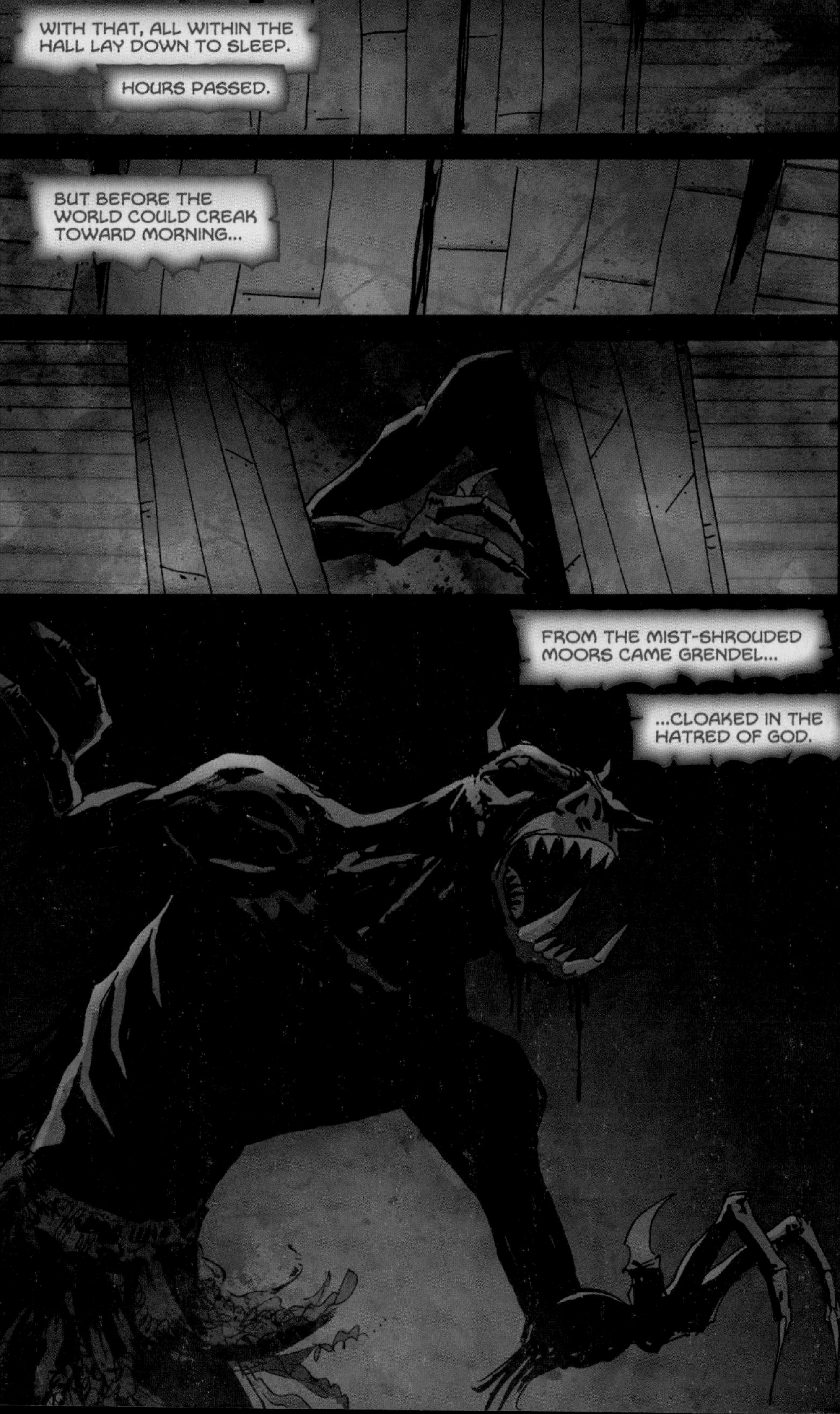
WITH THAT, ALL WITHIN THE HALL LAY DOWN TO SLEEP.
HOURS PASSED.
BUT BEFORE THE WORLD COULD CREAK TOWARD MORNING...
FROM THE MIST-SHROUDED MOORS CAME GRENDEL...
...CLOAKED IN THE HATRED OF GOD.

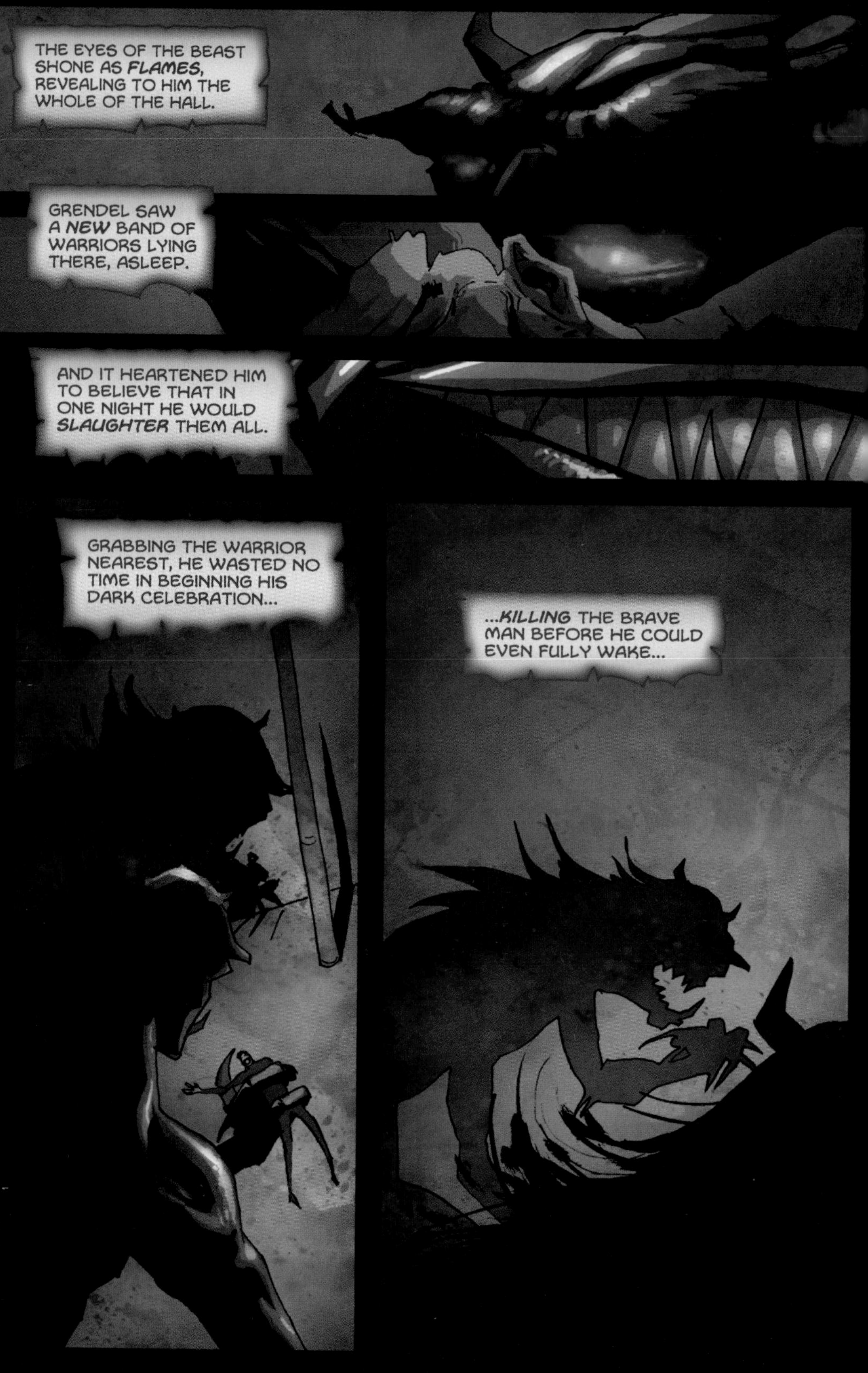
THE EYES OF THE BEAST SHONE AS FLAMES, REVEALING TO HIM THE WHOLE OF THE HALL.
GRENDEL SAW A NEW BAND OF WARRIORS LYING THERE, ASLEEP.
AND IT HEARTENED HIM TO BELIEVE THAT IN ONE NIGHT HE WOULD SLAUGHTER THEM ALL.
GRABBING THE WARRIOR NEAREST, HE WASTED NO TIME IN BEGINNING HIS DARK CELEBRATION...
...KILLING THE BRAVE MAN BEFORE HE COULD EVEN FULLY WAKE...

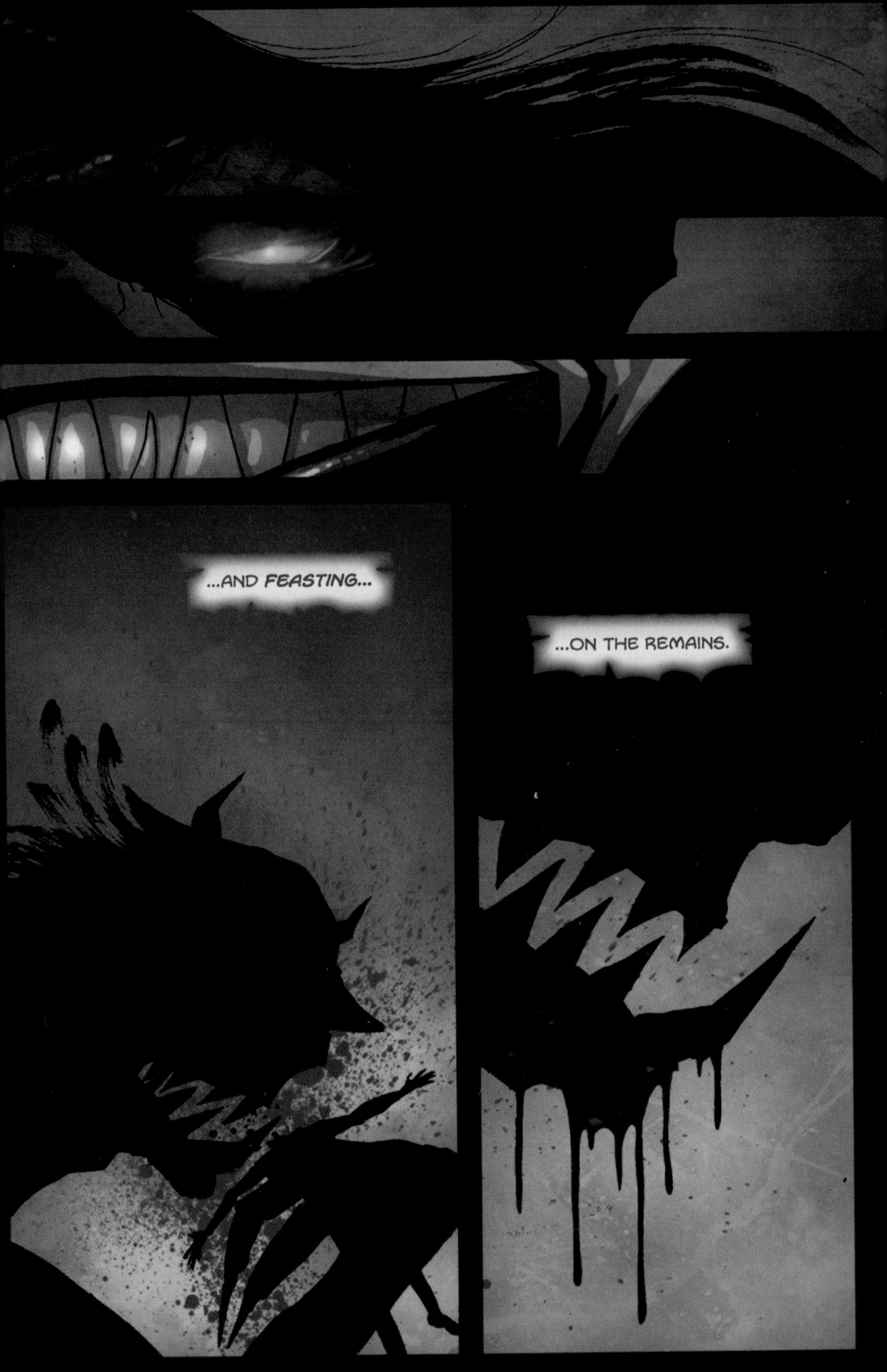
...AND FEASTING...
...ON THE REMAINS.

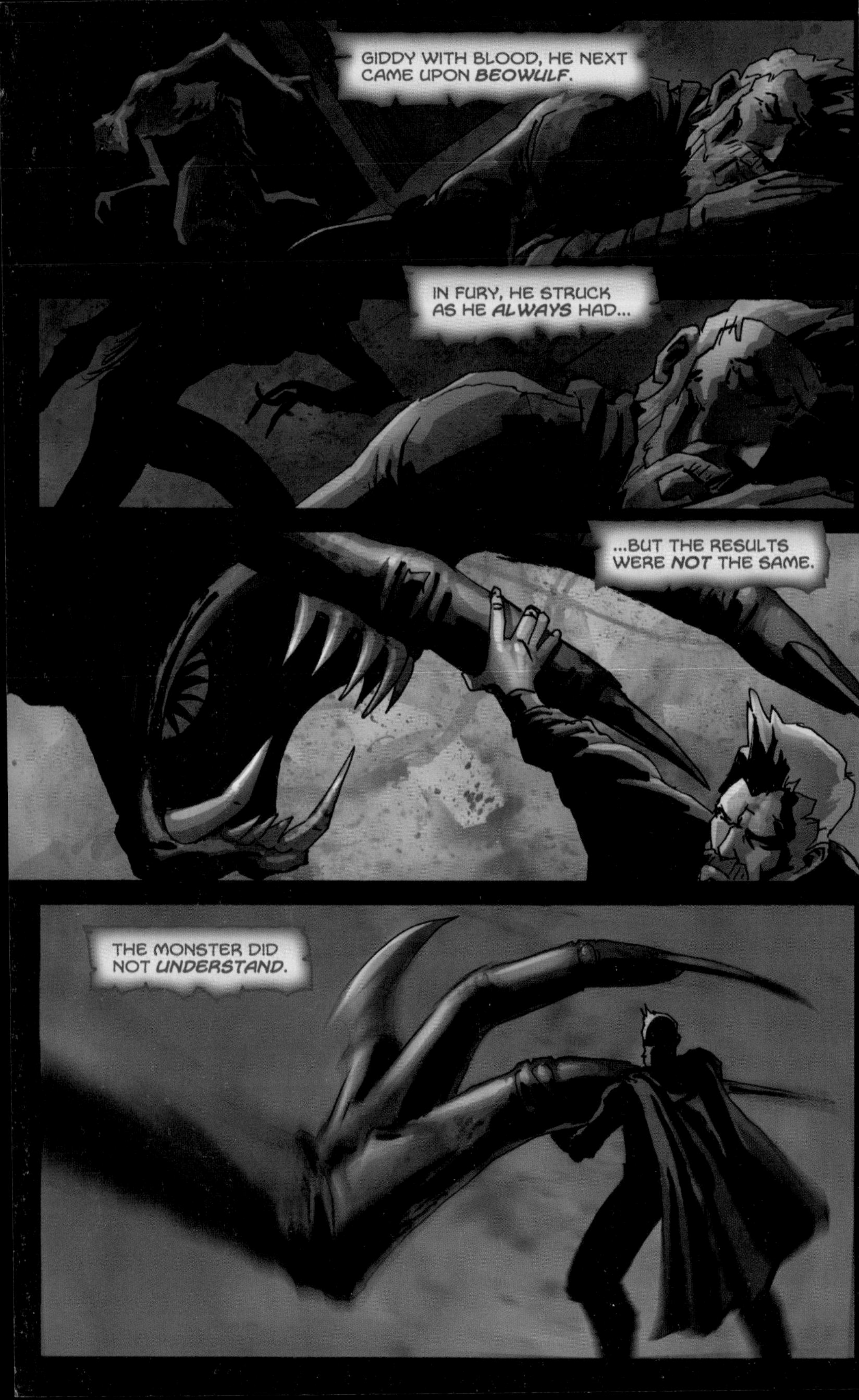
GIDDY WITH BLOOD, HE NEXT CAME UPON BEOWULF.
IN FURY, HE STRUCK AS HE ALWAYS HAD...
...BUT THE RESULTS WERE NOT THE SAME.
THE MONSTER DID NOT UNDERSTAND.

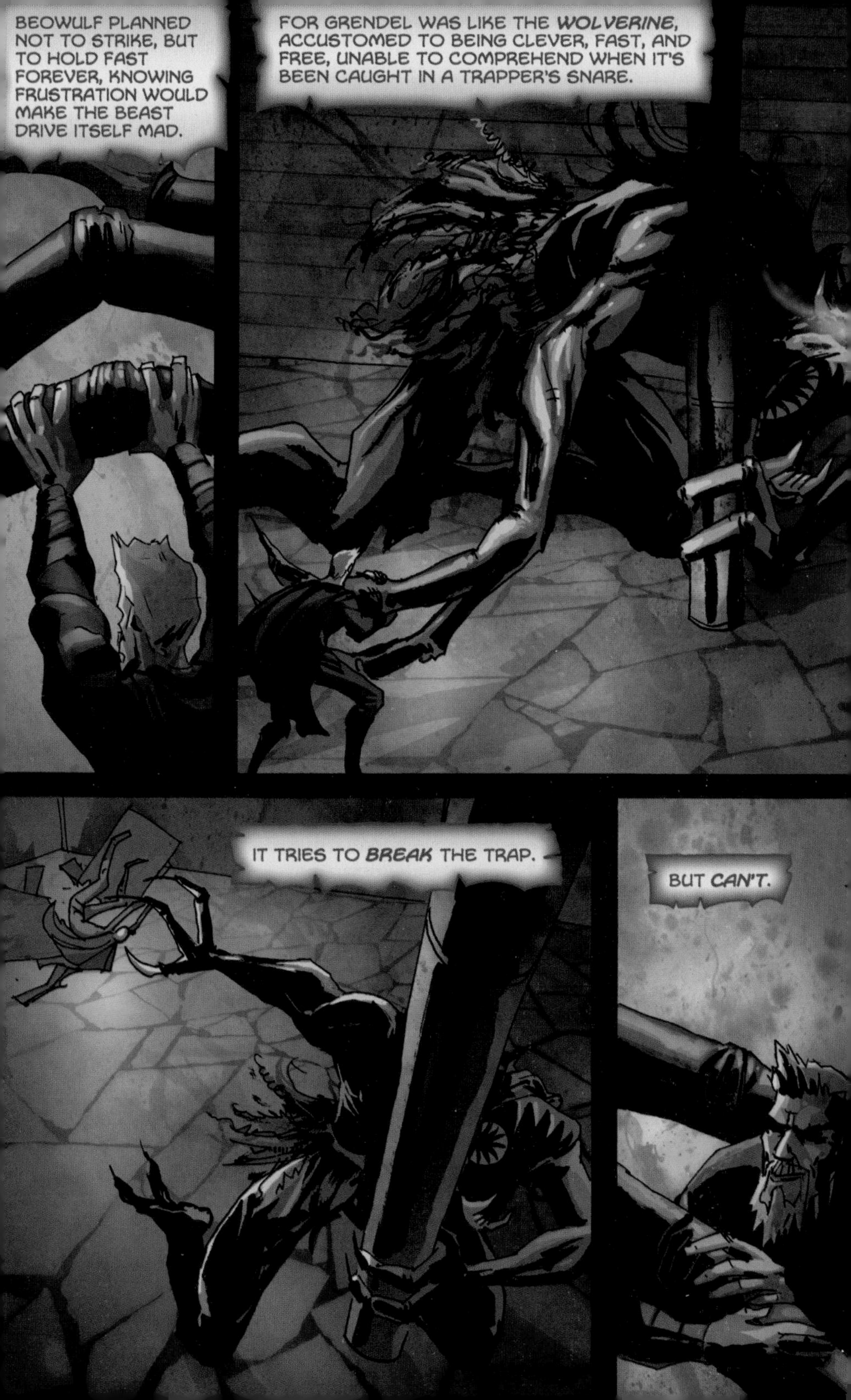
BEOWULF PLANNED NOT TO STRIKE, BUT TO HOLD FAST FOREVER, KNOWING FRUSTRATION WOULD MAKE THE BEAST DRIVE ITSELF MAD.
FOR GRENDEL WAS LIKE THE *WOLVERINE*, ACCUSTOMED TO BEING CLEVER, FAST, AND FREE, UNABLE TO COMPREHEND WHEN IT'S BEEN CAUGHT IN A TRAPPER'S SNARE.
IT TRIES TO *BREAK* THE TRAP.
BUT *CAN'T*.

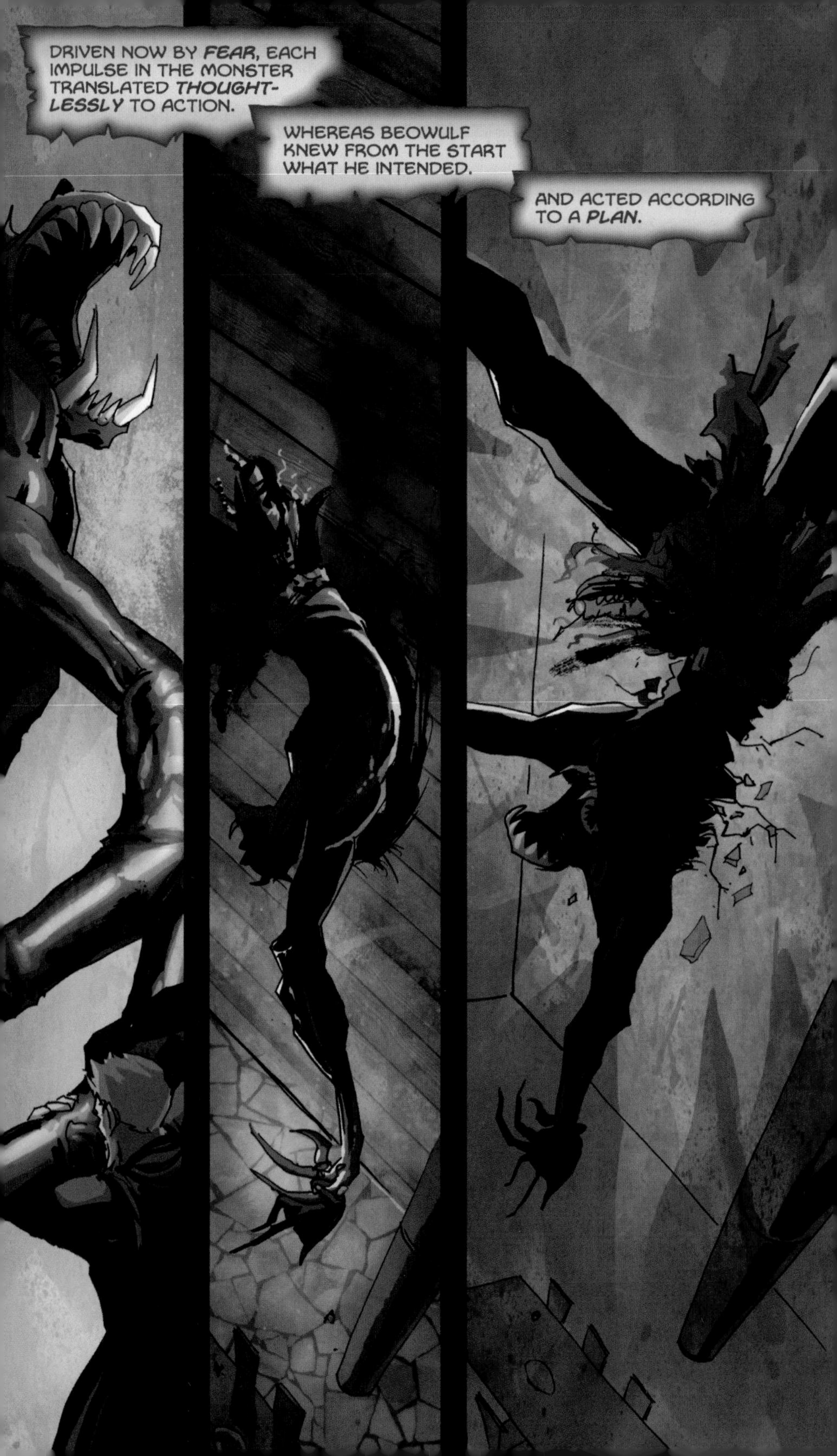
DRIVEN NOW BY *FEAR*, EACH IMPULSE IN THE MONSTER TRANSLATED *THOUGHT-LESSLY* TO ACTION.
WHEREAS BEOWULF KNEW FROM THE START WHAT HE INTENDED.
AND ACTED ACCORDING TO A *PLAN*.

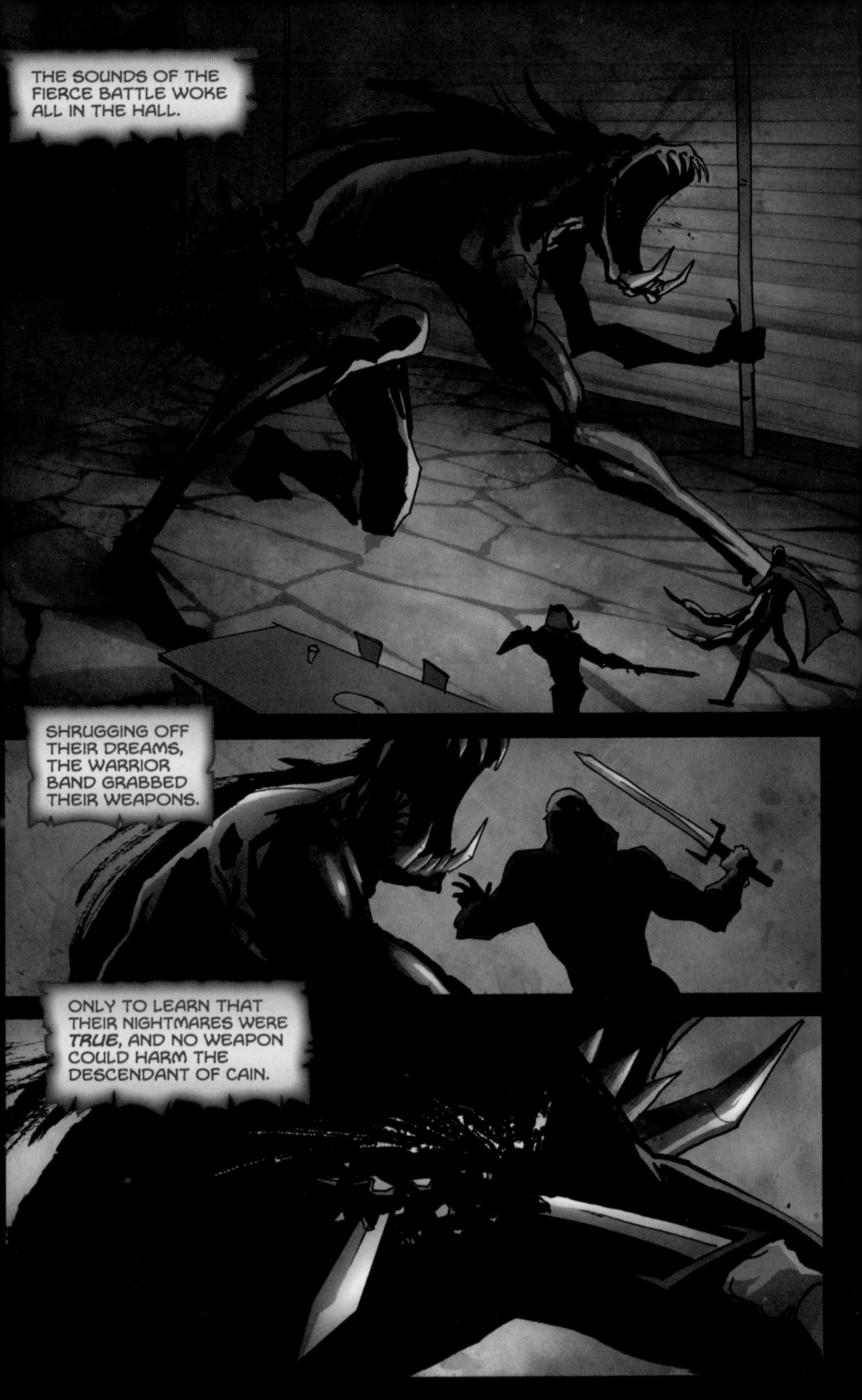
THE SOUNDS OF THE FIERCE BATTLE WOKE ALL IN THE HALL.
SHRUGGING OFF THEIR DREAMS, THE WARRIOR BAND GRABBED THEIR WEAPONS.
ONLY TO LEARN THAT THEIR NIGHTMARES WERE *TRUE*, AND NO WEAPON COULD HARM THE DESCENDANT OF CAIN.

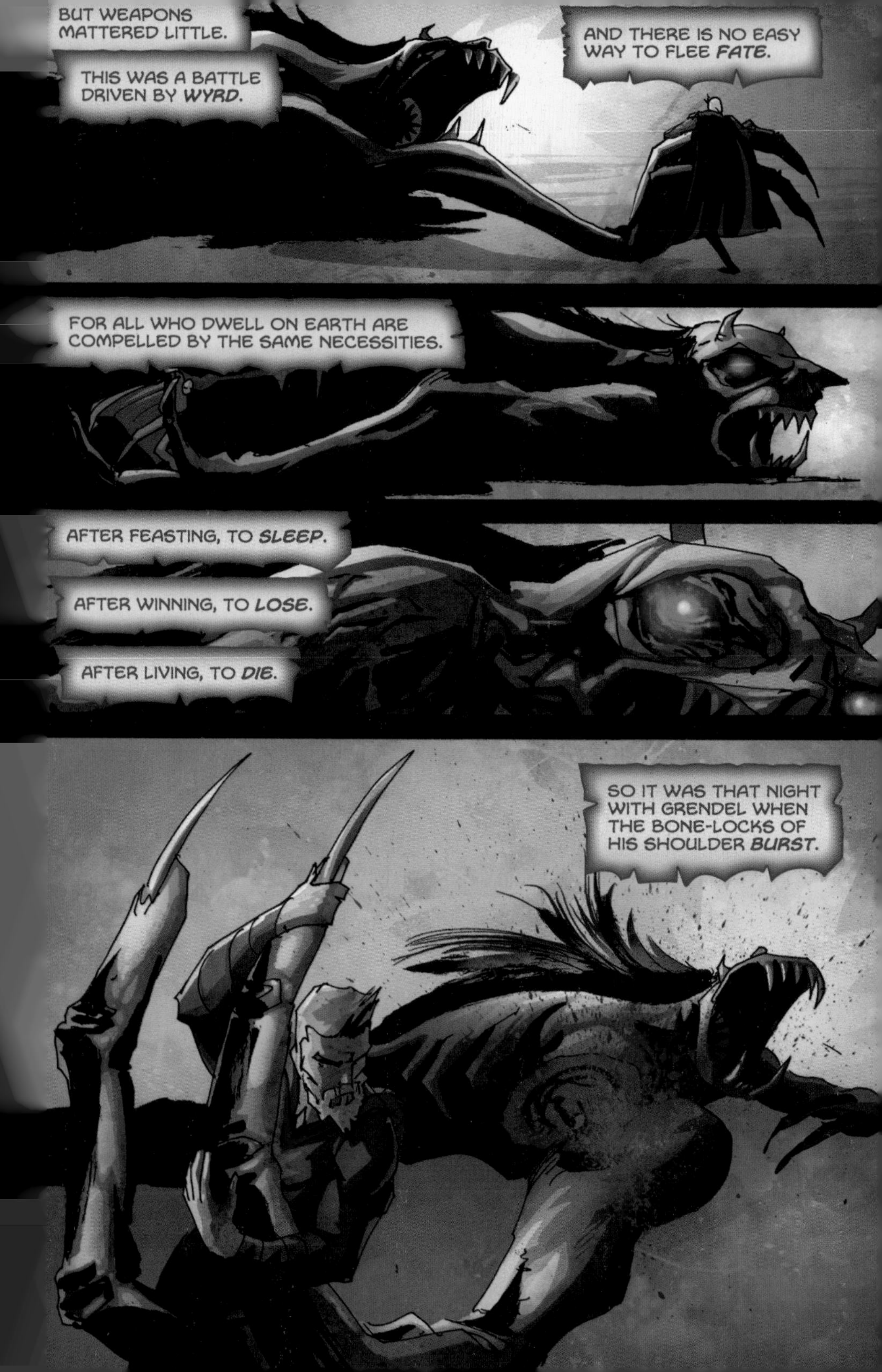
BUT WEAPONS MATTERED LITTLE.
THIS WAS A BATTLE DRIVEN BY WYRD.
AND THERE IS NO EASY WAY TO FLEE FATE.
FOR ALL WHO DWELL ON EARTH ARE COMPELLED BY THE SAME NECESSITIES.
AFTER FEASTING, TO SLEEP.
AFTER WINNING, TO LOSE.
AFTER LIVING, TO DIE.
SO IT WAS THAT NIGHT WITH GRENDEL WHEN THE BONE-LOCKS OF HIS SHOULDER BURST.

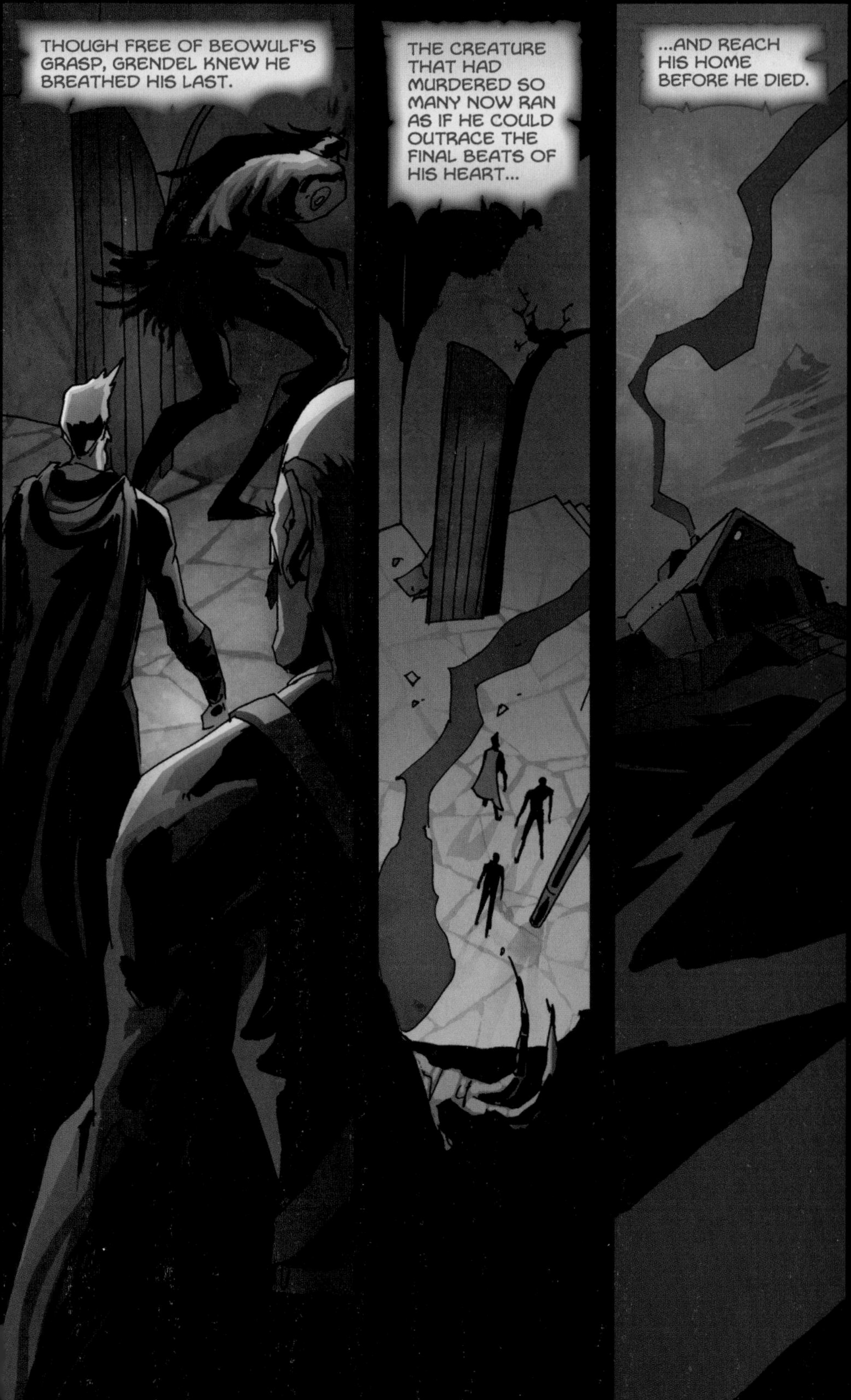
THOUGH FREE OF BEOWULF'S GRASP, GRENDEL KNEW HE BREATHED HIS LAST.
THE CREATURE THAT HAD MURDERED SO MANY NOW RAN AS IF HE COULD OUTRACE THE FINAL BEATS OF HIS HEART...
...AND REACH HIS HOME BEFORE HE DIED.

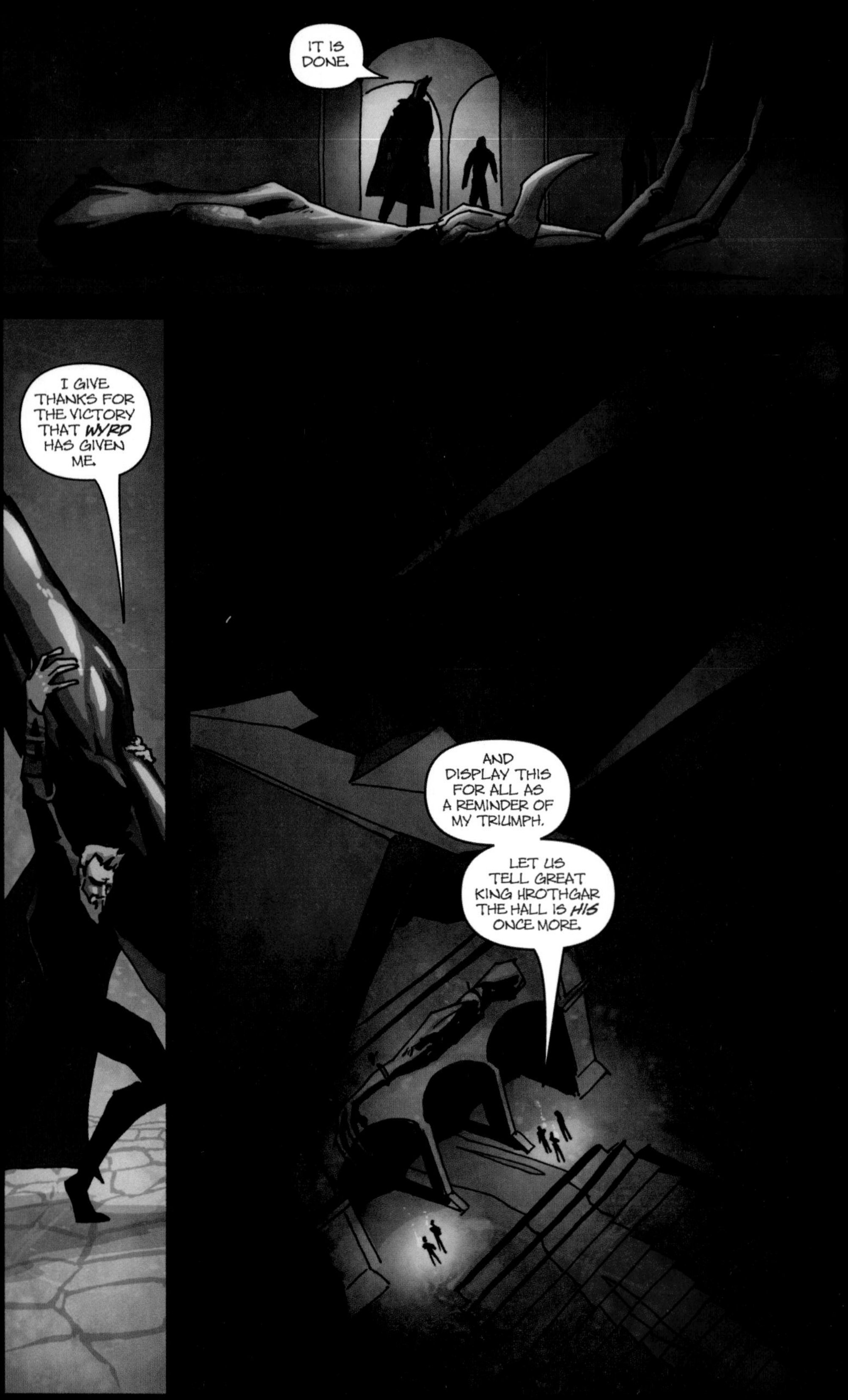
IT IS DONE.
I GIVE THANKS FOR THE VICTORY THAT *WYRD* HAS GIVEN ME.
AND DISPLAY THIS FOR ALL AS A REMINDER OF MY TRIUMPH.
LET US TELL GREAT KING HROTHGAR THE HALL IS *HIS* ONCE MORE.

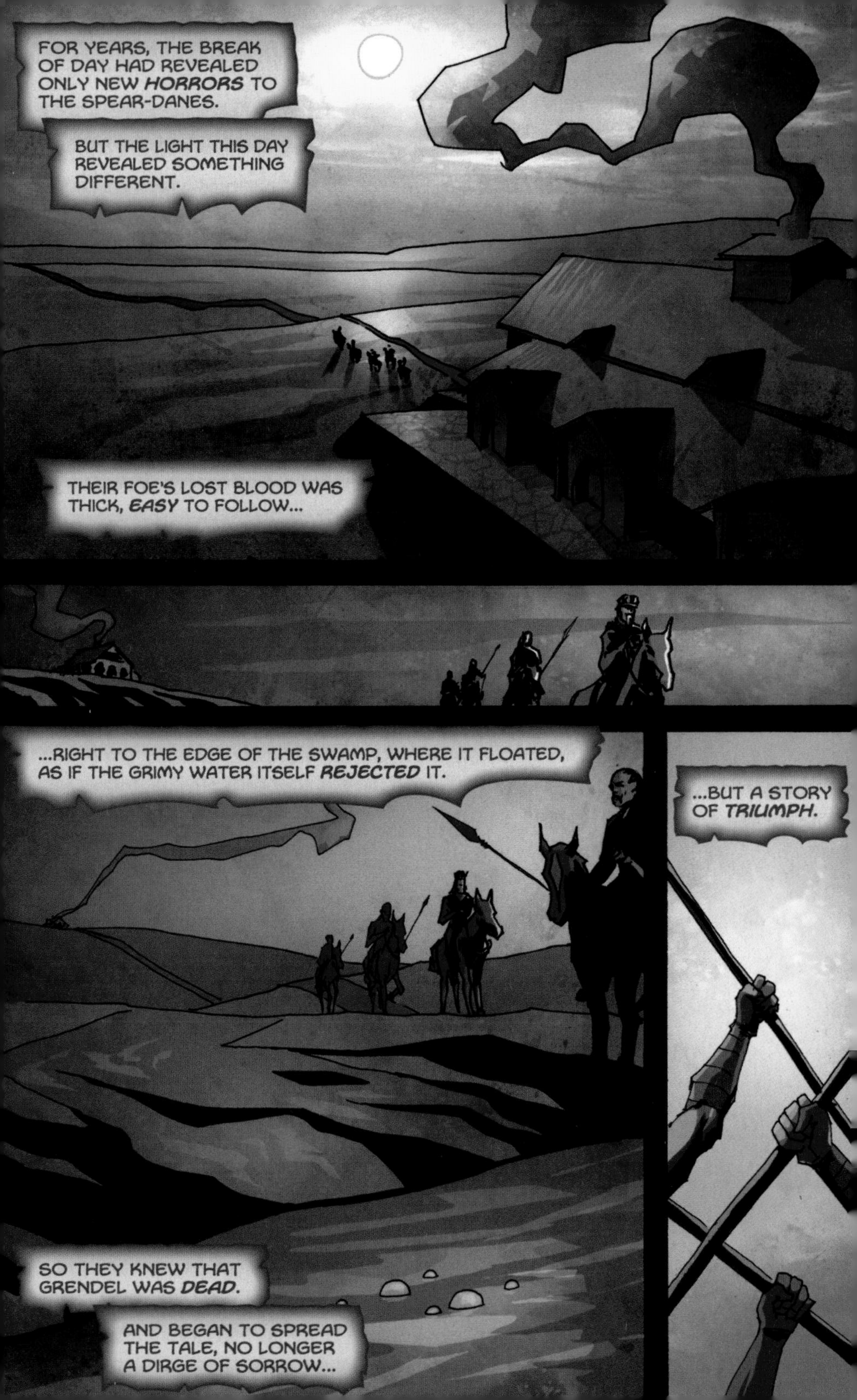
FOR YEARS, THE BREAK OF DAY HAD REVEALED ONLY NEW *HORRORS* TO THE SPEAR-DANES.
BUT THE LIGHT THIS DAY REVEALED SOMETHING DIFFERENT.
THEIR FOE'S LOST BLOOD WAS THICK, *EASY* TO FOLLOW...
...RIGHT TO THE EDGE OF THE SWAMP, WHERE IT FLOATED, AS IF THE GRIMY WATER ITSELF *REJECTED* IT.
SO THEY KNEW THAT GRENDEL WAS *DEAD*.
AND BEGAN TO SPREAD THE TALE, NO LONGER A DIRGE OF SORROW...
...BUT A STORY OF *TRIUMPH*.

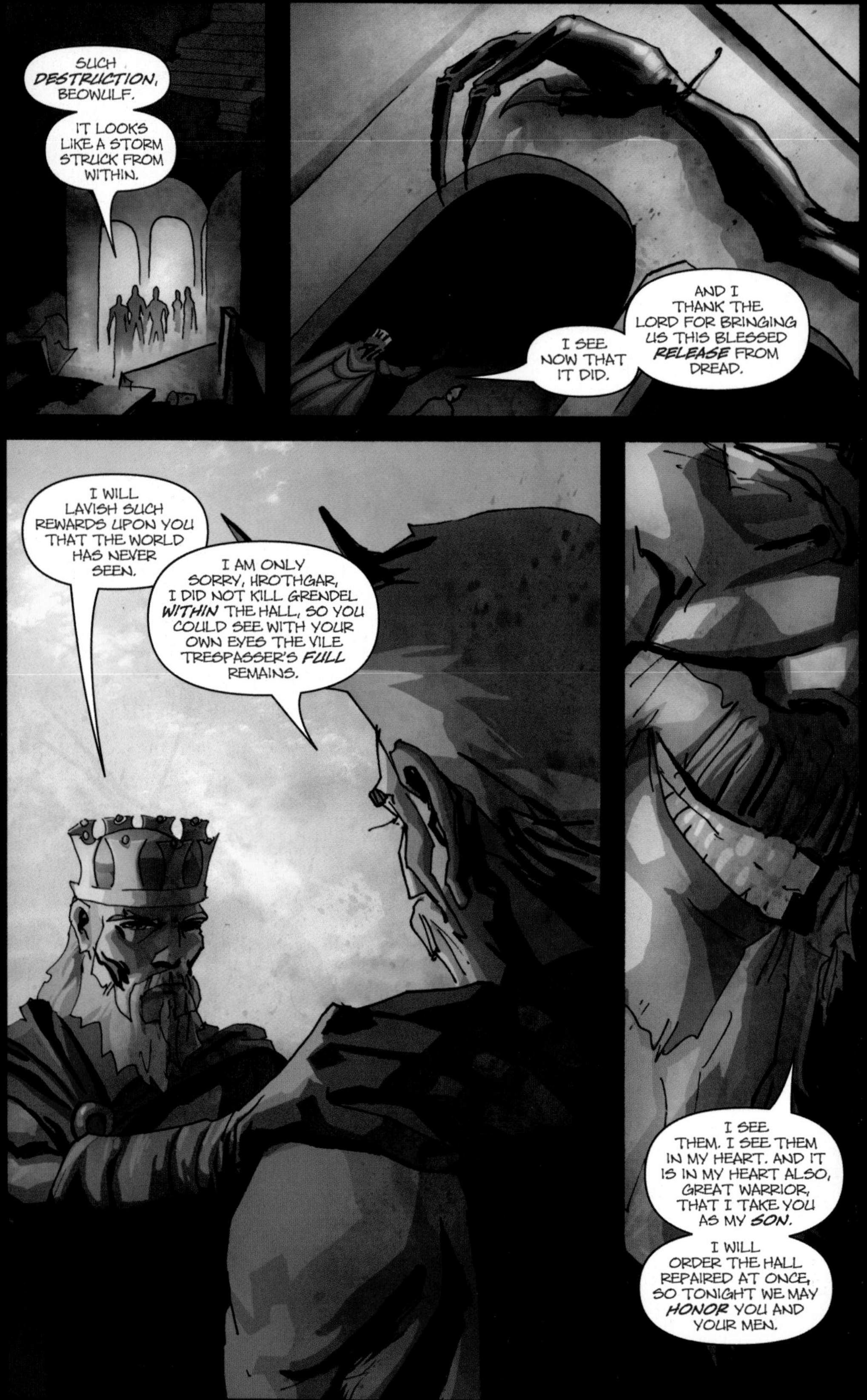
SUCH DESTRUCTION, BEOWULF.
IT LOOKS LIKE A STORM STRUCK FROM WITHIN.
I SEE NOW THAT IT DID.
AND I THANK THE LORD FOR BRINGING US THIS BLESSED RELEASE FROM DREAD.
I WILL LAVISH SUCH REWARDS UPON YOU THAT THE WORLD HAS NEVER SEEN.
I AM ONLY SORRY, HROTHGAR, I DID NOT KILL GRENDEL WITHIN THE HALL, SO YOU COULD SEE WITH YOUR OWN EYES THE VILE TRESPASSER'S FULL REMAINS.
I SEE THEM. I SEE THEM IN MY HEART. AND IT IS IN MY HEART ALSO, GREAT WARRIOR, THAT I TAKE YOU AS MY SON.
I WILL ORDER THE HALL REPAIRED AT ONCE, SO TONIGHT WE MAY HONOR YOU AND YOUR MEN.

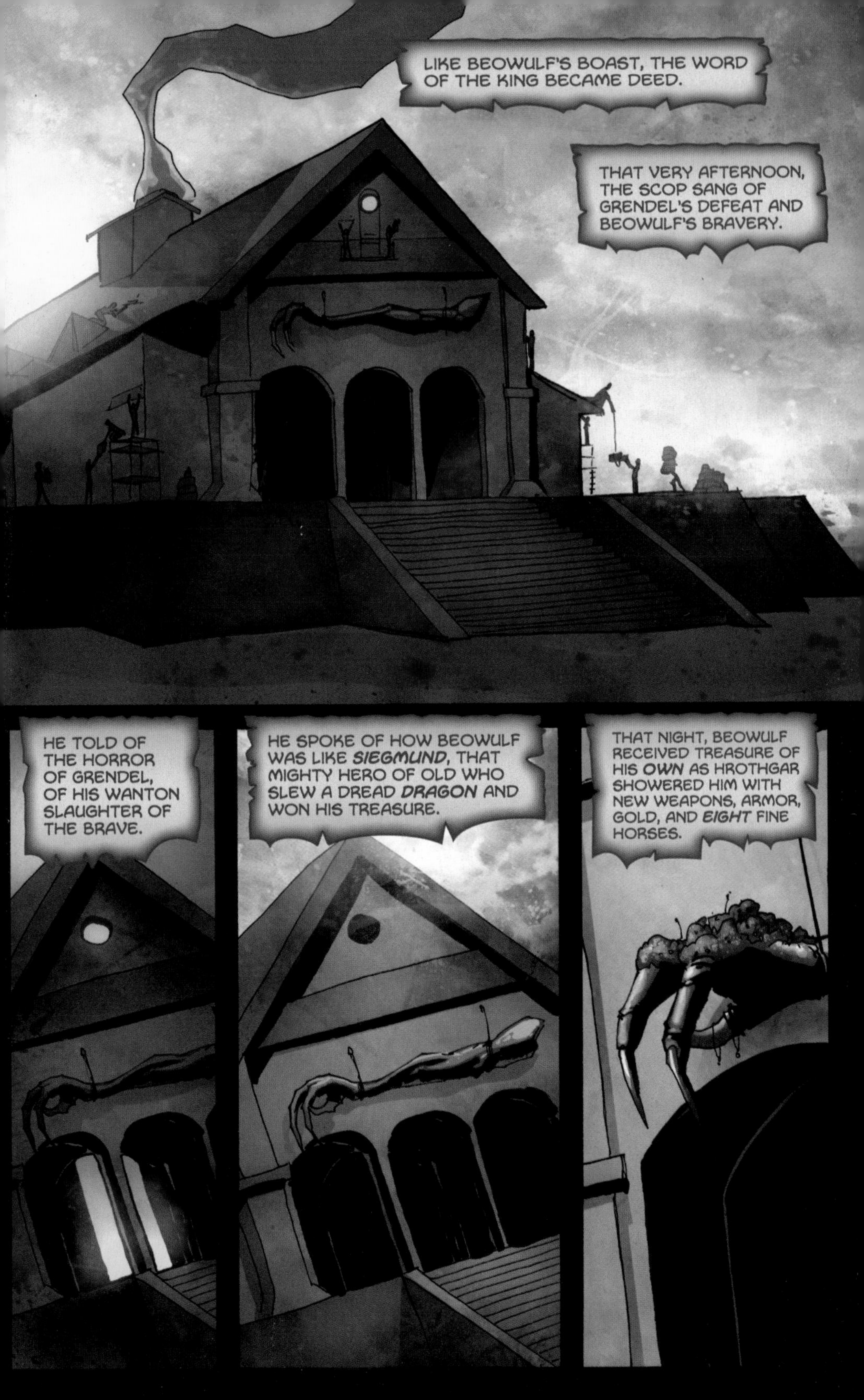
LIKE BEOWULF'S BOAST, THE WORD OF THE KING BECAME DEED.
THAT VERY AFTERNOON, THE SCOP SANG OF GRENDEL'S DEFEAT AND BEOWULF'S BRAVERY.
HE TOLD OF THE HORROR OF GRENDEL, OF HIS WANTON SLAUGHTER OF THE BRAVE.
HE SPOKE OF HOW BEOWULF WAS LIKE *SIEGMUND*, THAT MIGHTY HERO OF OLD WHO SLEW A DREAD *DRAGON* AND WON HIS TREASURE.
THAT NIGHT, BEOWULF RECEIVED TREASURE OF HIS *OWN* AS HROTHGAR SHOWERED HIM WITH NEW WEAPONS, ARMOR, GOLD, AND *EIGHT* FINE HORSES.

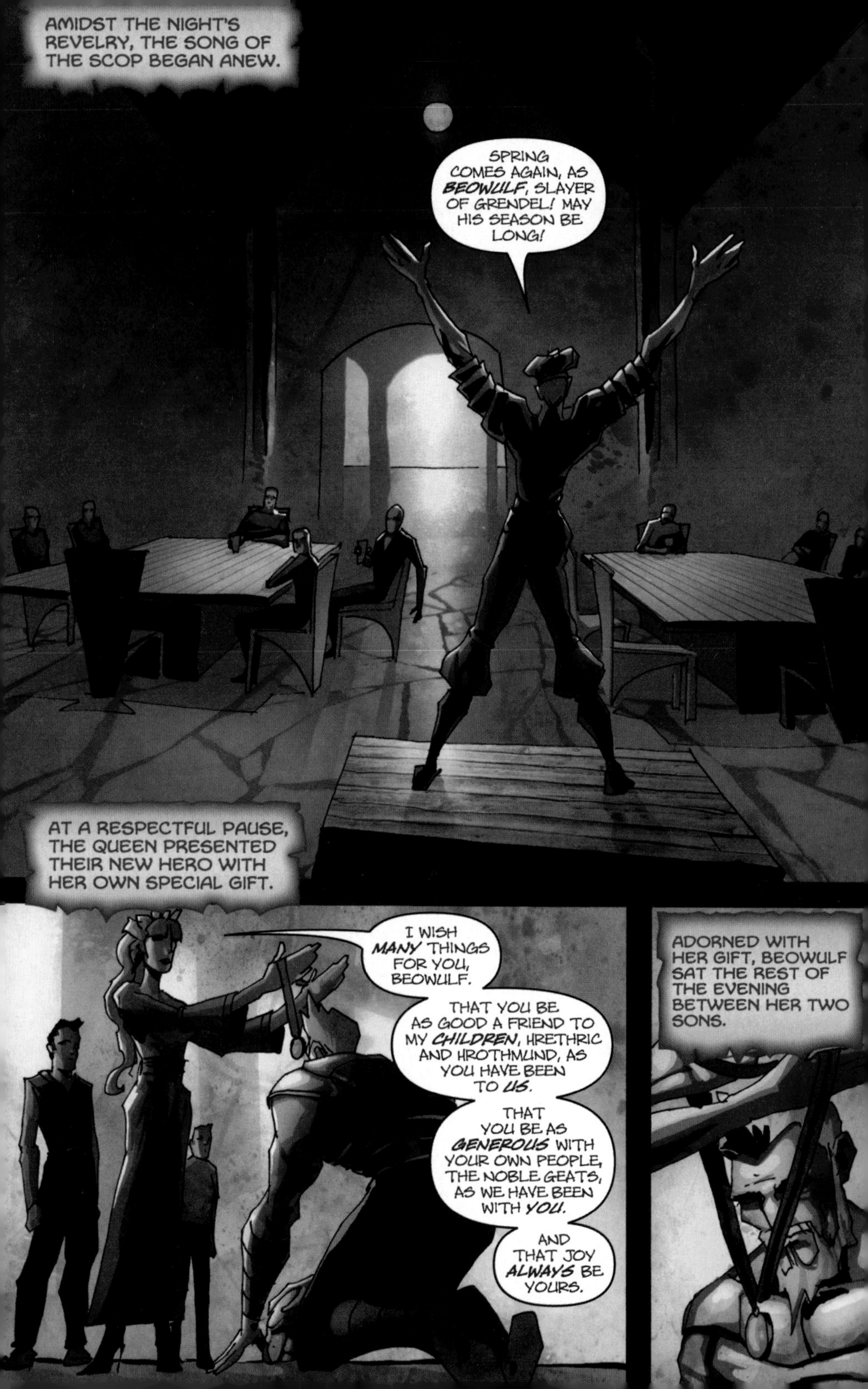
AMIDST THE NIGHT'S REVELRY, THE SONG OF THE SCOP BEGAN ANEW.
SPRING COMES AGAIN, AS BEOWULF, SLAYER OF GRENDEL! MAY HIS SEASON BE LONG!
AT A RESPECTFUL PAUSE, THE QUEEN PRESENTED THEIR NEW HERO WITH HER OWN SPECIAL GIFT.
I WISH MANY THINGS FOR YOU, BEOWULF.
THAT YOU BE AS GOOD A FRIEND TO MY CHILDREN, HRETHRIC AND HROTHMUND, AS YOU HAVE BEEN TO US.
THAT YOU BE AS GENEROUS WITH YOUR OWN PEOPLE, THE NOBLE GEATS, AS WE HAVE BEEN WITH YOU.
AND THAT JOY ALWAYS BE YOURS.
ADORNED WITH HER GIFT, BEOWULF SAT THE REST OF THE EVENING BETWEEN HER TWO SONS.

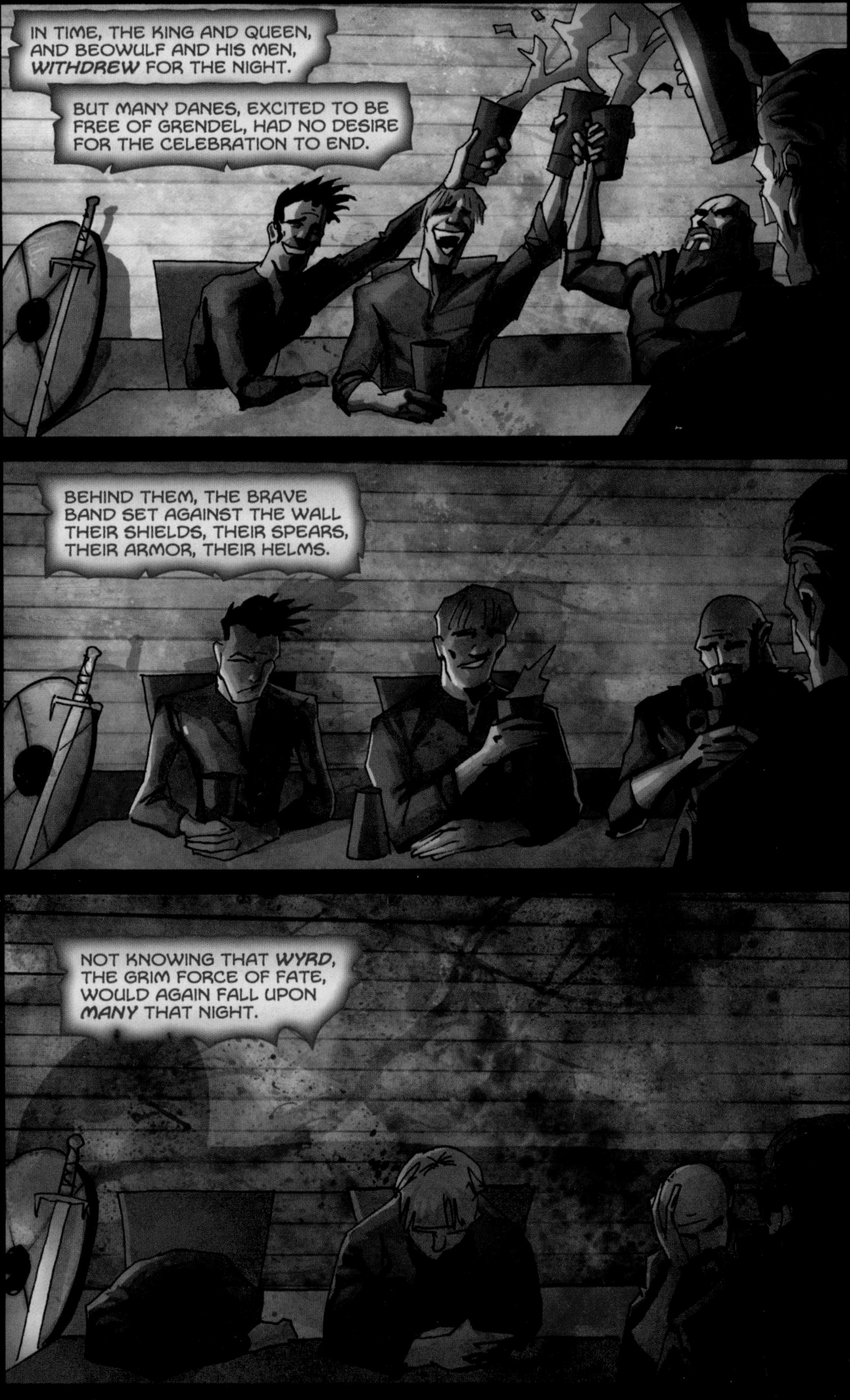
IN TIME, THE KING AND QUEEN, AND BEOWULF AND HIS MEN, *WITHDREW* FOR THE NIGHT.
BUT MANY DANES, EXCITED TO BE FREE OF GRENDEL, HAD NO DESIRE FOR THE CELEBRATION TO END.
BEHIND THEM, THE BRAVE BAND SET AGAINST THE WALL THEIR SHIELDS, THEIR SPEARS, THEIR ARMOR, THEIR HELMS.
NOT KNOWING THAT *WYRD*, THE GRIM FORCE OF FATE, WOULD AGAIN FALL UPON *MANY* THAT NIGHT.

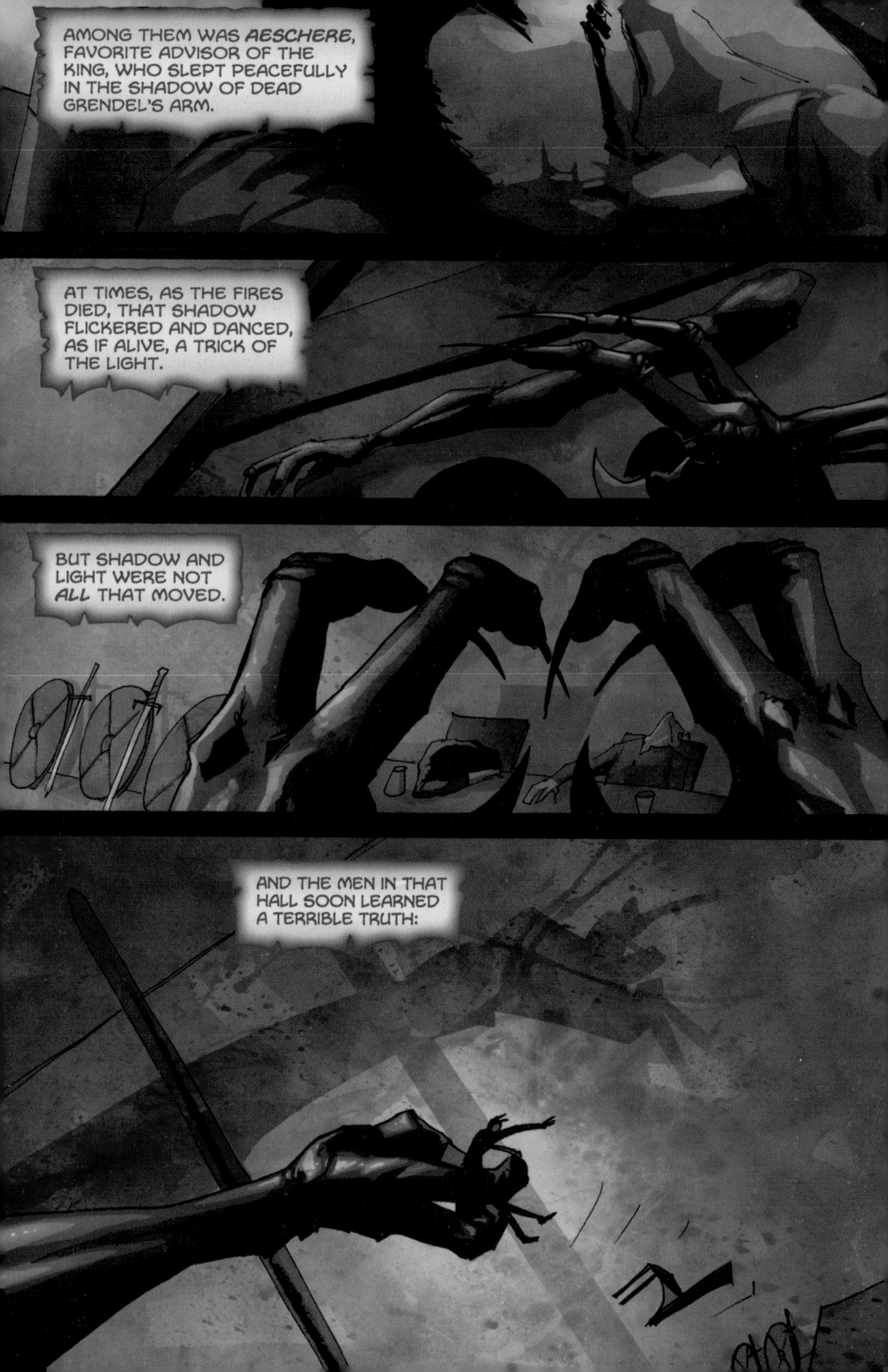
AMONG THEM WAS *AESCHERE*, FAVORITE ADVISOR OF THE KING, WHO SLEPT PEACEFULLY IN THE SHADOW OF DEAD GRENDEL'S ARM.
AT TIMES, AS THE FIRES DIED, THAT SHADOW FLICKERED AND DANCED, AS IF ALIVE, A TRICK OF THE LIGHT.
BUT SHADOW AND LIGHT WERE NOT *ALL* THAT MOVED.
AND THE MEN IN THAT HALL SOON LEARNED A TERRIBLE TRUTH:

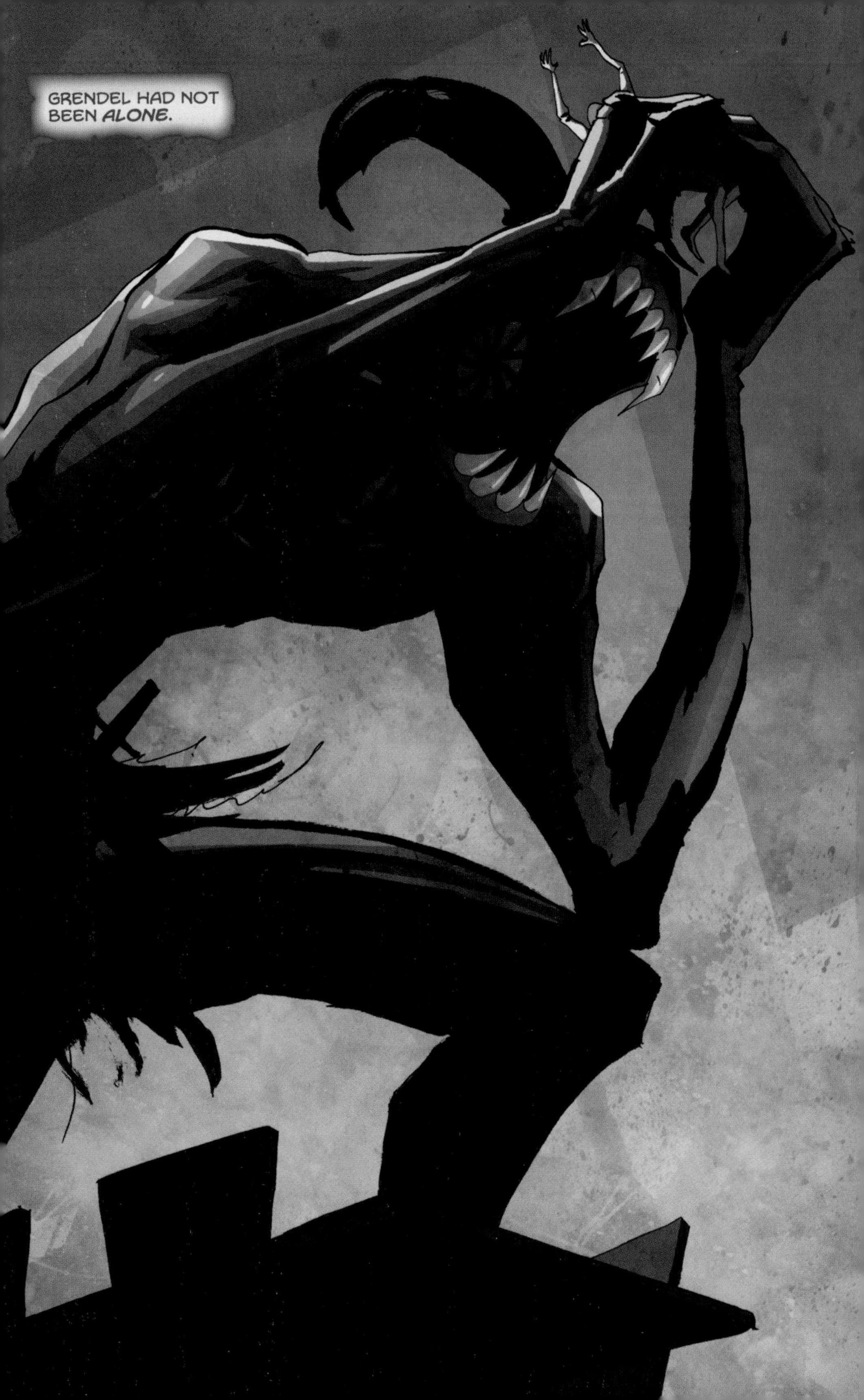
GRENDEL HAD NOT BEEN ALONE.

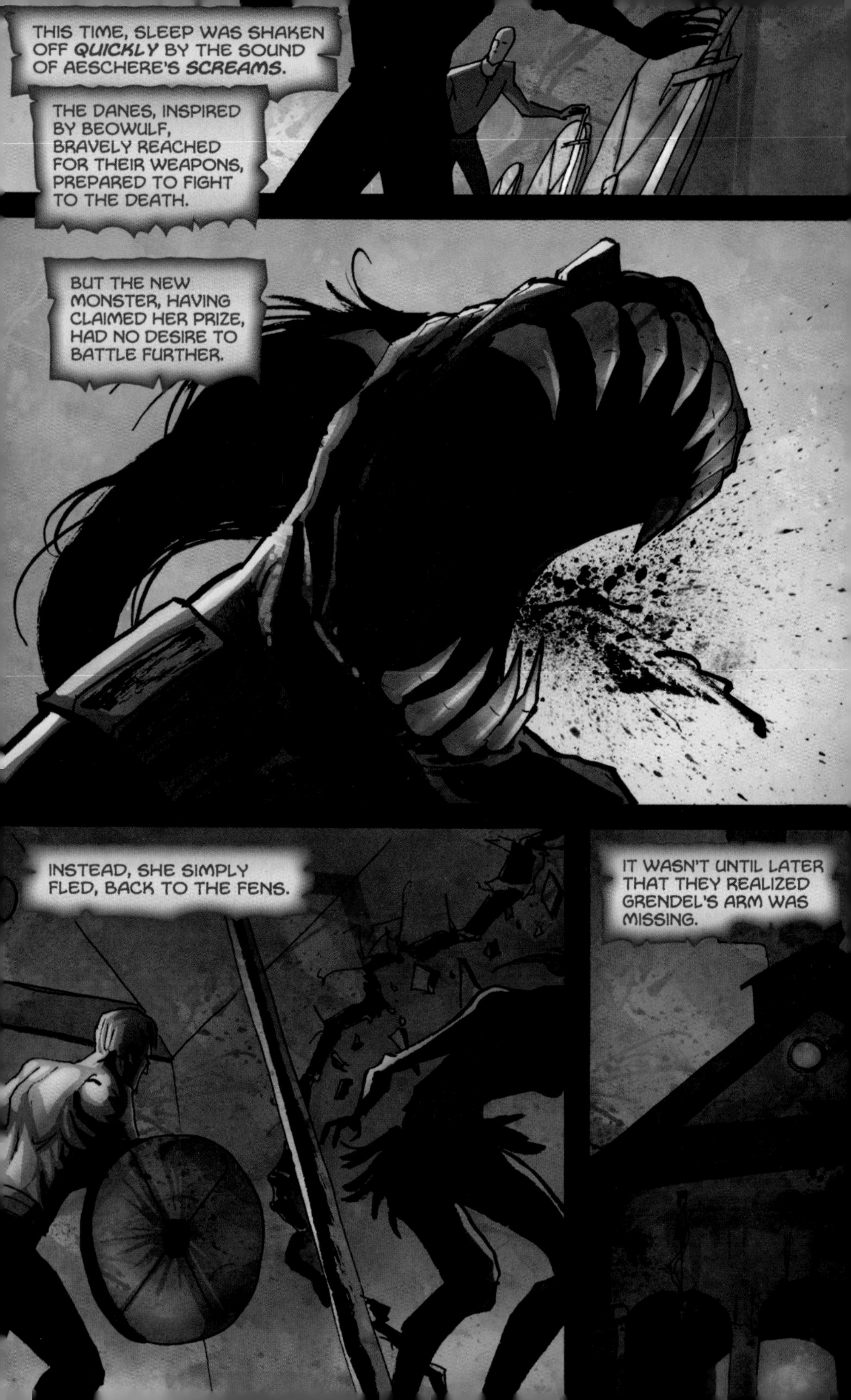
THIS TIME, SLEEP WAS SHAKEN OFF QUICKLY BY THE SOUND OF AESCHERE'S SCREAMS.
THE DANES, INSPIRED BY BEOWULF, BRAVELY REACHED FOR THEIR WEAPONS, PREPARED TO FIGHT TO THE DEATH.
BUT THE NEW MONSTER, HAVING CLAIMED HER PRIZE, HAD NO DESIRE TO BATTLE FURTHER.
INSTEAD, SHE SIMPLY FLED, BACK TO THE FENS.
IT WASN'T UNTIL LATER THAT THEY REALIZED GRENDEL'S ARM WAS MISSING.

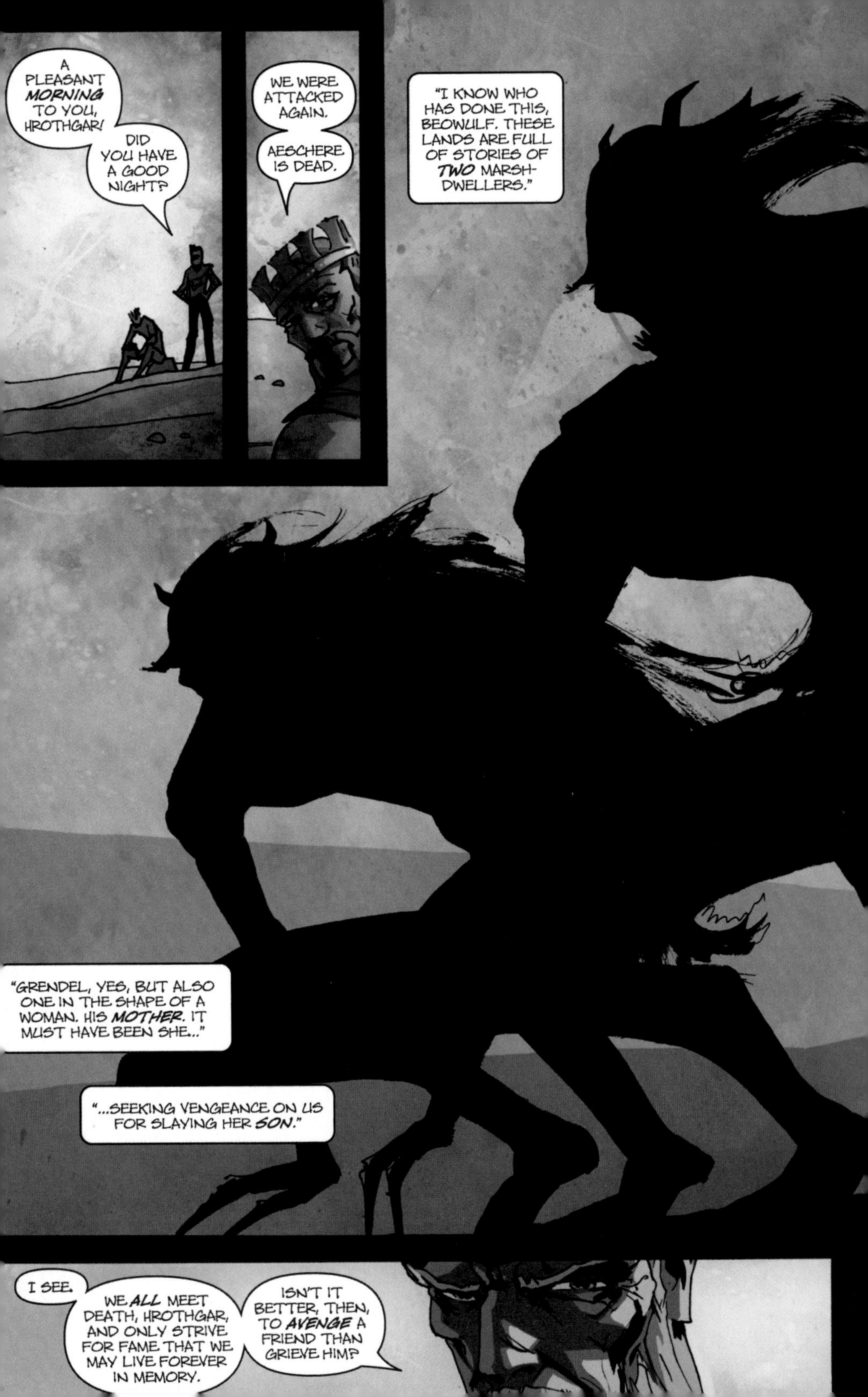
A PLEASANT MORNING TO YOU, HROTHGAR!
DID YOU HAVE A GOOD NIGHT?
WE WERE ATTACKED AGAIN.
AESCHERE IS DEAD.
"I KNOW WHO HAS DONE THIS, BEOWULF. THESE LANDS ARE FULL OF STORIES OF TWO MARSH-DWELLERS."
"GRENDEL, YES, BUT ALSO ONE IN THE SHAPE OF A WOMAN. HIS MOTHER. IT MUST HAVE BEEN SHE..."
"...SEEKING VENGEANCE ON US FOR SLAYING HER SON."
I SEE.
WE ALL MEET DEATH, HROTHGAR, AND ONLY STRIVE FOR FAME THAT WE MAY LIVE FOREVER IN MEMORY.
ISN'T IT BETTER, THEN, TO AVENGE A FRIEND THAN GRIEVE HIM?

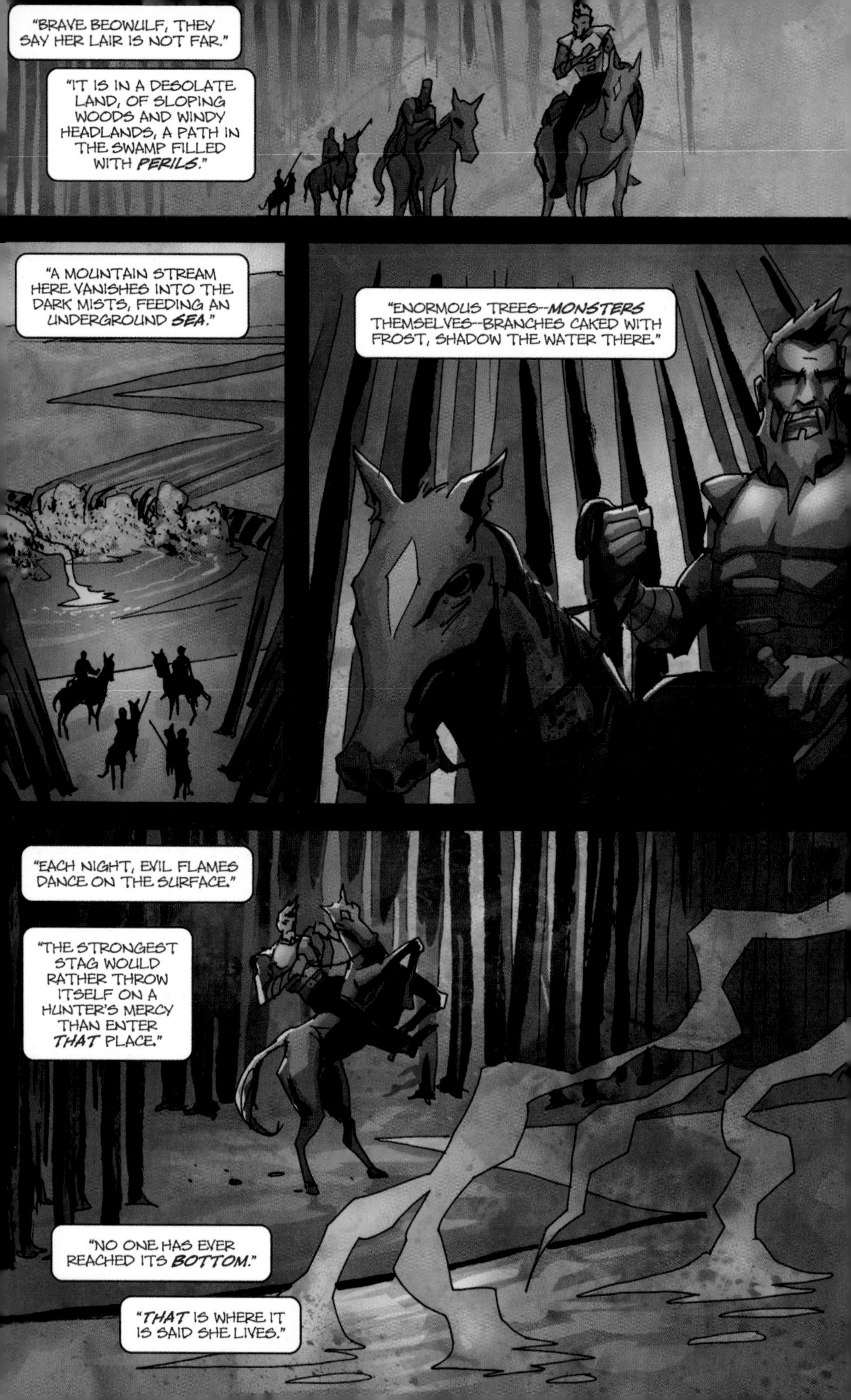
"BRAVE BEOWULF, THEY SAY HER LAIR IS NOT FAR."
"IT IS IN A DESOLATE LAND, OF SLOPING WOODS AND WINDY HEADLANDS, A PATH IN THE SWAMP FILLED WITH *PERILS*."
"A MOUNTAIN STREAM HERE VANISHES INTO THE DARK MISTS, FEEDING AN UNDERGROUND *SEA*."
"ENORMOUS TREES--*MONSTERS* THEMSELVES--BRANCHES CAKED WITH FROST, SHADOW THE WATER THERE."
"EACH NIGHT, EVIL FLAMES DANCE ON THE SURFACE."
"THE STRONGEST STAG WOULD RATHER THROW ITSELF ON A HUNTER'S MERCY THAN ENTER *THAT* PLACE."
"NO ONE HAS EVER REACHED ITS *BOTTOM*."
"*THAT* IS WHERE IT IS SAID SHE LIVES."

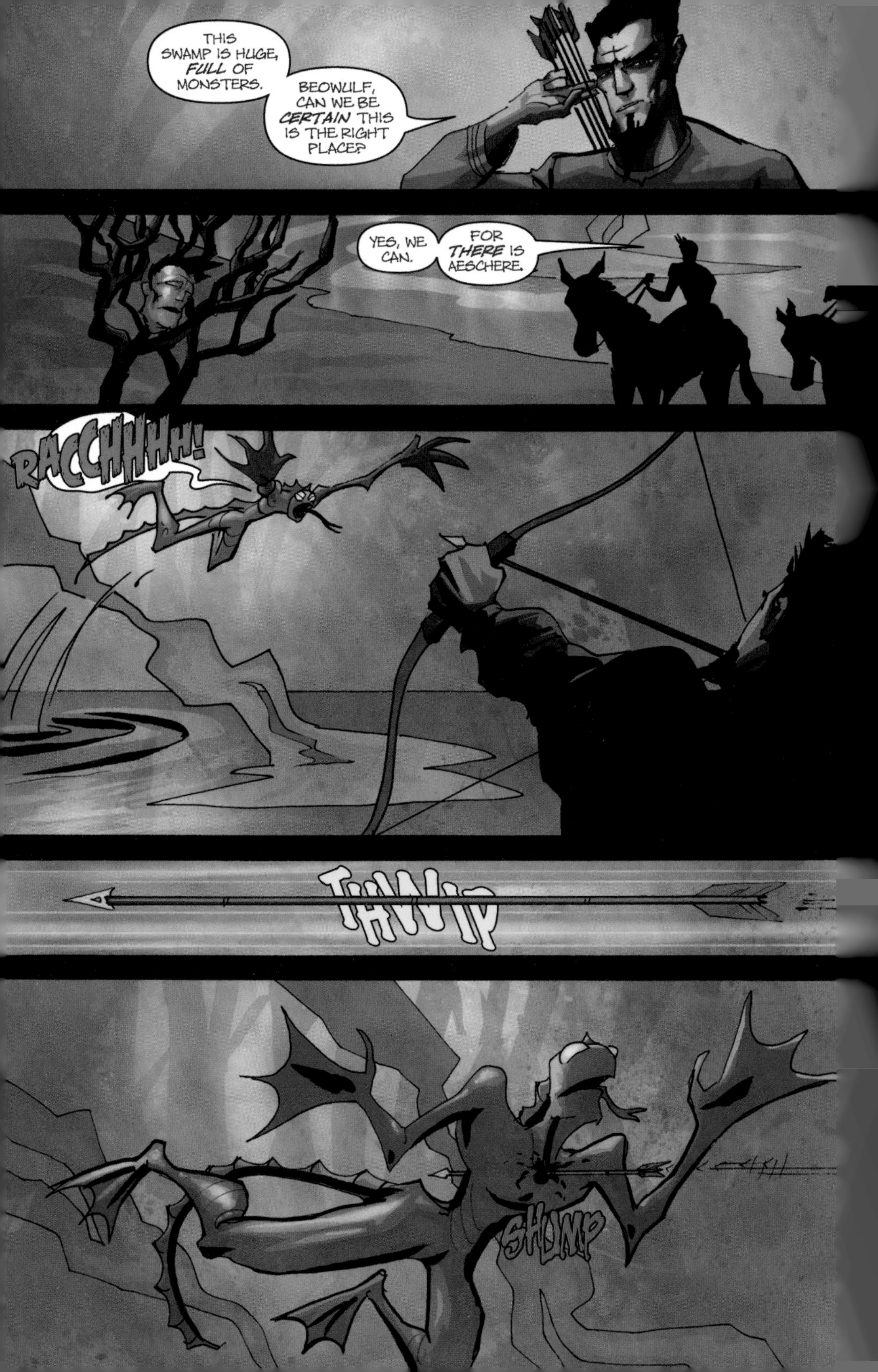

THIS SWAMP IS HUGE, FULL OF MONSTERS.
BEOWULF, CAN WE BE CERTAIN THIS IS THE RIGHT PLACE?
YES, WE CAN.
FOR THERE IS AESCHERE.
RACCHHHH!
THWIP
SHUMP

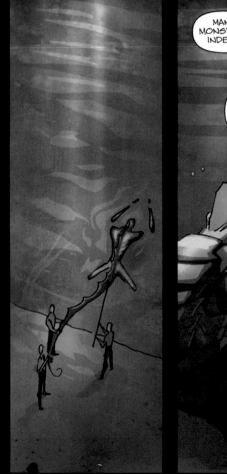

MANY MONSTERS INDEED.

THIS POOL IS THEIR SOURCE.

SEE HOW THEY WRITHE BELOW?

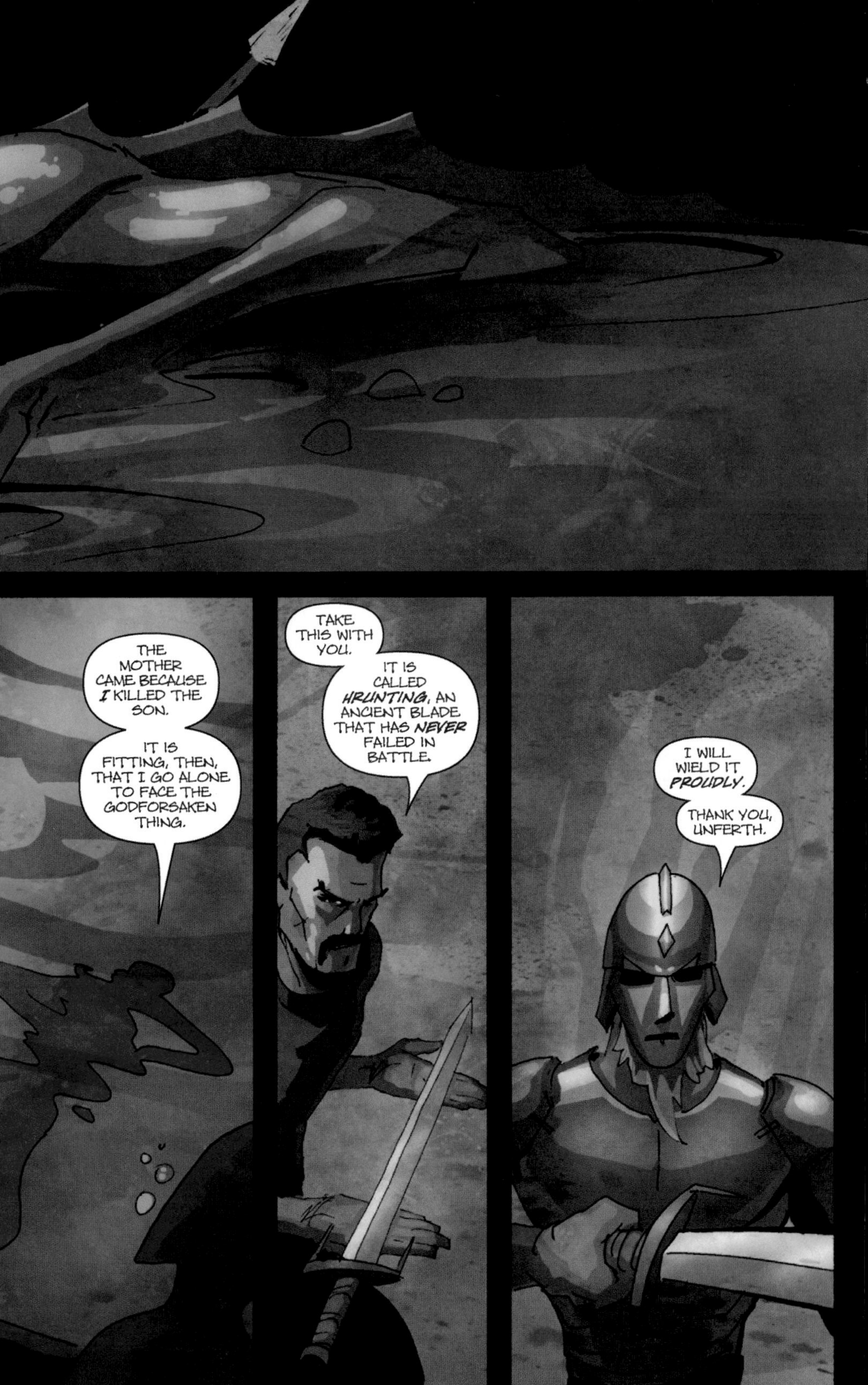
THE MOTHER CAME BECAUSE I KILLED THE SON.
IT IS FITTING, THEN, THAT I GO ALONE TO FACE THE GODFORSAKEN THING.
TAKE THIS WITH YOU.
IT IS CALLED HRUNTING, AN ANCIENT BLADE THAT HAS NEVER FAILED IN BATTLE.
I WILL WIELD IT PROUDLY.
THANK YOU, UNFERTH.

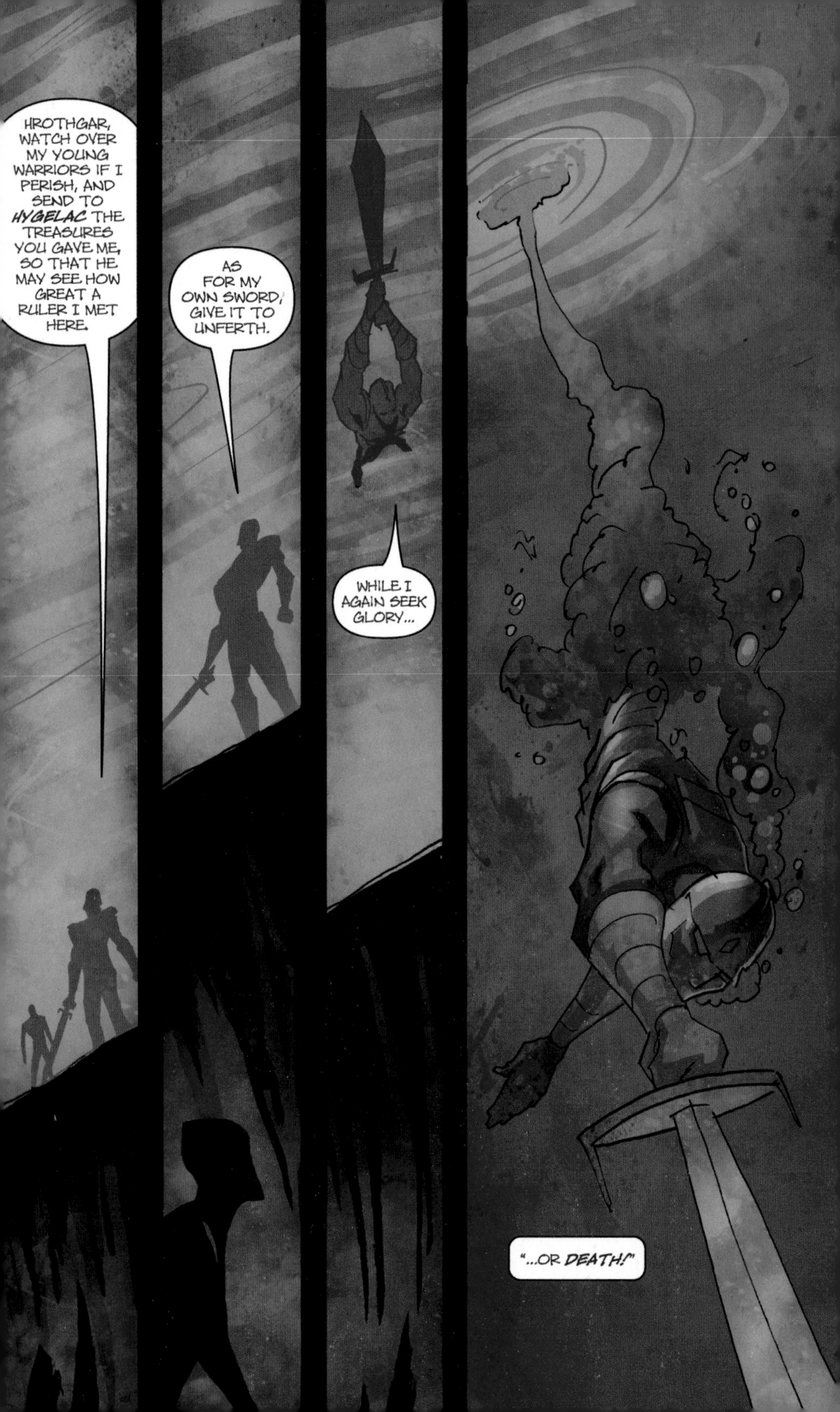
HROTHGAR, WATCH OVER MY YOUNG WARRIORS IF I PERISH, AND SEND TO *HYGELAC* THE TREASURES YOU GAVE ME, SO THAT HE MAY SEE HOW GREAT A RULER I MET HERE.
AS FOR MY OWN SWORD, GIVE IT TO UNFERTH.
WHILE I AGAIN SEEK GLORY...
"...OR *DEATH!*"

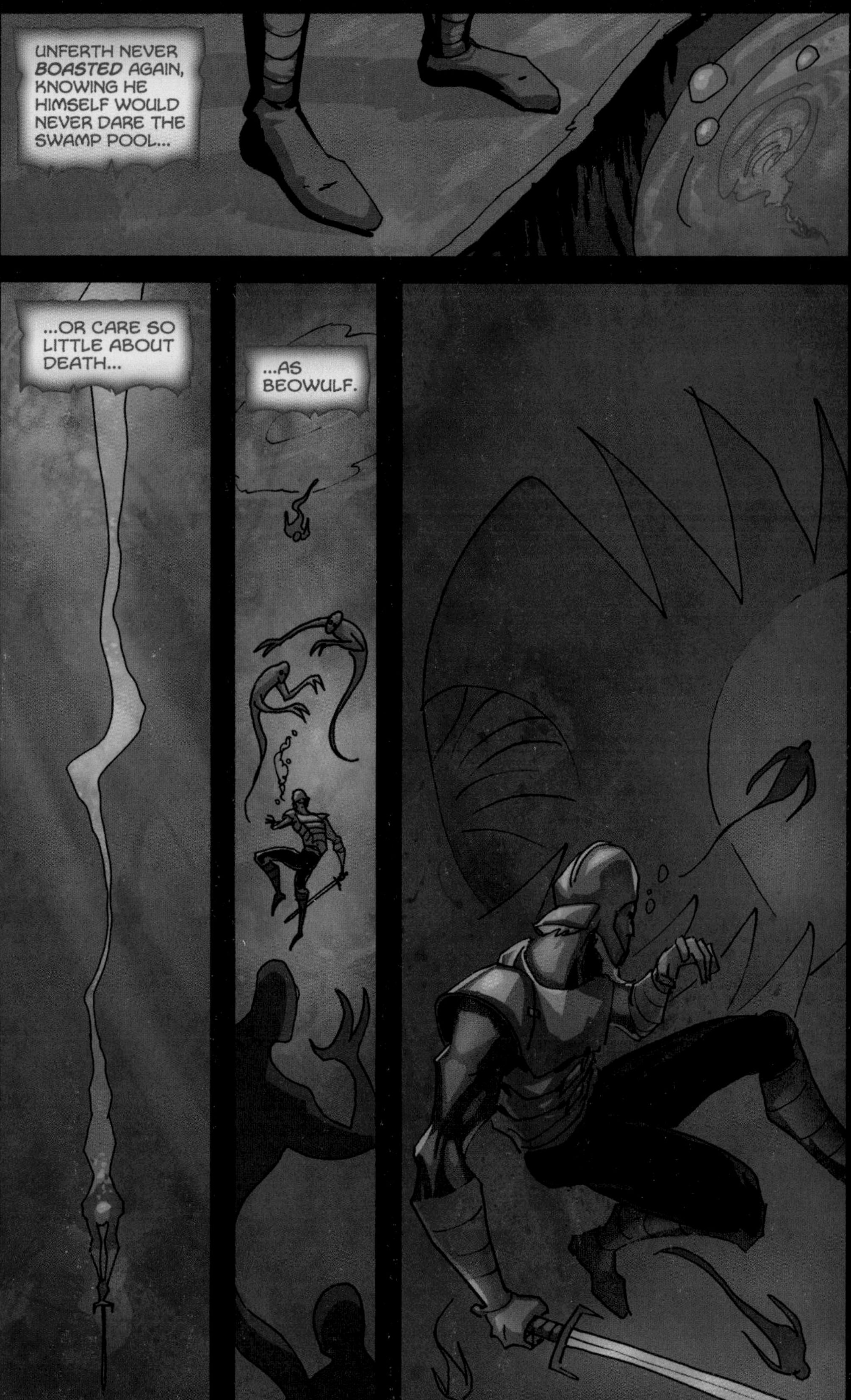
UNFERTH NEVER *BOASTED* AGAIN, KNOWING HE HIMSELF WOULD NEVER DARE THE SWAMP POOL...
...OR CARE SO LITTLE ABOUT DEATH...
...AS BEOWULF.

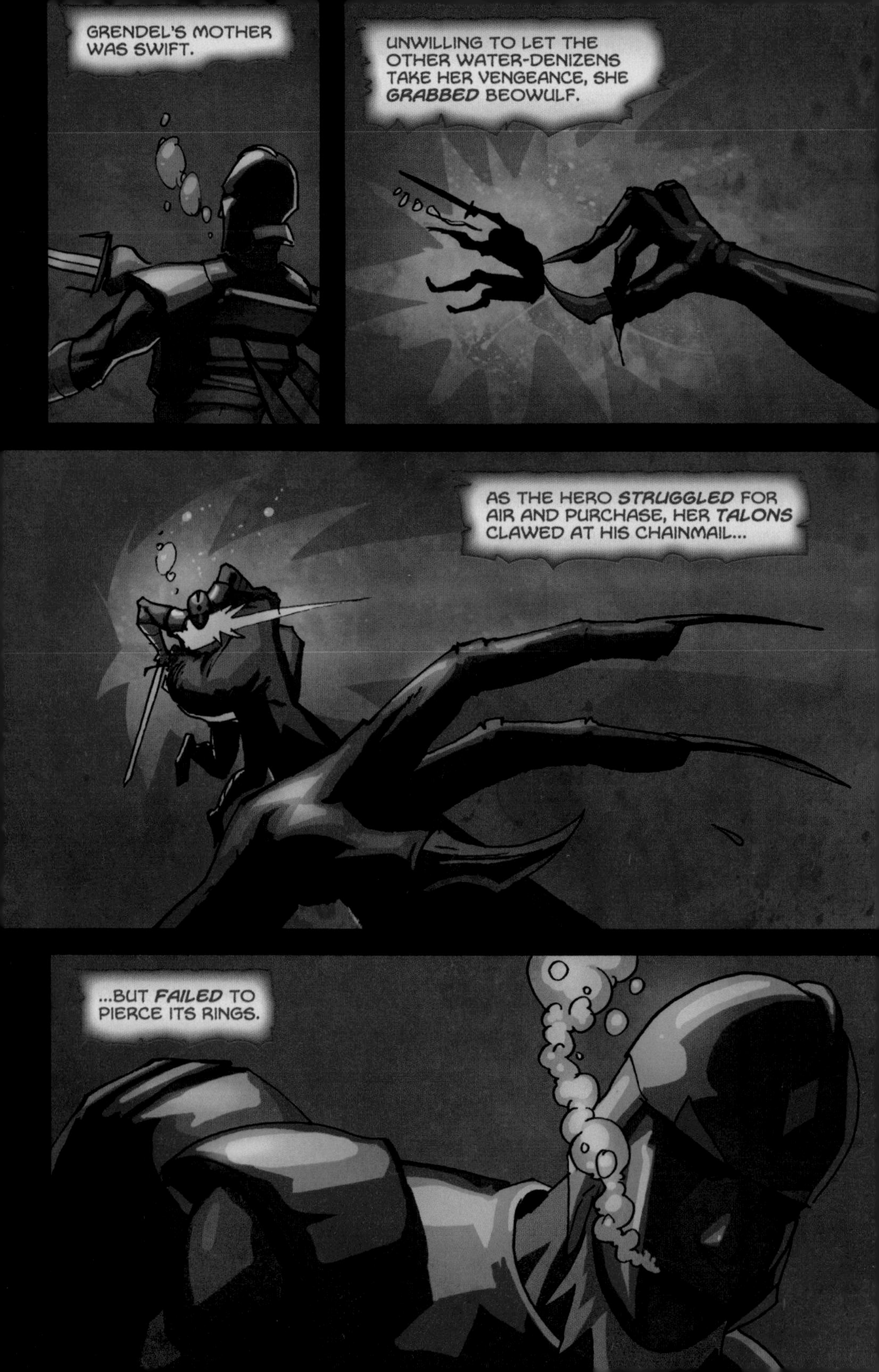
GRENDEL'S MOTHER WAS SWIFT.
UNWILLING TO LET THE OTHER WATER-DENIZENS TAKE HER VENGEANCE, SHE *GRABBED* BEOWULF.
AS THE HERO *STRUGGLED* FOR AIR AND PURCHASE, HER *TALONS* CLAWED AT HIS CHAINMAIL...
...BUT *FAILED* TO PIERCE ITS RINGS.

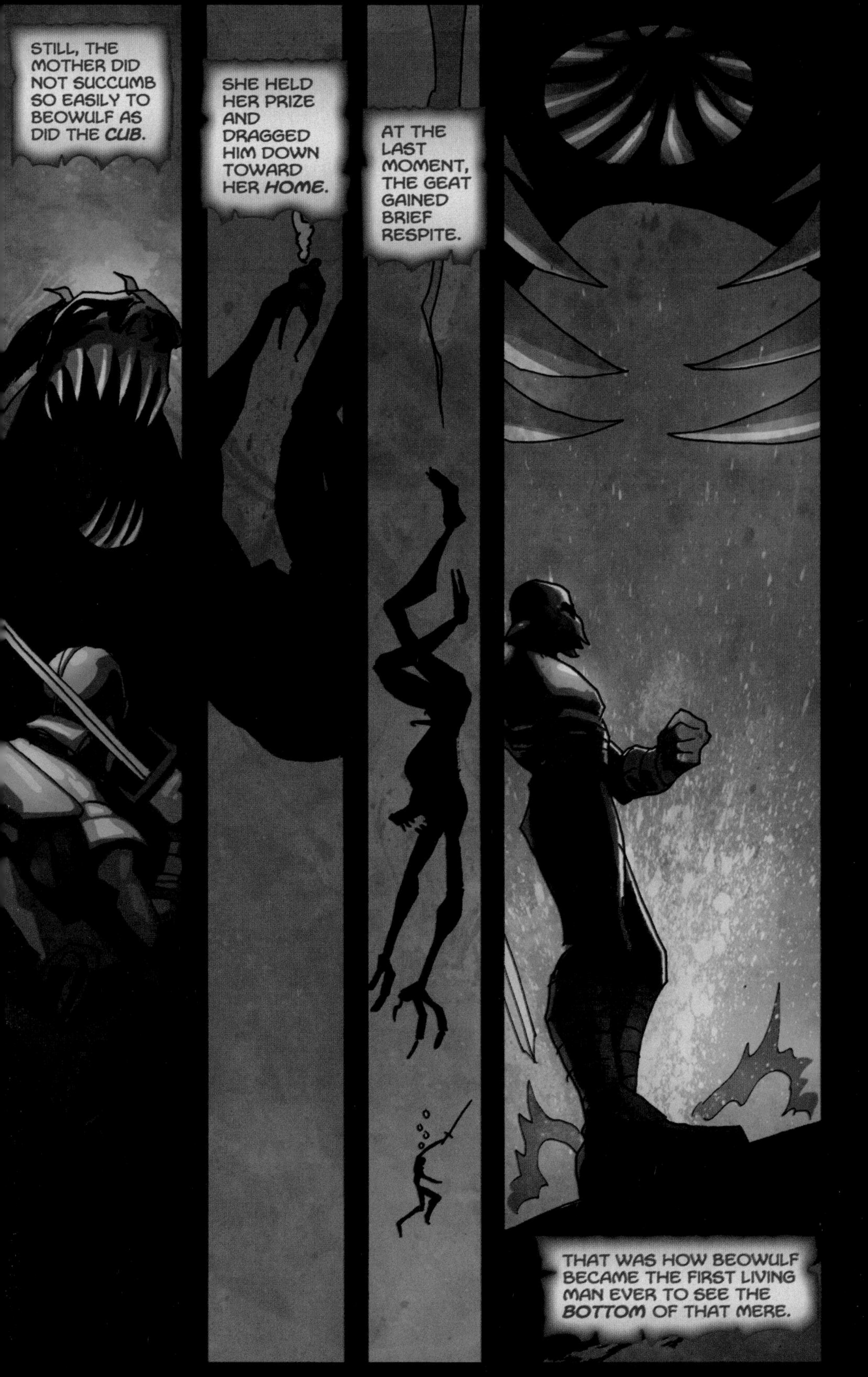
STILL, THE MOTHER DID NOT SUCCUMB SO EASILY TO BEOWULF AS DID THE *CUB*.
SHE HELD HER PRIZE AND DRAGGED HIM DOWN TOWARD HER *HOME*.
AT THE LAST MOMENT, THE GEAT GAINED BRIEF RESPITE.
THAT WAS HOW BEOWULF BECAME THE FIRST LIVING MAN EVER TO SEE THE *BOTTOM* OF THAT MERE.

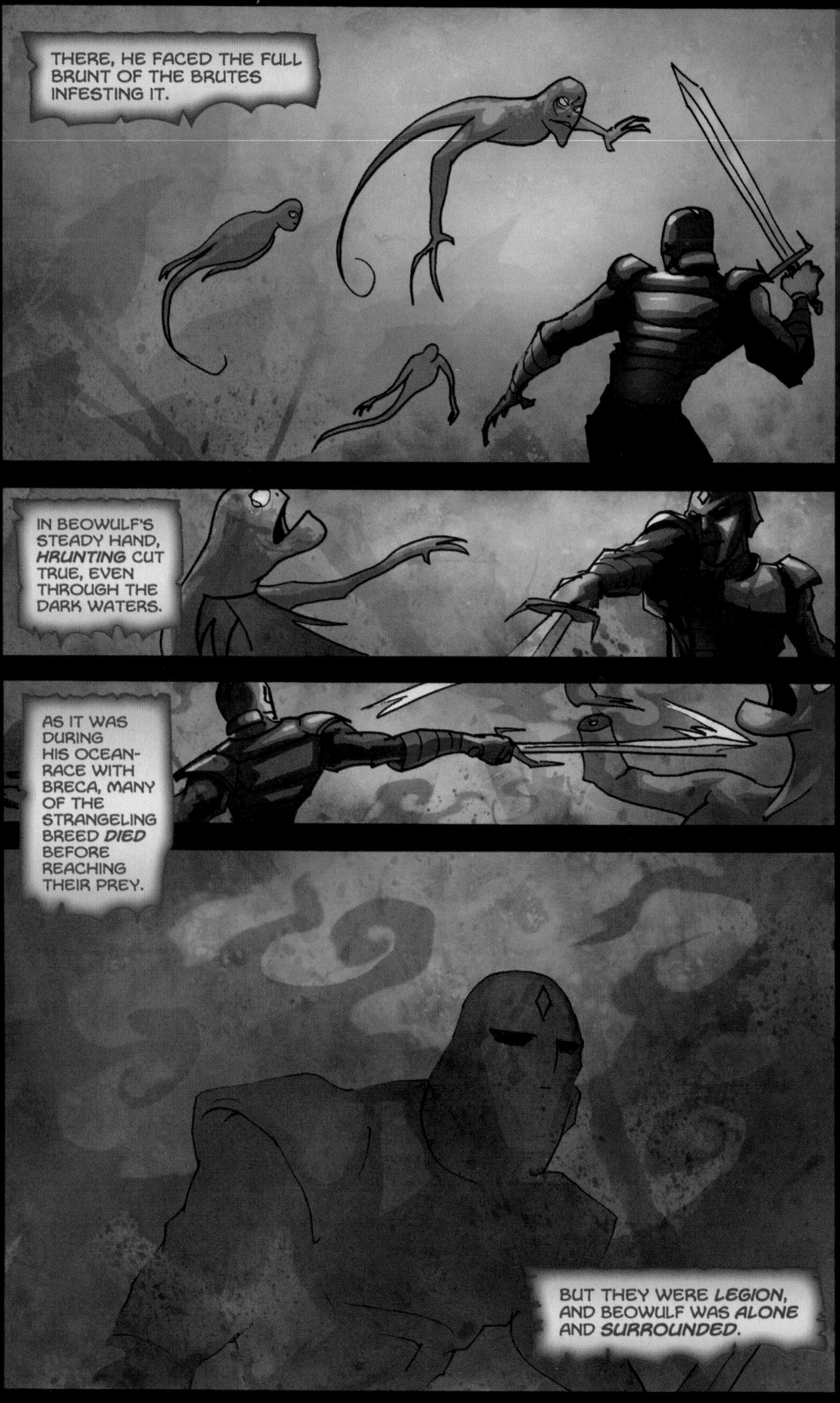
THERE, HE FACED THE FULL BRUNT OF THE BRUTES INFESTING IT.
IN BEOWULF'S STEADY HAND, HRUNTING CUT TRUE, EVEN THROUGH THE DARK WATERS.
AS IT WAS DURING HIS OCEAN-RACE WITH BRECA, MANY OF THE STRANGELING BREED DIED BEFORE REACHING THEIR PREY.
BUT THEY WERE LEGION, AND BEOWULF WAS ALONE AND SURROUNDED.

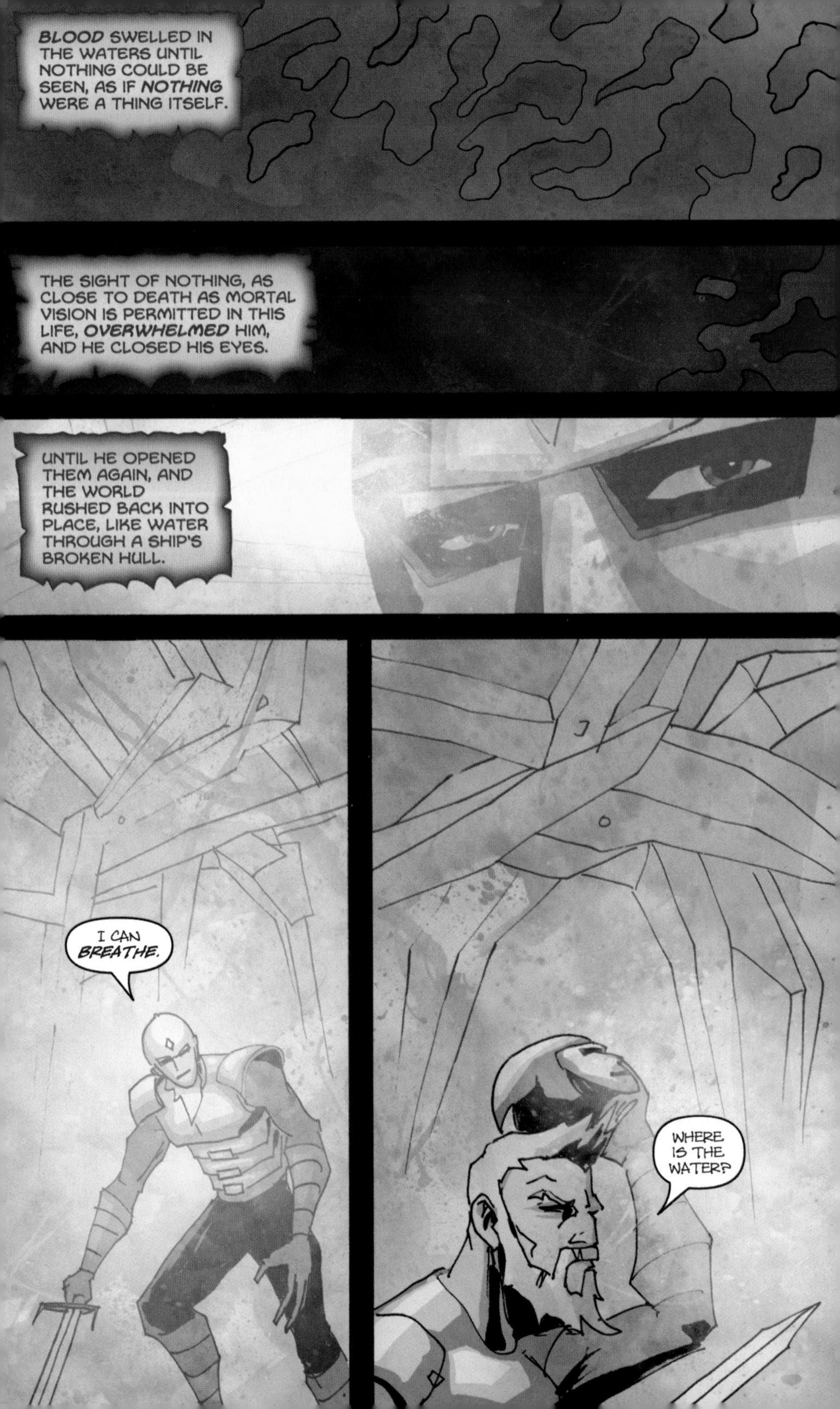
BLOOD SWELLED IN THE WATERS UNTIL NOTHING COULD BE SEEN, AS IF NOTHING WERE A THING ITSELF.
THE SIGHT OF NOTHING, AS CLOSE TO DEATH AS MORTAL VISION IS PERMITTED IN THIS LIFE, OVERWHELMED HIM, AND HE CLOSED HIS EYES.
UNTIL HE OPENED THEM AGAIN, AND THE WORLD RUSHED BACK INTO PLACE, LIKE WATER THROUGH A SHIP'S BROKEN HULL.
I CAN BREATHE.
WHERE IS THE WATER?

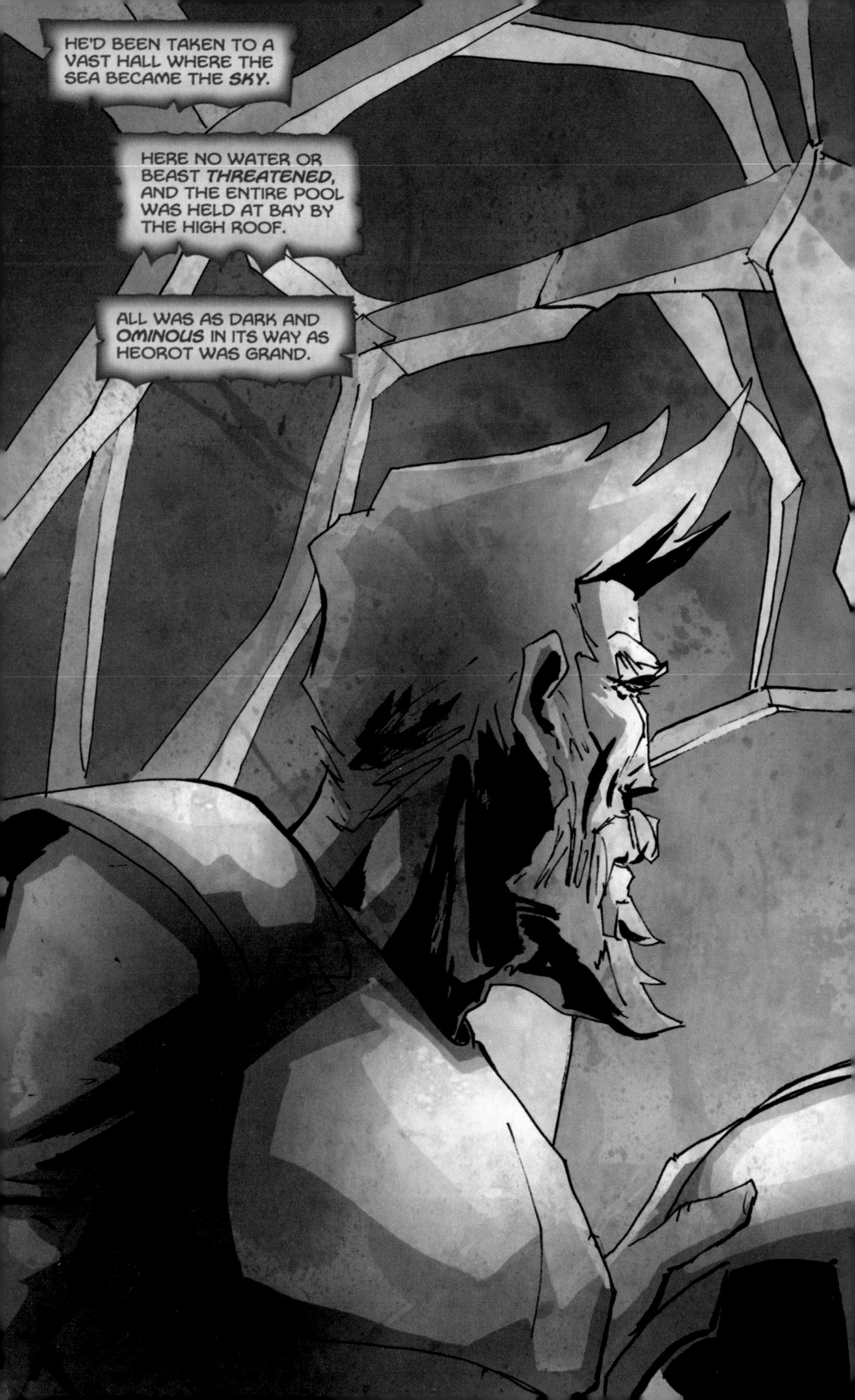
HE'D BEEN TAKEN TO A VAST HALL WHERE THE SEA BECAME THE SKY.
HERE NO WATER OR BEAST THREATENED, AND THE ENTIRE POOL WAS HELD AT BAY BY THE HIGH ROOF.
ALL WAS AS DARK AND OMINOUS IN ITS WAY AS HEOROT WAS GRAND.

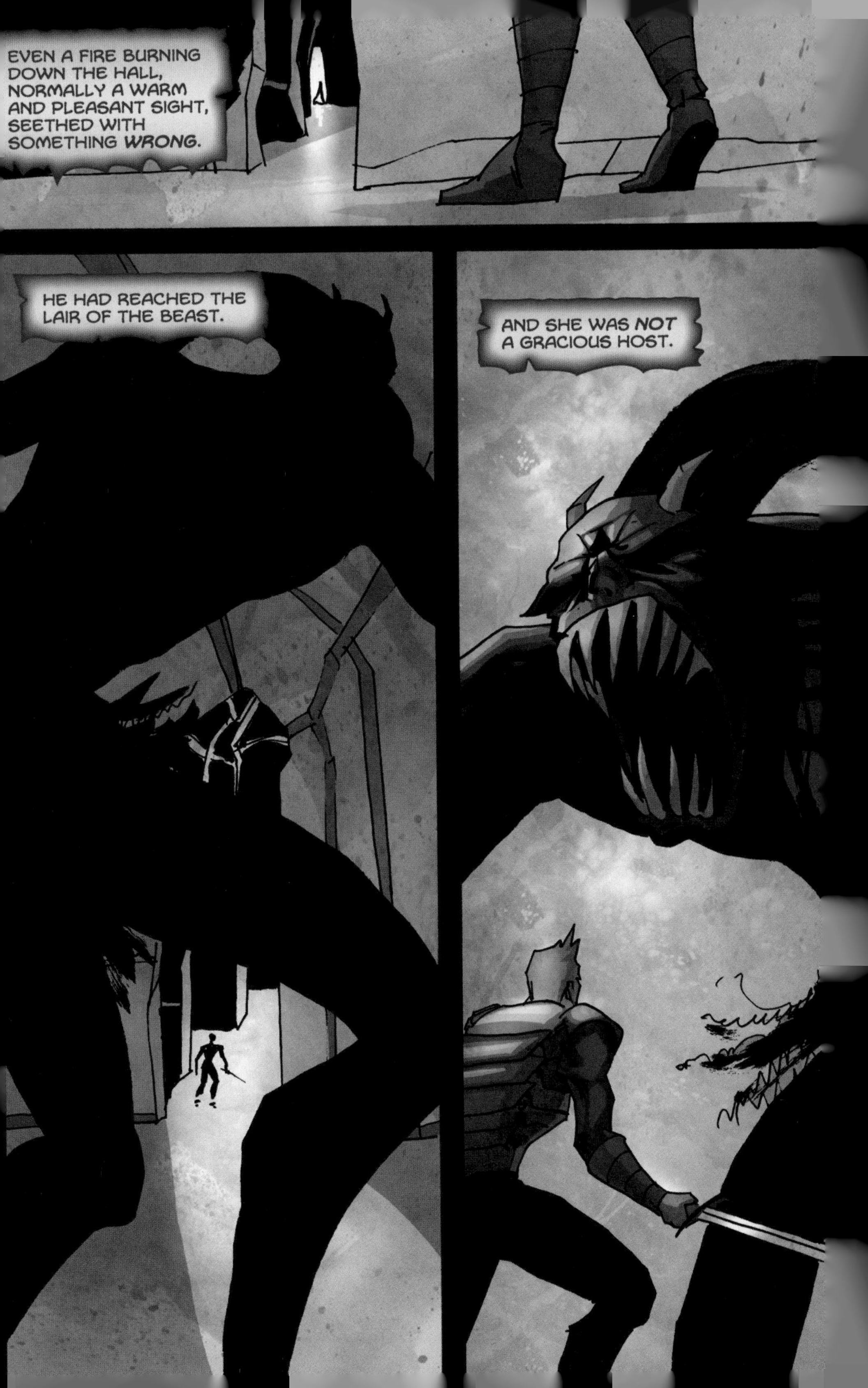
EVEN A FIRE BURNING DOWN THE HALL, NORMALLY A WARM AND PLEASANT SIGHT, SEETHED WITH SOMETHING WRONG.
HE HAD REACHED THE LAIR OF THE BEAST.
AND SHE WAS NOT A GRACIOUS HOST.

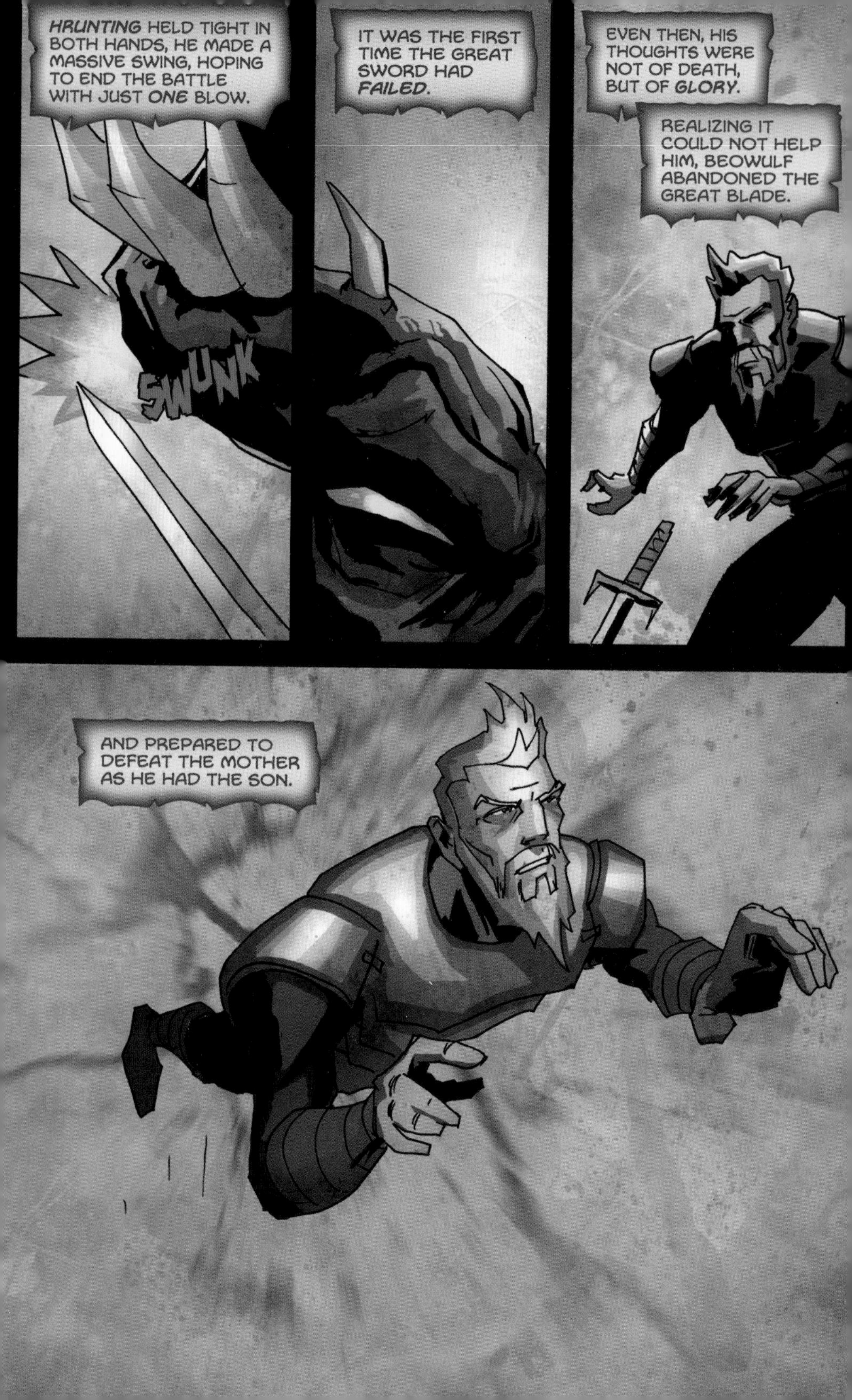
HRUNTING HELD TIGHT IN BOTH HANDS, HE MADE A MASSIVE SWING, HOPING TO END THE BATTLE WITH JUST ONE BLOW.
SWUNK
IT WAS THE FIRST TIME THE GREAT SWORD HAD FAILED.
EVEN THEN, HIS THOUGHTS WERE NOT OF DEATH, BUT OF GLORY.
REALIZING IT COULD NOT HELP HIM, BEOWULF ABANDONED THE GREAT BLADE.
AND PREPARED TO DEFEAT THE MOTHER AS HE HAD THE SON.

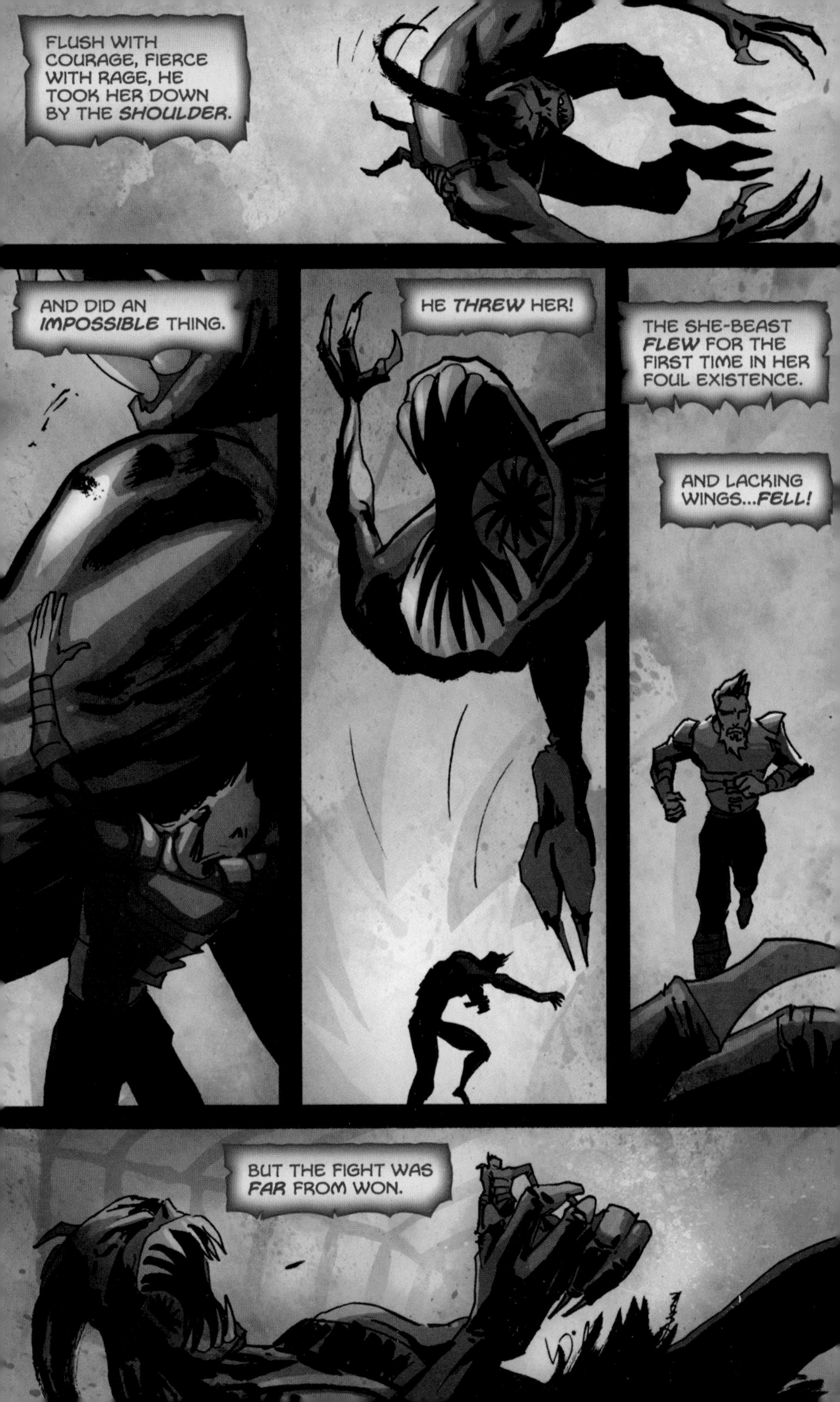
FLUSH WITH COURAGE, FIERCE WITH RAGE, HE TOOK HER DOWN BY THE *SHOULDER*.
AND DID AN *IMPOSSIBLE* THING.
HE *THREW* HER!
THE SHE-BEAST *FLEW* FOR THE FIRST TIME IN HER FOUL EXISTENCE.
AND LACKING WINGS...*FELL!*
BUT THE FIGHT WAS *FAR* FROM WON.

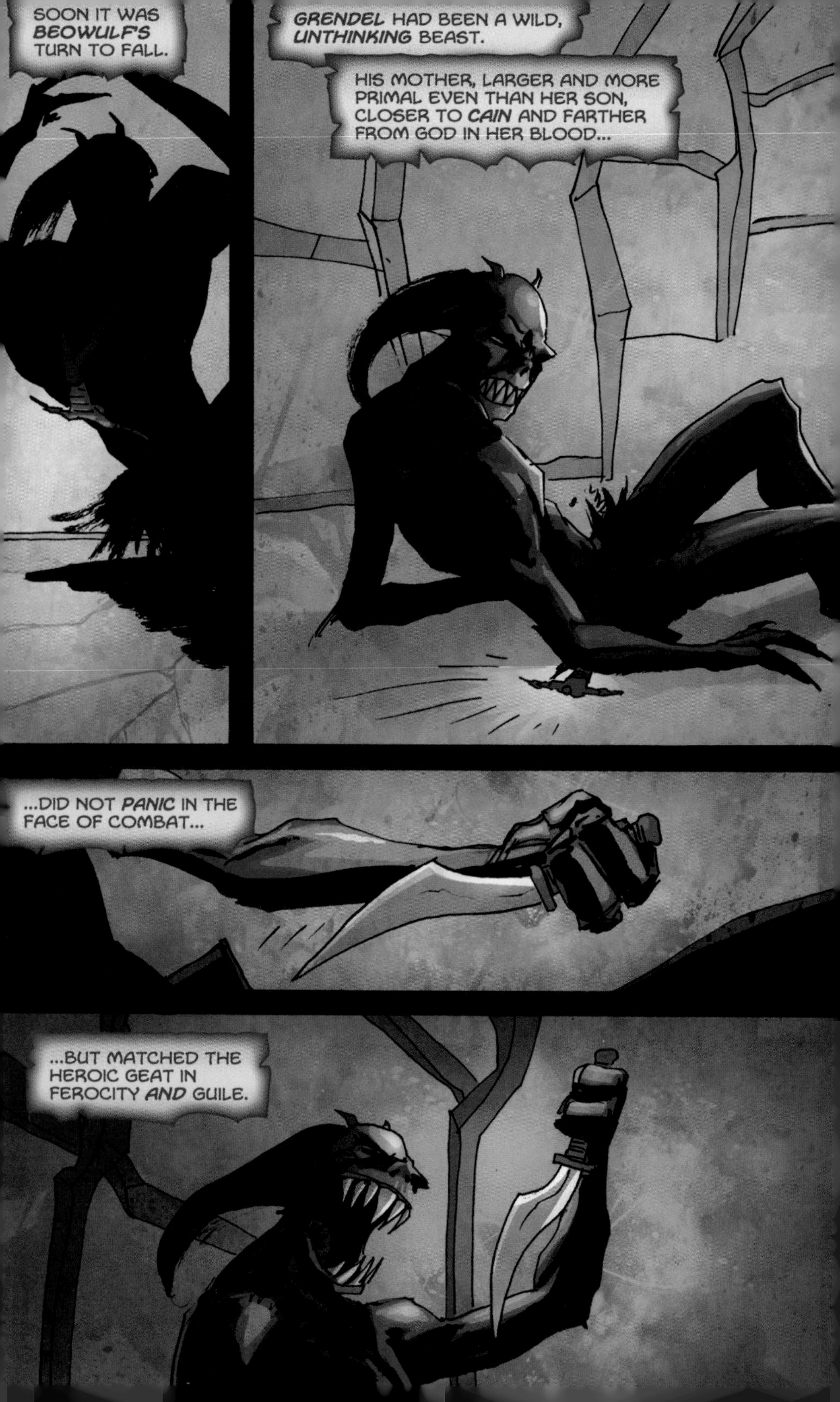
SOON IT WAS BEOWULF'S TURN TO FALL.
GRENDEL HAD BEEN A WILD, UNTHINKING BEAST.
HIS MOTHER, LARGER AND MORE PRIMAL EVEN THAN HER SON, CLOSER TO CAIN AND FARTHER FROM GOD IN HER BLOOD...
...DID NOT PANIC IN THE FACE OF COMBAT...
...BUT MATCHED THE HEROIC GEAT IN FEROCITY AND GUILE.

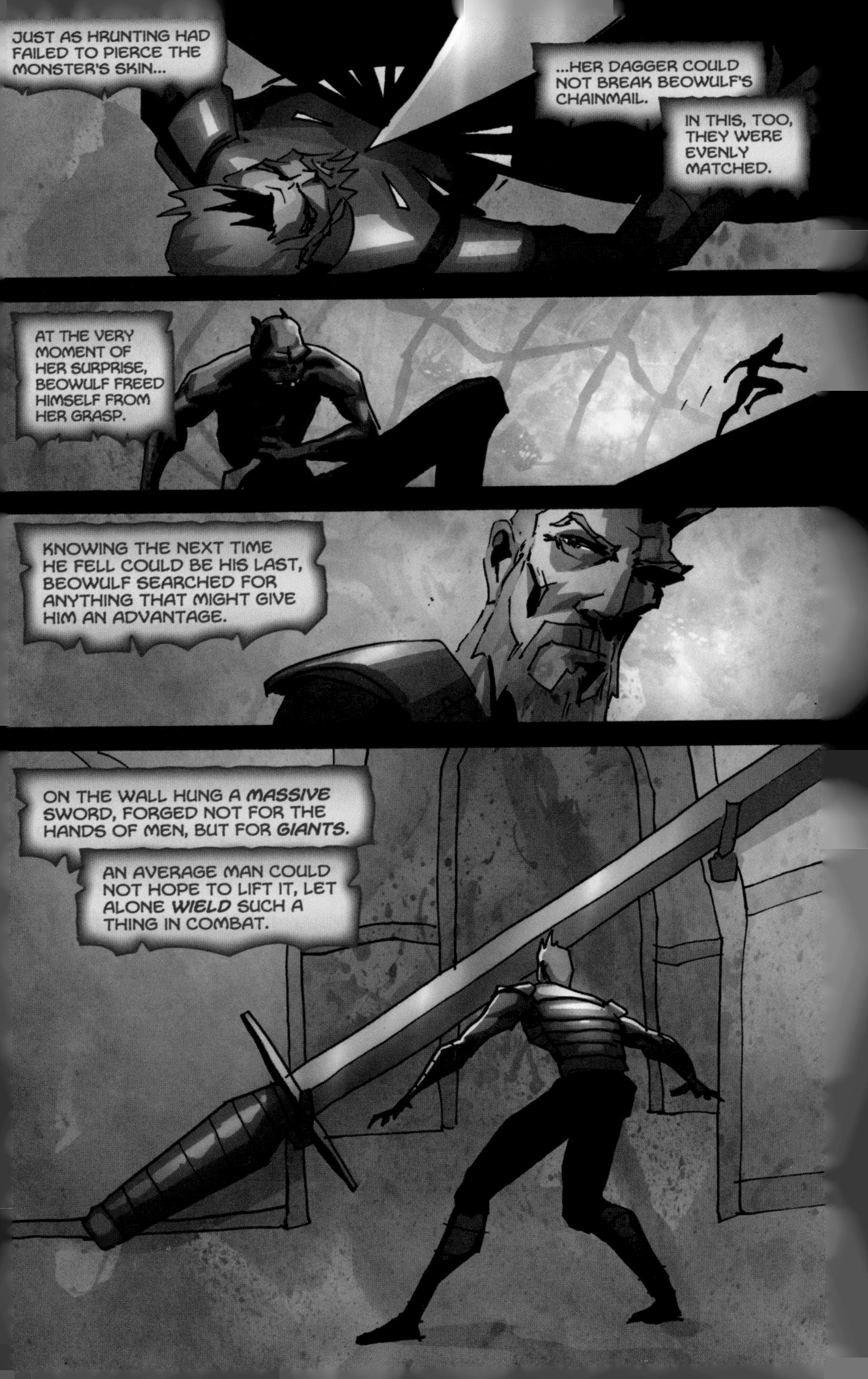
JUST AS HRUNTING HAD FAILED TO PIERCE THE MONSTER'S SKIN...
...HER DAGGER COULD NOT BREAK BEOWULF'S CHAINMAIL.
IN THIS, TOO, THEY WERE EVENLY MATCHED.
AT THE VERY MOMENT OF HER SURPRISE, BEOWULF FREED HIMSELF FROM HER GRASP.
KNOWING THE NEXT TIME HE FELL COULD BE HIS LAST, BEOWULF SEARCHED FOR ANYTHING THAT MIGHT GIVE HIM AN ADVANTAGE.
ON THE WALL HUNG A *MASSIVE* SWORD, FORGED NOT FOR THE HANDS OF MEN, BUT FOR *GIANTS*.
AN AVERAGE MAN COULD NOT HOPE TO LIFT IT, LET ALONE *WIELD* SUCH A THING IN COMBAT.

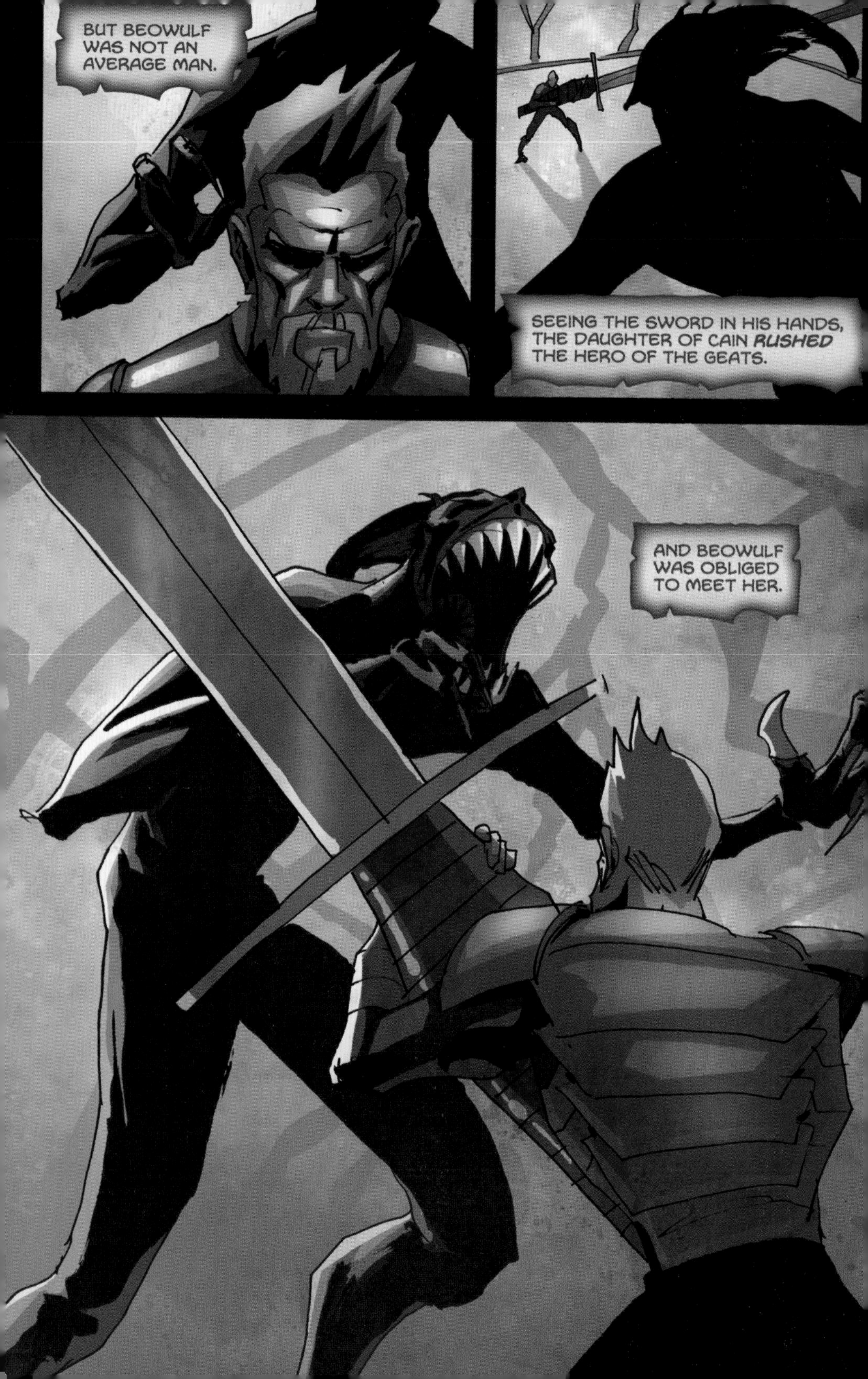
BUT BEOWULF WAS NOT AN AVERAGE MAN.
SEEING THE SWORD IN HIS HANDS, THE DAUGHTER OF CAIN *RUSHED* THE HERO OF THE GEATS.
AND BEOWULF WAS OBLIGED TO MEET HER.

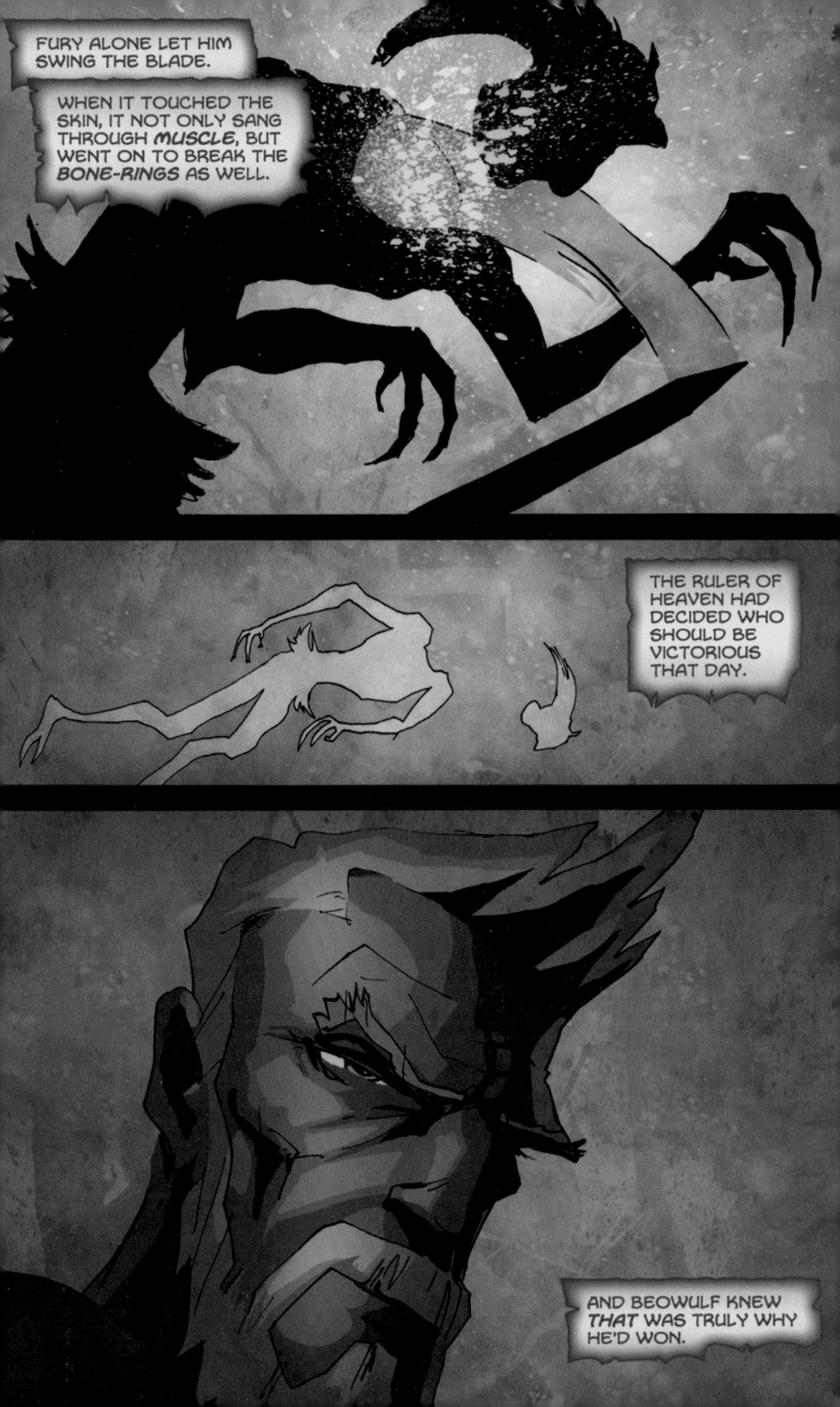
FURY ALONE LET HIM SWING THE BLADE.
WHEN IT TOUCHED THE SKIN, IT NOT ONLY SANG THROUGH *MUSCLE*, BUT WENT ON TO BREAK THE *BONE-RINGS* AS WELL.
THE RULER OF HEAVEN HAD DECIDED WHO SHOULD BE VICTORIOUS THAT DAY.
AND BEOWULF KNEW *THAT* WAS TRULY WHY HE'D WON.

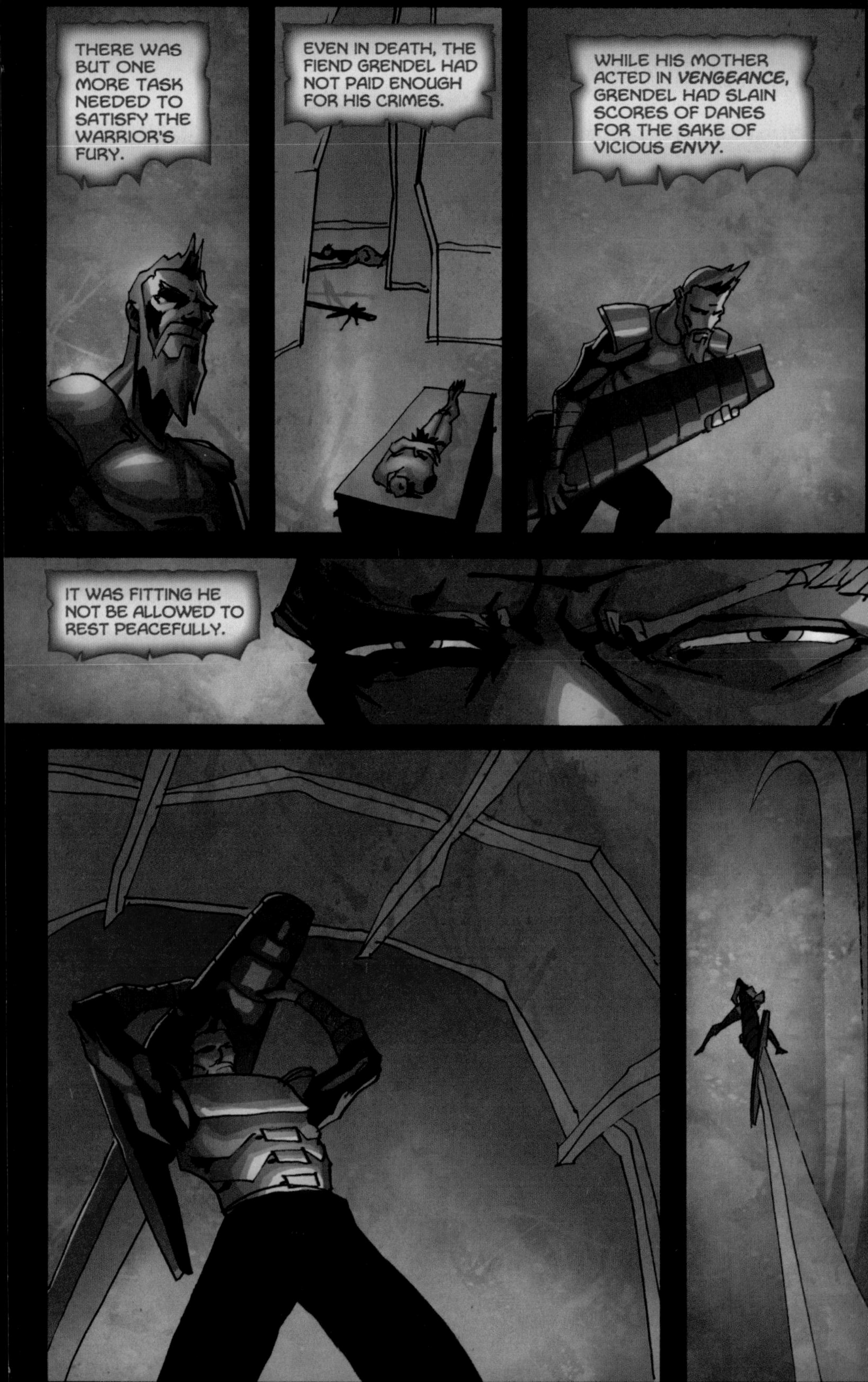
THERE WAS BUT ONE MORE TASK NEEDED TO SATISFY THE WARRIOR'S FURY.
EVEN IN DEATH, THE FIEND GRENDEL HAD NOT PAID ENOUGH FOR HIS CRIMES.
WHILE HIS MOTHER ACTED IN VENGEANCE, GRENDEL HAD SLAIN SCORES OF DANES FOR THE SAKE OF VICIOUS ENVY.
IT WAS FITTING HE NOT BE ALLOWED TO REST PEACEFULLY.

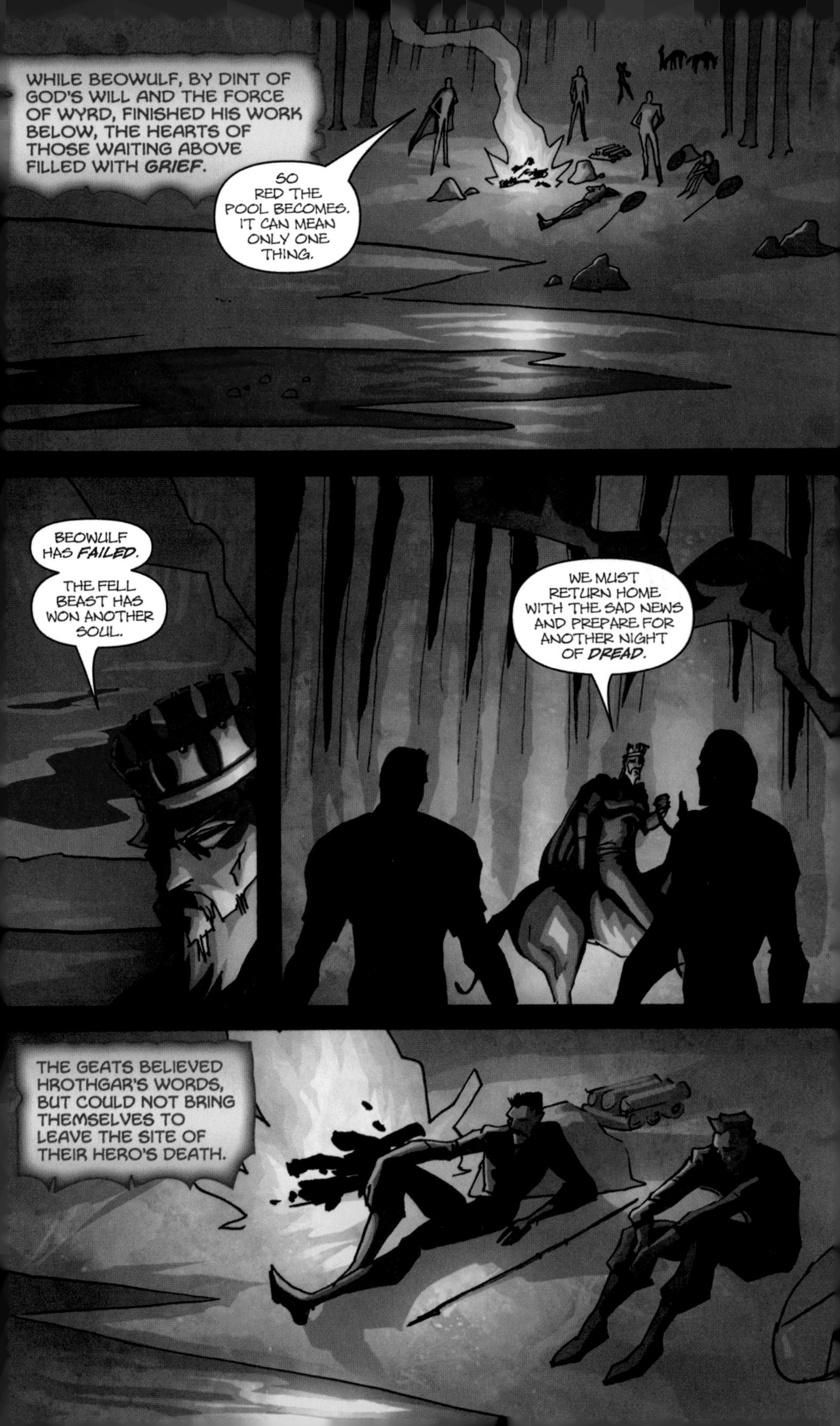

WHILE BEOWULF, BY DINT OF GOD'S WILL AND THE FORCE OF WYRD, FINISHED HIS WORK BELOW, THE HEARTS OF THOSE WAITING ABOVE FILLED WITH GRIEF.
SO RED THE POOL BECOMES. IT CAN MEAN ONLY ONE THING.
BEOWULF HAS FAILED.
THE FELL BEAST HAS WON ANOTHER SOUL.
WE MUST RETURN HOME WITH THE SAD NEWS AND PREPARE FOR ANOTHER NIGHT OF DREAD.
THE GEATS BELIEVED HROTHGAR'S WORDS, BUT COULD NOT BRING THEMSELVES TO LEAVE THE SITE OF THEIR HERO'S DEATH.

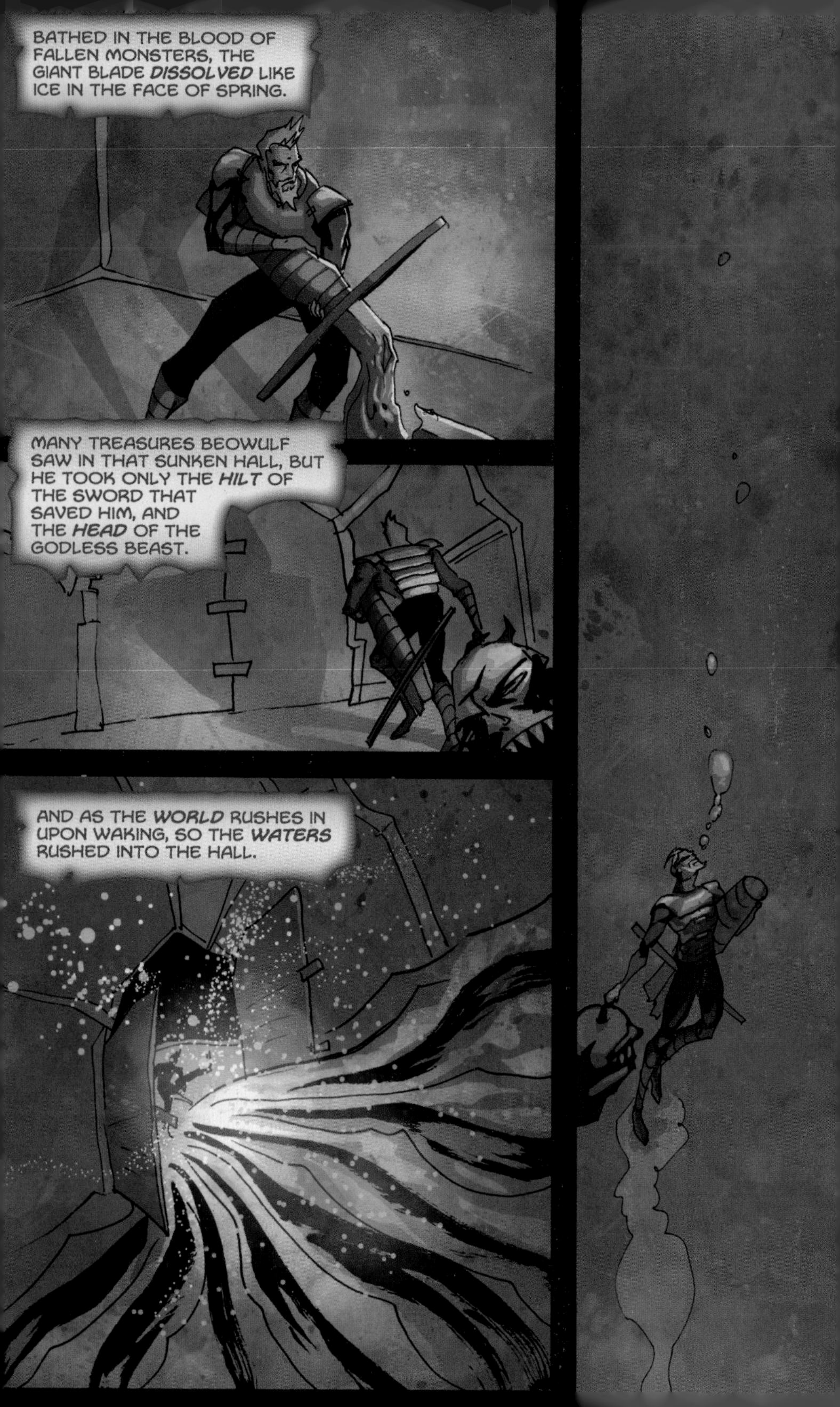
BATHED IN THE BLOOD OF FALLEN MONSTERS, THE GIANT BLADE DISSOLVED LIKE ICE IN THE FACE OF SPRING.
MANY TREASURES BEOWULF SAW IN THAT SUNKEN HALL, BUT HE TOOK ONLY THE HILT OF THE SWORD THAT SAVED HIM, AND THE HEAD OF THE GODLESS BEAST.
AND AS THE WORLD RUSHES IN UPON WAKING, SO THE WATERS RUSHED INTO THE HALL.

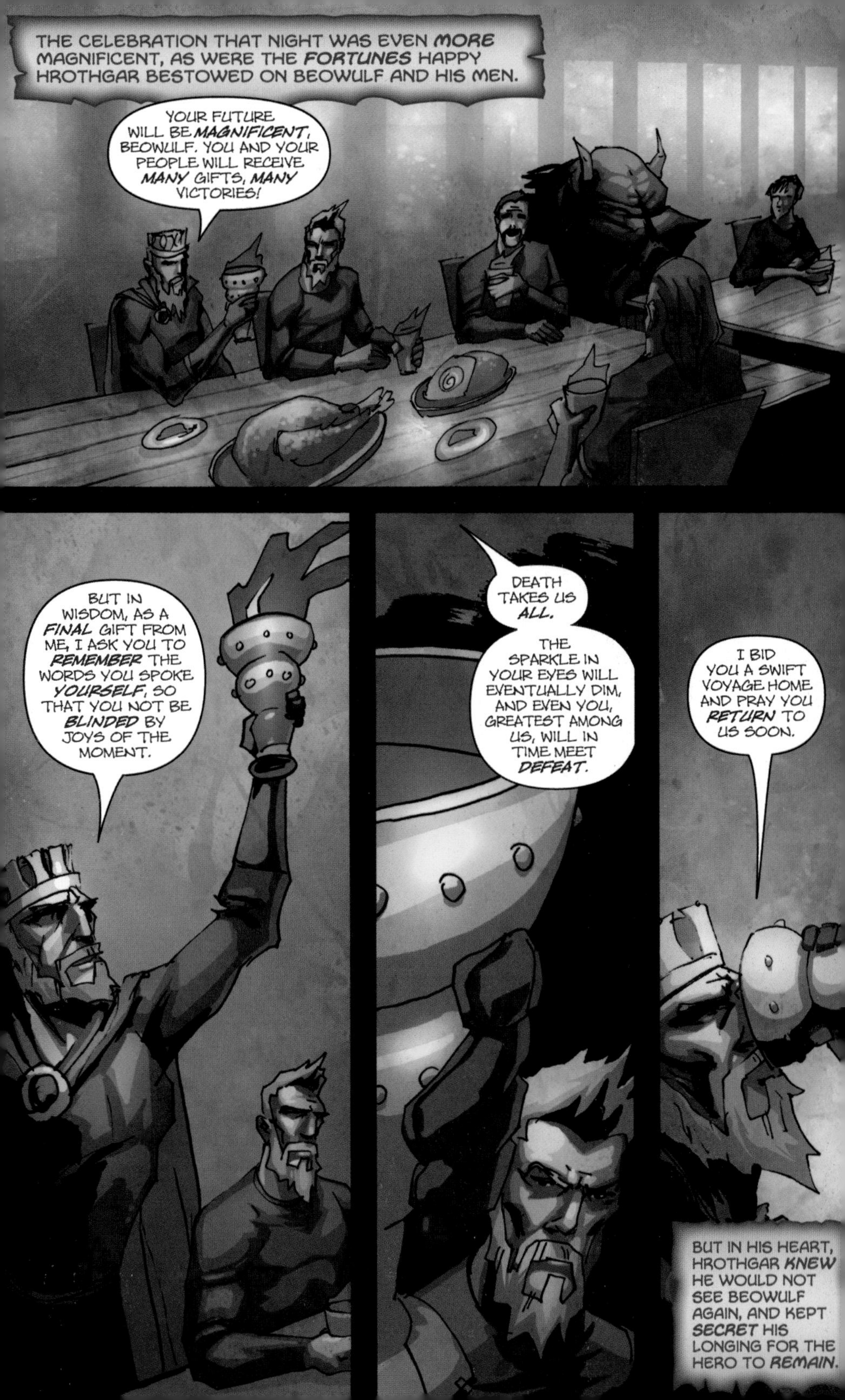
THE CELEBRATION THAT NIGHT WAS EVEN MORE MAGNIFICENT, AS WERE THE FORTUNES HAPPY HROTHGAR BESTOWED ON BEOWULF AND HIS MEN.
YOUR FUTURE WILL BE MAGNIFICENT, BEOWULF. YOU AND YOUR PEOPLE WILL RECEIVE MANY GIFTS, MANY VICTORIES!
BUT IN WISDOM, AS A FINAL GIFT FROM ME, I ASK YOU TO REMEMBER THE WORDS YOU SPOKE YOURSELF, SO THAT YOU NOT BE BLINDED BY JOYS OF THE MOMENT.
DEATH TAKES US ALL.
THE SPARKLE IN YOUR EYES WILL EVENTUALLY DIM, AND EVEN YOU, GREATEST AMONG US, WILL IN TIME MEET DEFEAT.
I BID YOU A SWIFT VOYAGE HOME AND PRAY YOU RETURN TO US SOON.
BUT IN HIS HEART, HROTHGAR KNEW HE WOULD NOT SEE BEOWULF AGAIN, AND KEPT SECRET HIS LONGING FOR THE HERO TO REMAIN.

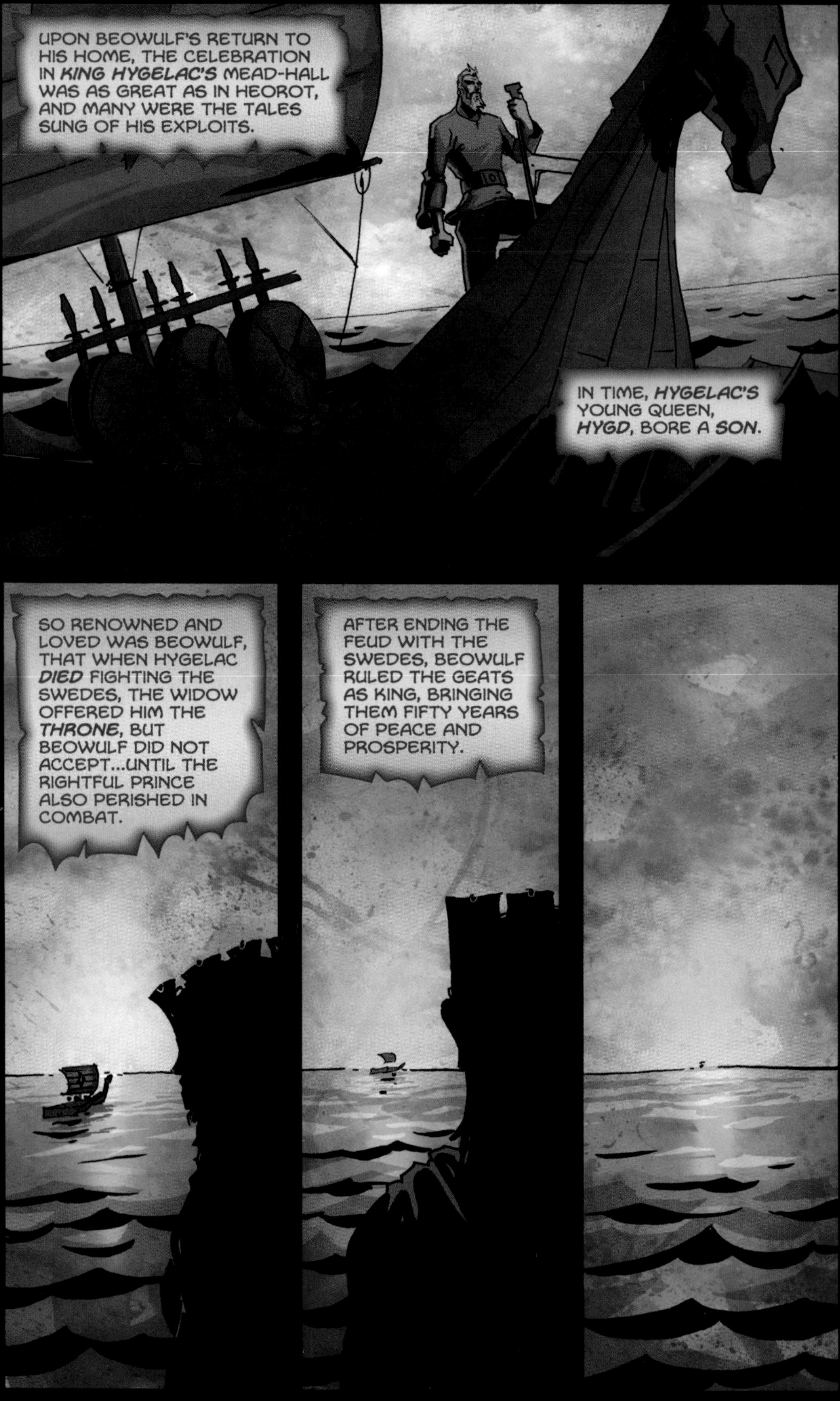
UPON BEOWULF'S RETURN TO HIS HOME, THE CELEBRATION IN *KING HYGELAC'S* MEAD-HALL WAS AS GREAT AS IN HEOROT, AND MANY WERE THE TALES SUNG OF HIS EXPLOITS.
IN TIME, *HYGELAC'S* YOUNG QUEEN, *HYGD*, BORE A *SON*.
SO RENOWNED AND LOVED WAS BEOWULF, THAT WHEN HYGELAC *DIED* FIGHTING THE SWEDES, THE WIDOW OFFERED HIM THE *THRONE*, BUT BEOWULF DID NOT ACCEPT...UNTIL THE RIGHTFUL PRINCE ALSO PERISHED IN COMBAT.
AFTER ENDING THE FEUD WITH THE SWEDES, BEOWULF RULED THE GEATS AS KING, BRINGING THEM FIFTY YEARS OF PEACE AND PROSPERITY.

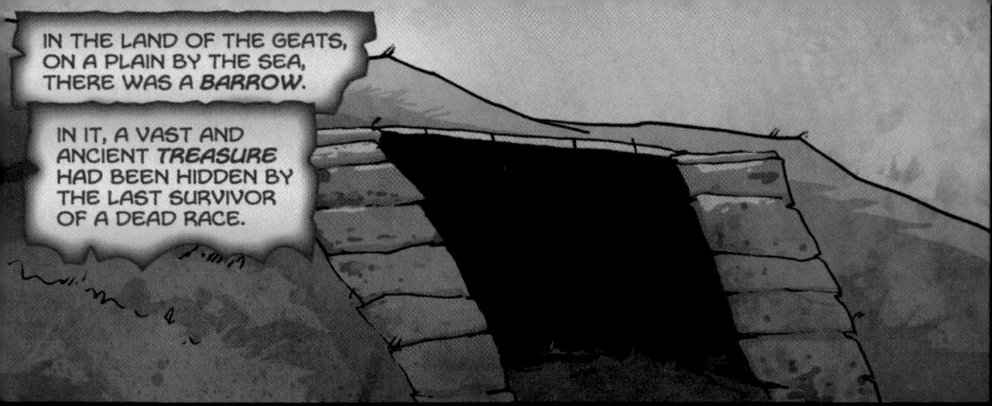
IN THE LAND OF THE GEATS, ON A PLAIN BY THE SEA, THERE WAS A *BARROW*.
IN IT, A VAST AND ANCIENT *TREASURE* HAD BEEN HIDDEN BY THE LAST SURVIVOR OF A DEAD RACE.

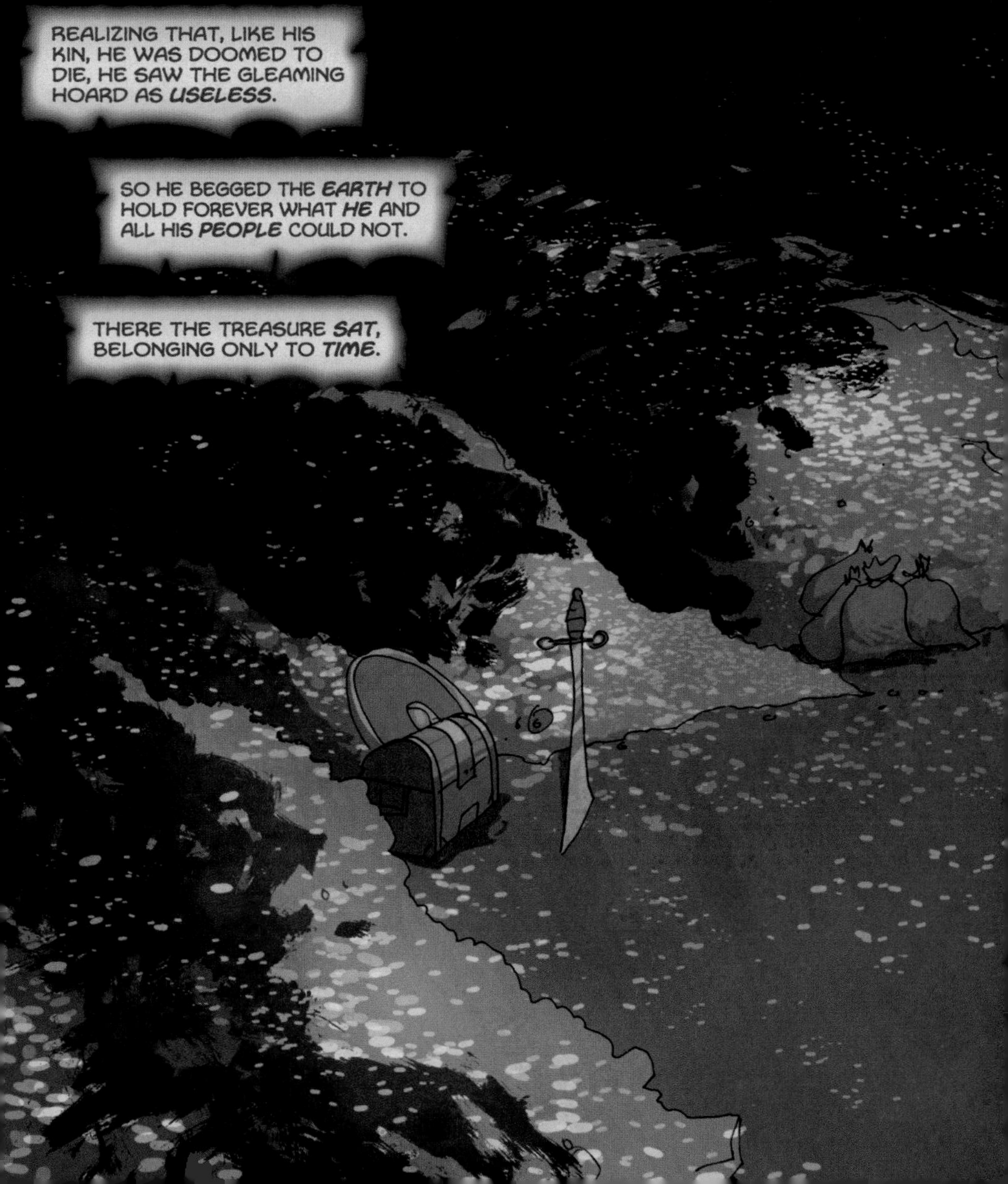
REALIZING THAT, LIKE HIS KIN, HE WAS DOOMED TO DIE, HE SAW THE GLEAMING HOARD AS *USELESS*.
SO HE BEGGED THE *EARTH* TO HOLD FOREVER WHAT *HE* AND ALL HIS *PEOPLE* COULD NOT.
THERE THE TREASURE *SAT*, BELONGING ONLY TO *TIME*.

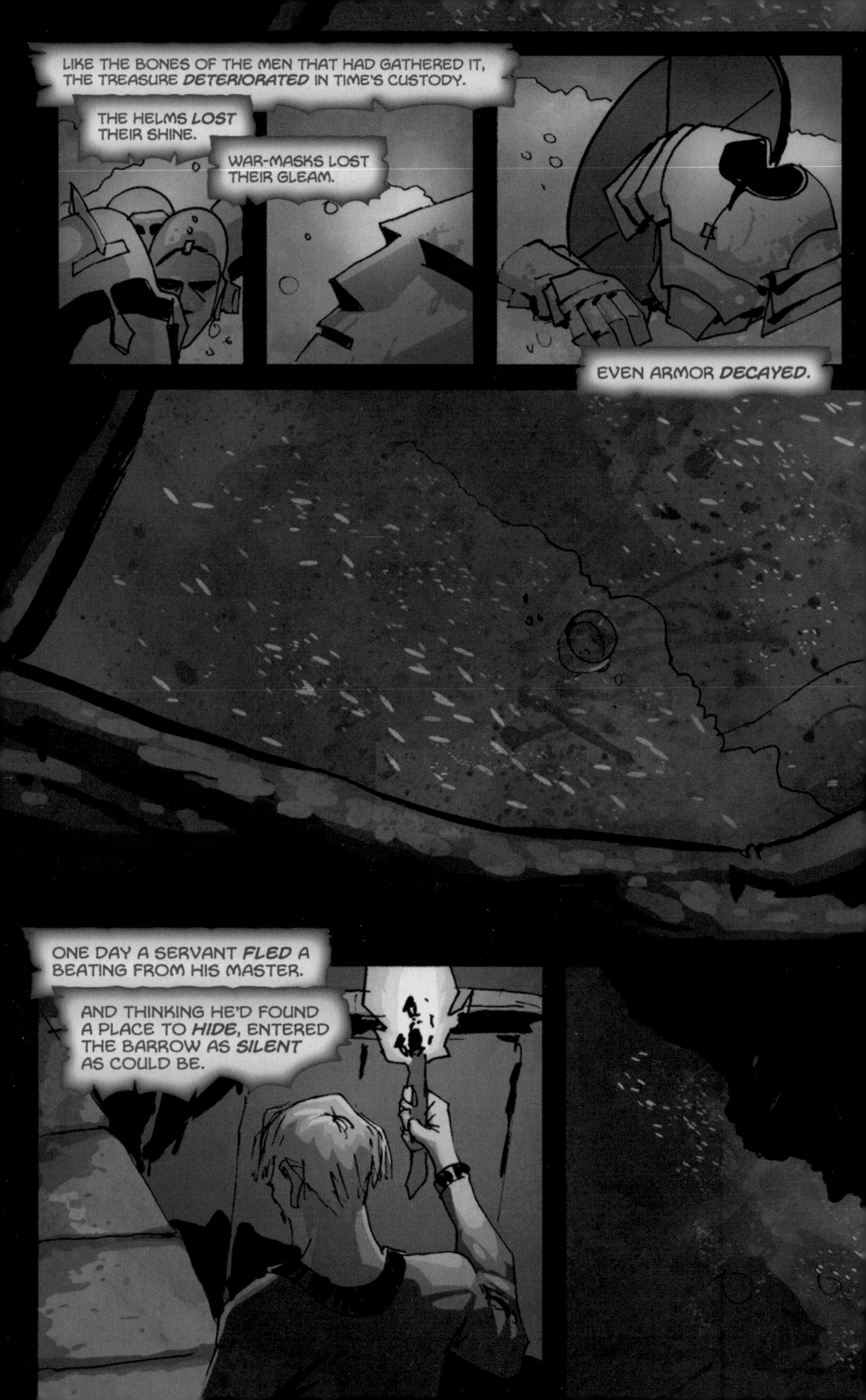
LIKE THE BONES OF THE MEN THAT HAD GATHERED IT, THE TREASURE DETERIORATED IN TIME'S CUSTODY.
THE HELMS LOST THEIR SHINE.
WAR-MASKS LOST THEIR GLEAM.
EVEN ARMOR DECAYED.
ONE DAY A SERVANT FLED A BEATING FROM HIS MASTER.
AND THINKING HE'D FOUND A PLACE TO HIDE, ENTERED THE BARROW AS SILENT AS COULD BE.

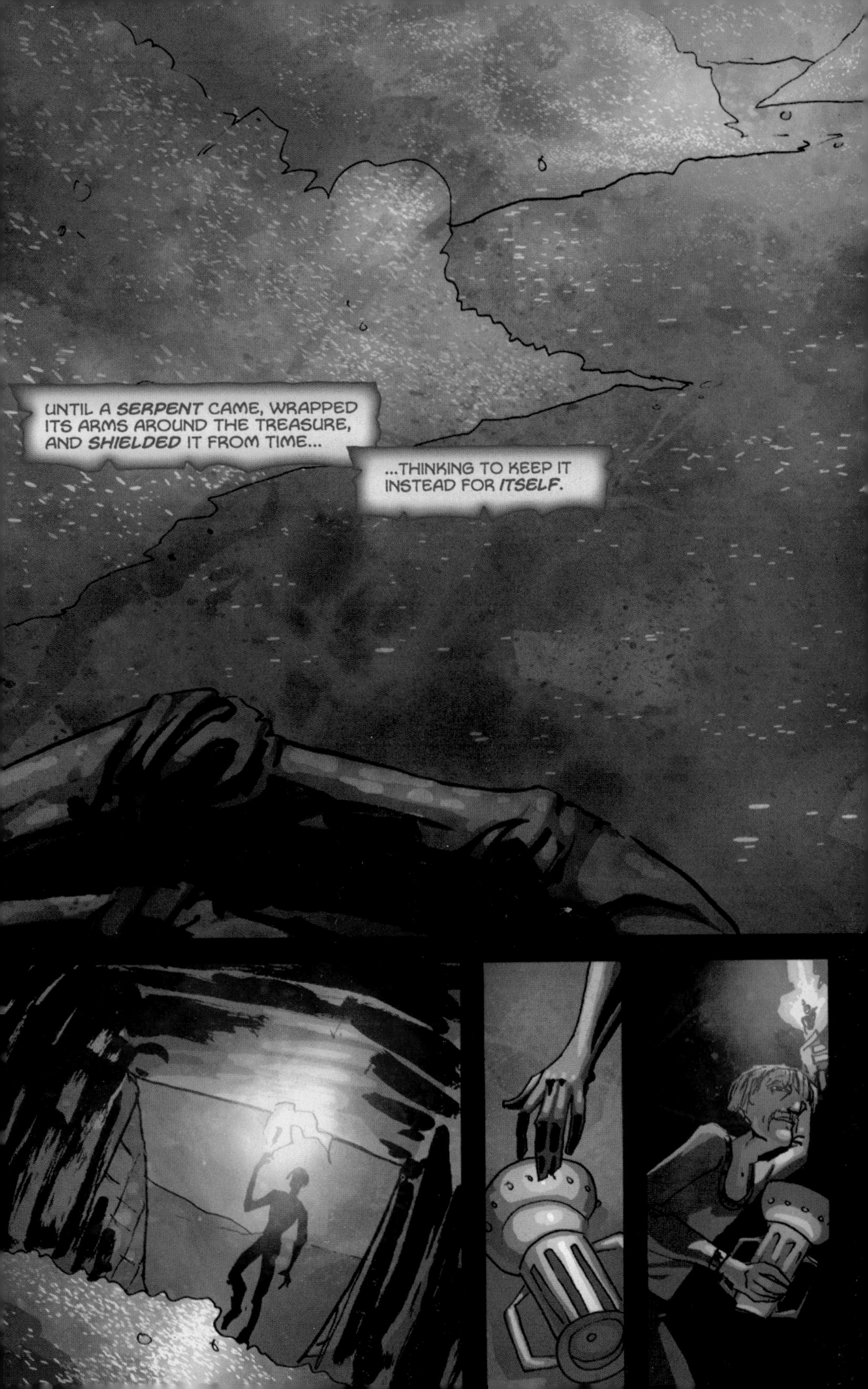
UNTIL A SERPENT CAME, WRAPPED ITS ARMS AROUND THE TREASURE, AND SHIELDED IT FROM TIME...
...THINKING TO KEEP IT INSTEAD FOR ITSELF.

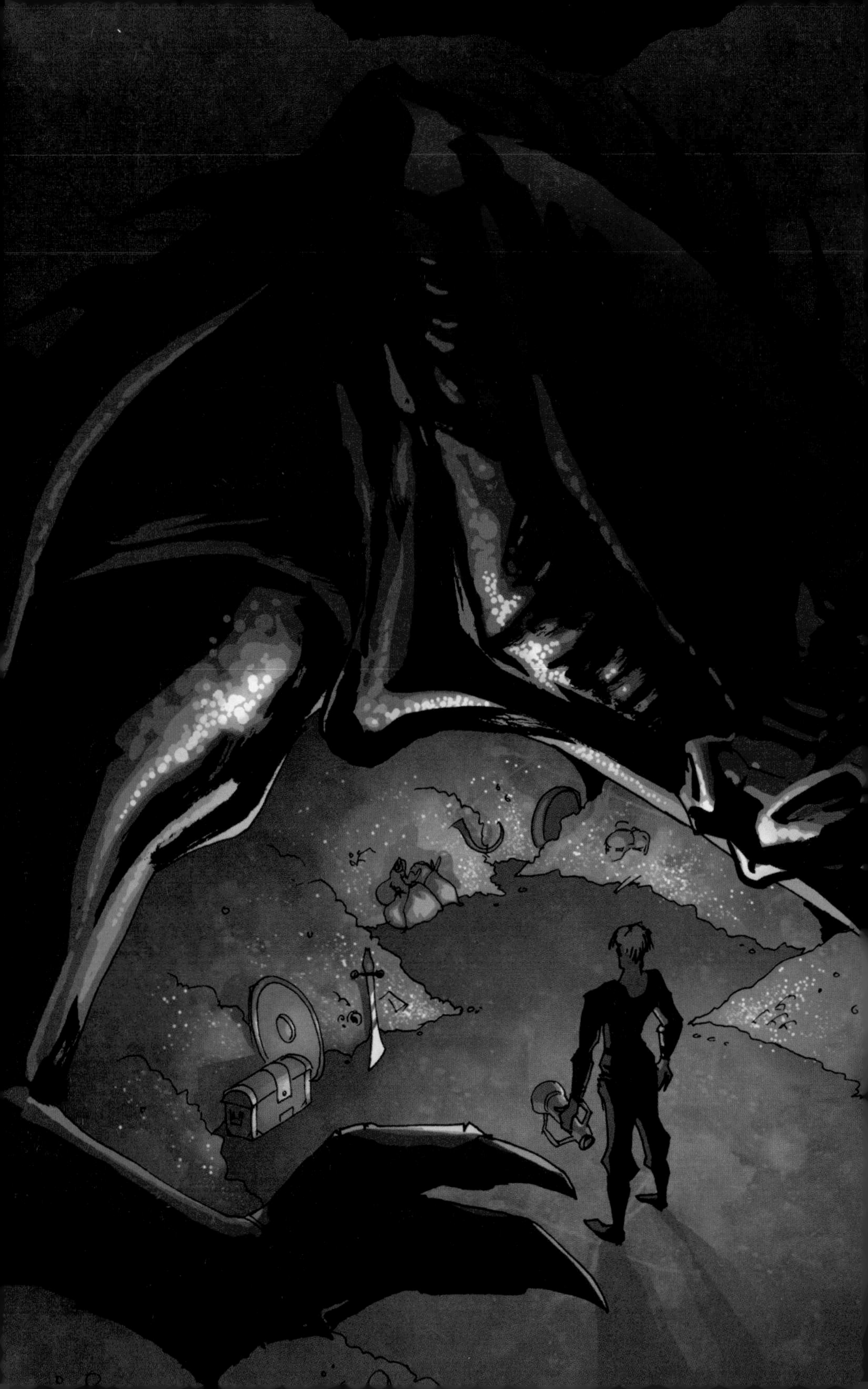

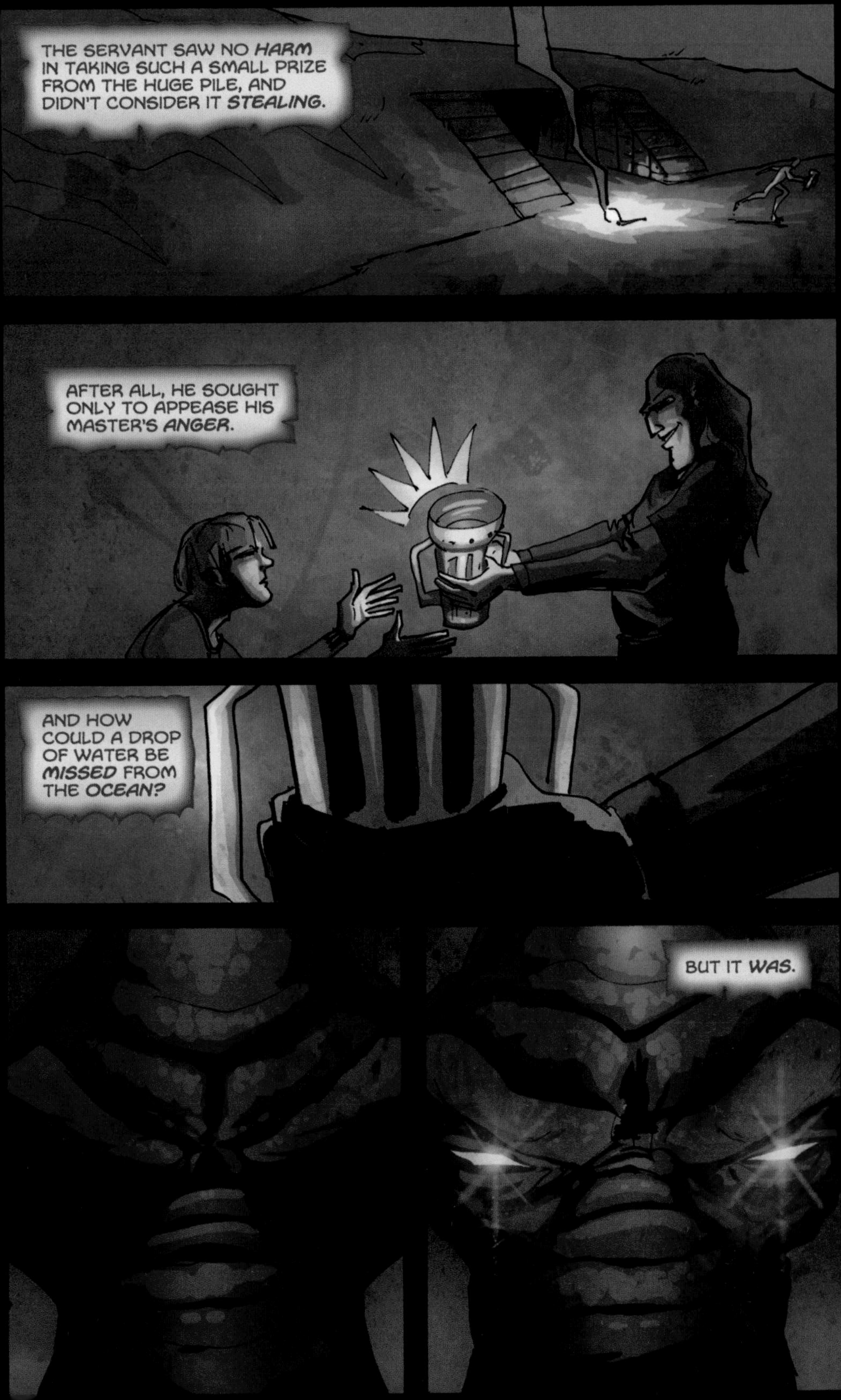
THE SERVANT SAW NO HARM IN TAKING SUCH A SMALL PRIZE FROM THE HUGE PILE, AND DIDN'T CONSIDER IT STEALING.
AFTER ALL, HE SOUGHT ONLY TO APPEASE HIS MASTER'S ANGER.
AND HOW COULD A DROP OF WATER BE MISSED FROM THE OCEAN?
BUT IT WAS.

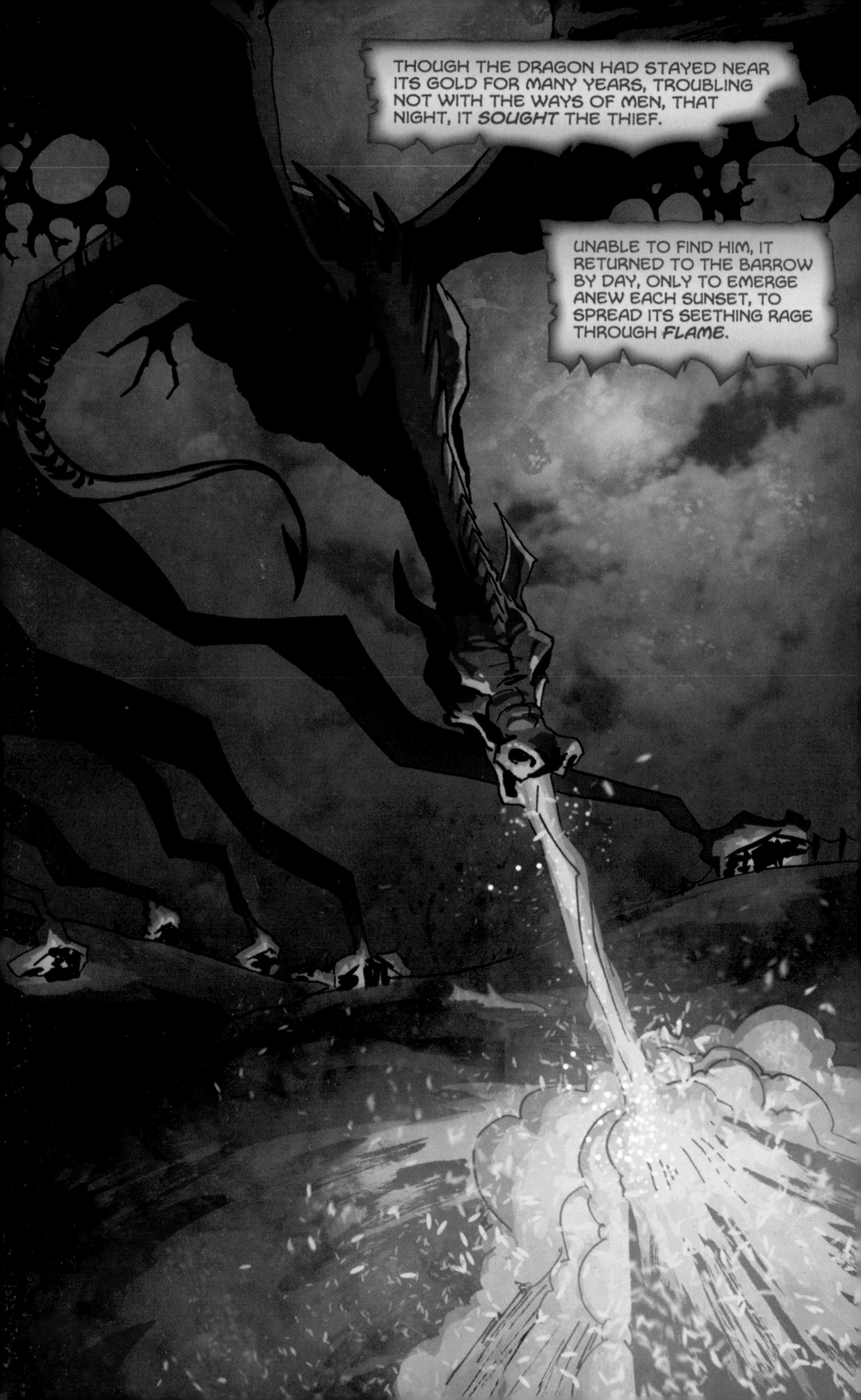
THOUGH THE DRAGON HAD STAYED NEAR ITS GOLD FOR MANY YEARS, TROUBLING NOT WITH THE WAYS OF MEN, THAT NIGHT, IT *SOUGHT* THE THIEF.
UNABLE TO FIND HIM, IT RETURNED TO THE BARROW BY DAY, ONLY TO EMERGE ANEW EACH SUNSET, TO SPREAD ITS SEETHING RAGE THROUGH *FLAME*.

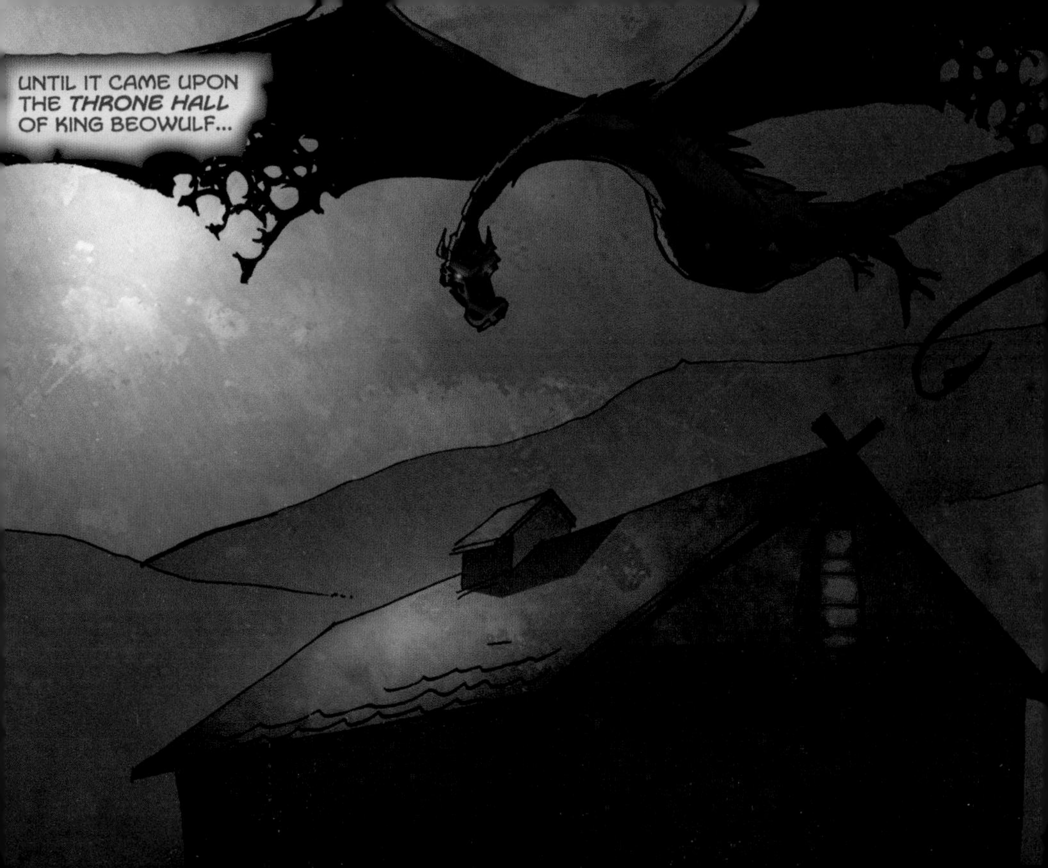
UNTIL IT CAME UPON THE *THRONE HALL* OF KING BEOWULF...

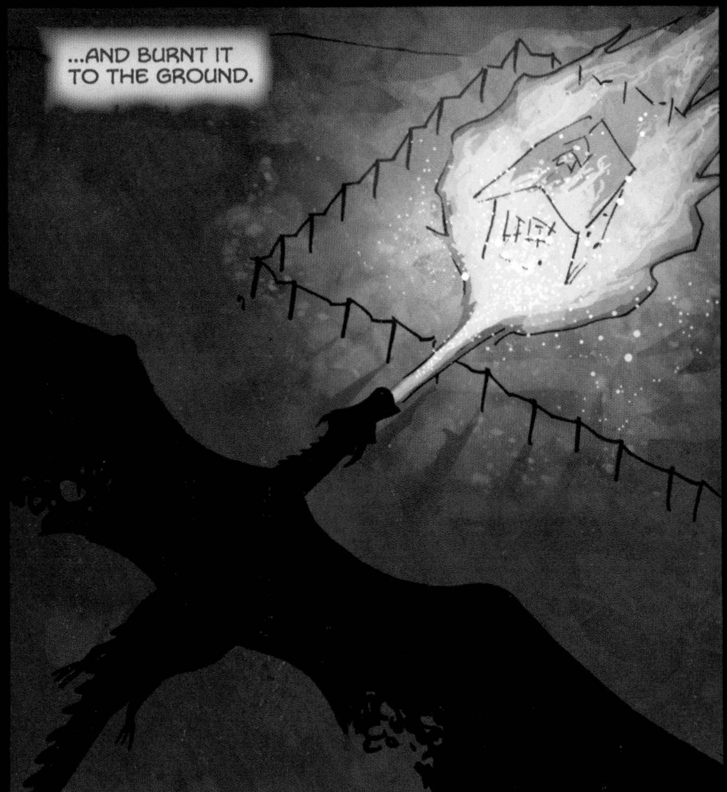
...AND BURNT IT TO THE GROUND.

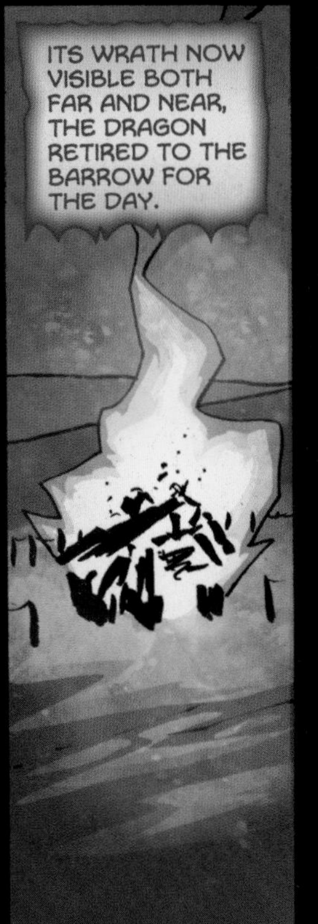
ITS WRATH NOW VISIBLE BOTH FAR AND NEAR, THE DRAGON RETIRED TO THE BARROW FOR THE DAY.

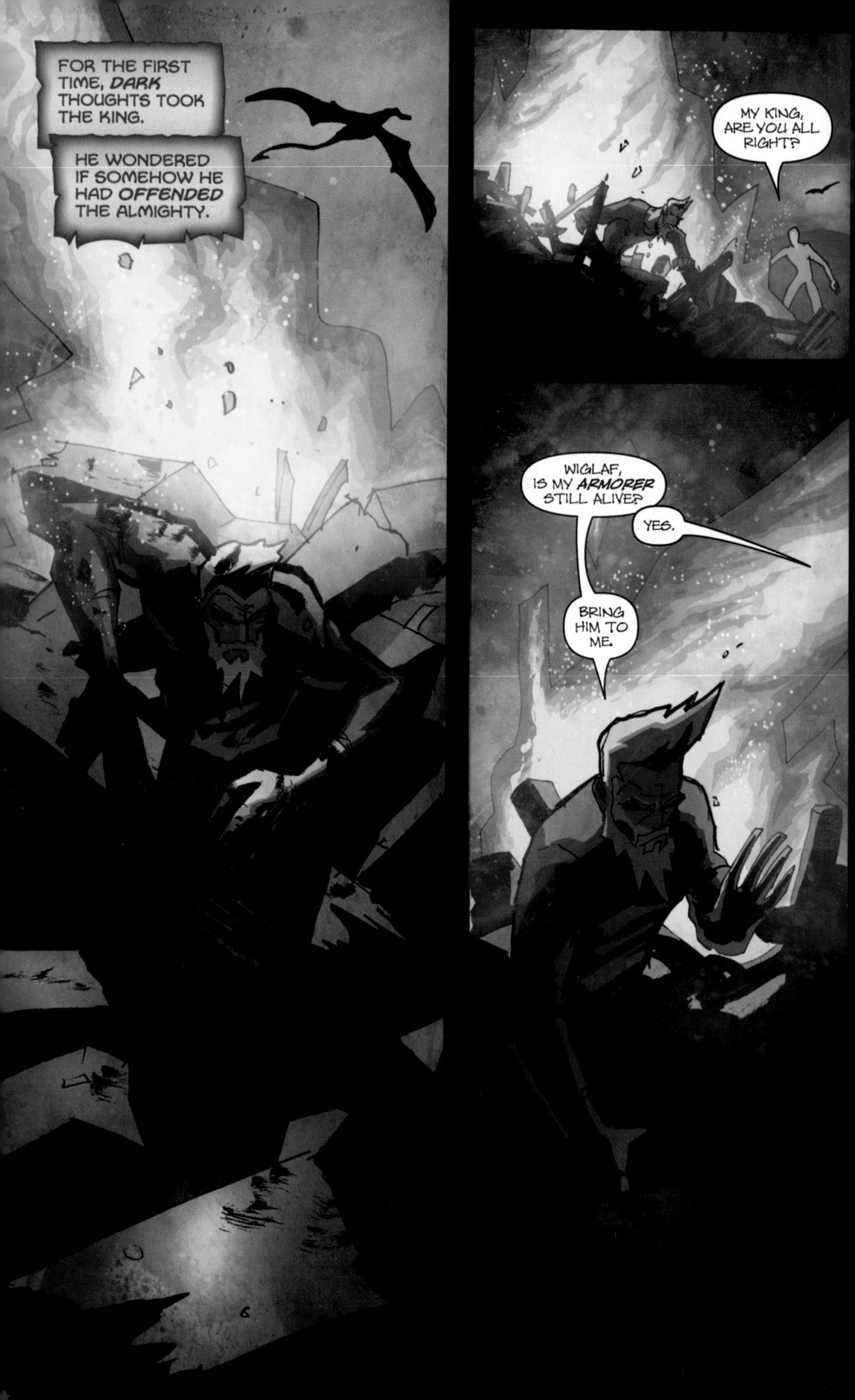
FOR THE FIRST TIME, DARK THOUGHTS TOOK THE KING.
HE WONDERED IF SOMEHOW HE HAD OFFENDED THE ALMIGHTY.
MY KING, ARE YOU ALL RIGHT?
WIGLAF, IS MY ARMORER STILL ALIVE?
YES.
BRING HIM TO ME.

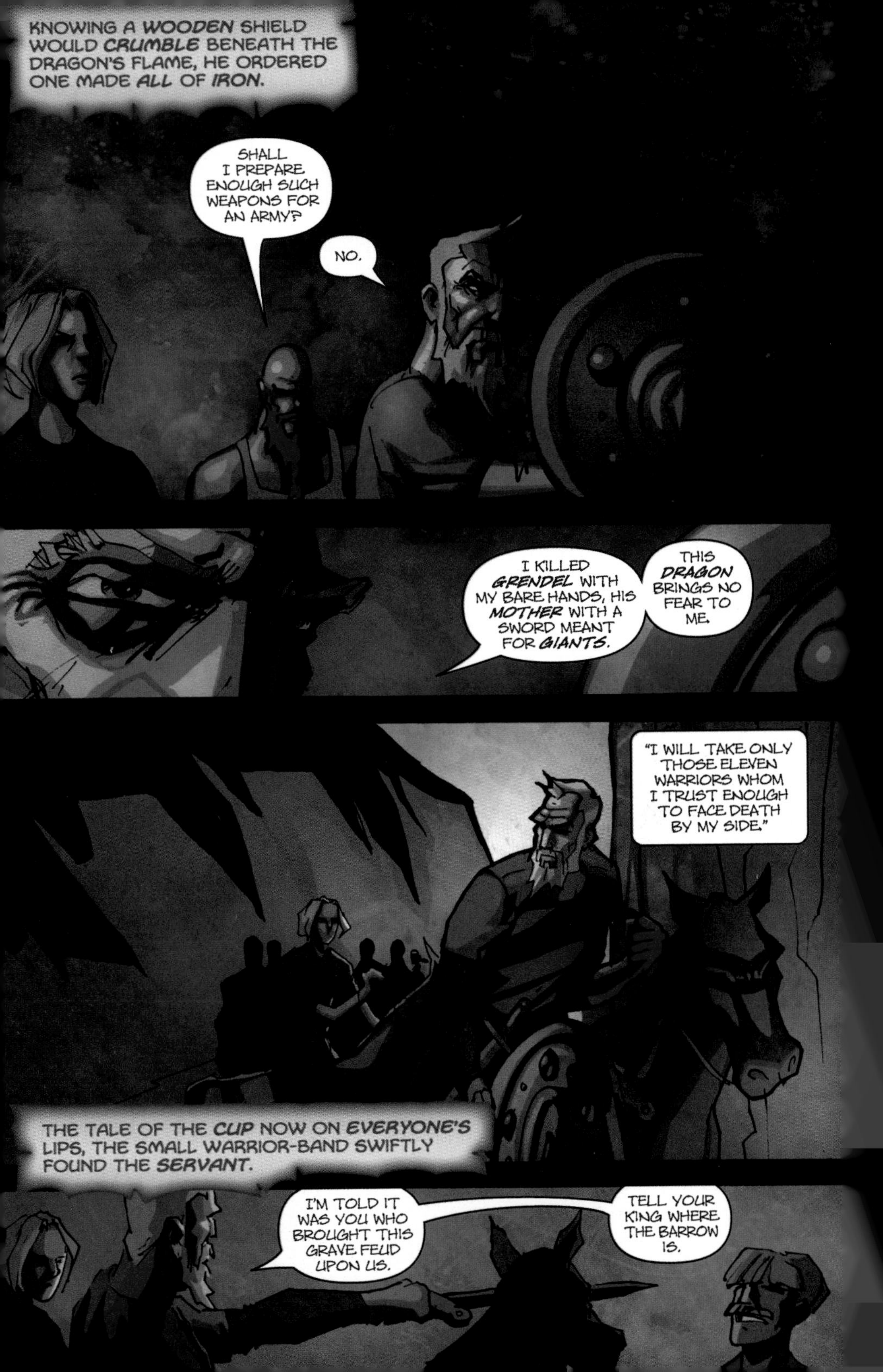
KNOWING A WOODEN SHIELD WOULD CRUMBLE BENEATH THE DRAGON'S FLAME, HE ORDERED ONE MADE ALL OF IRON.
SHALL I PREPARE ENOUGH SUCH WEAPONS FOR AN ARMY?
NO.
I KILLED GRENDEL WITH MY BARE HANDS, HIS MOTHER WITH A SWORD MEANT FOR GIANTS.
THIS DRAGON BRINGS NO FEAR TO ME.
"I WILL TAKE ONLY THOSE ELEVEN WARRIORS WHOM I TRUST ENOUGH TO FACE DEATH BY MY SIDE."
THE TALE OF THE CUP NOW ON EVERYONE'S LIPS, THE SMALL WARRIOR-BAND SWIFTLY FOUND THE SERVANT.
I'M TOLD IT WAS YOU WHO BROUGHT THIS GRAVE FEUD UPON US.
TELL YOUR KING WHERE THE BARROW IS.

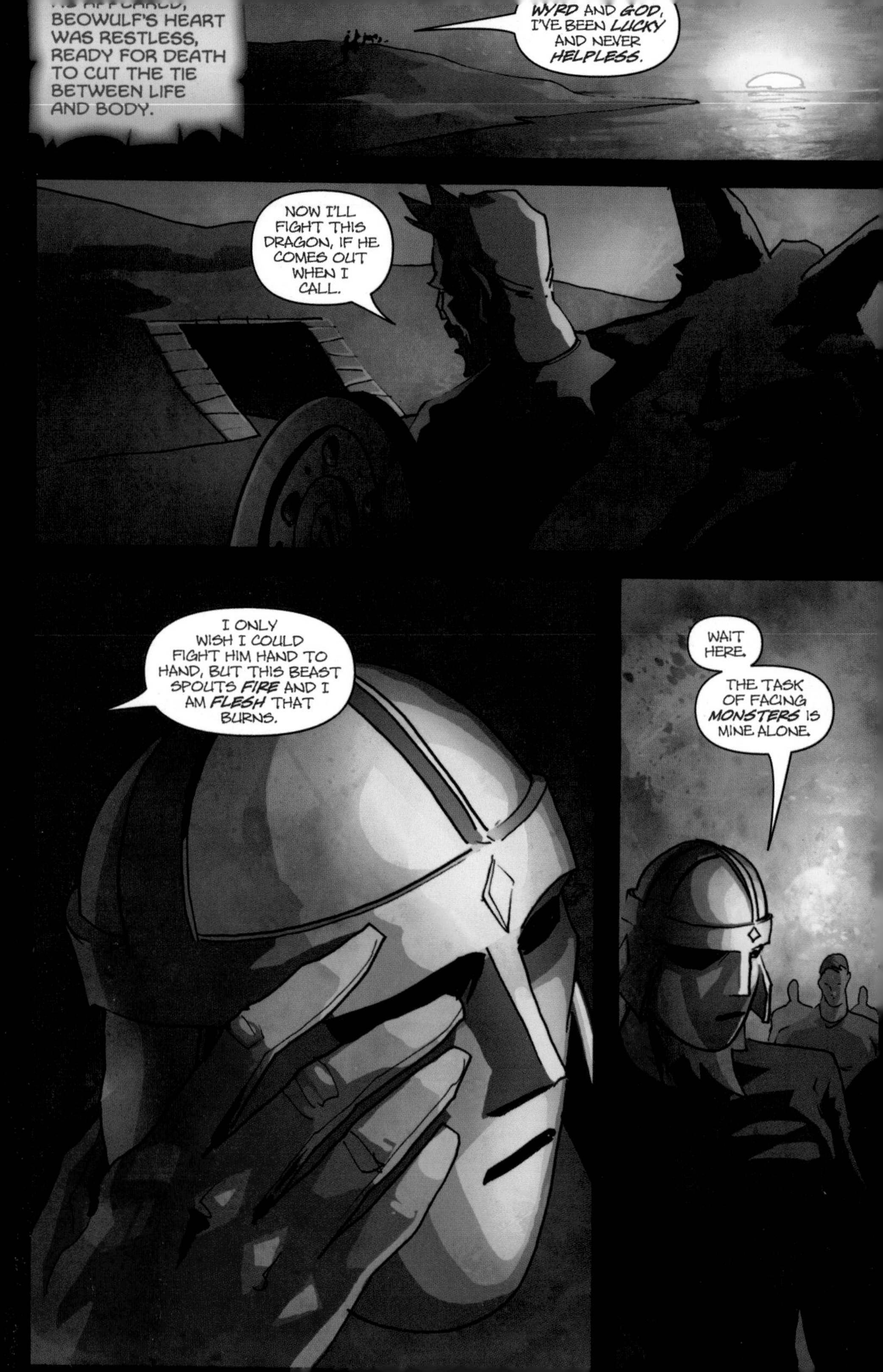
BEOWULF'S HEART WAS RESTLESS, READY FOR DEATH TO CUT THE TIE BETWEEN LIFE AND BODY.
WYRD AND GOD, I'VE BEEN LUCKY AND NEVER HELPLESS.
NOW I'LL FIGHT THIS DRAGON, IF HE COMES OUT WHEN I CALL.
I ONLY WISH I COULD FIGHT HIM HAND TO HAND, BUT THIS BEAST SPOUTS FIRE AND I AM FLESH THAT BURNS.
WAIT HERE.
THE TASK OF FACING MONSTERS IS MINE ALONE.

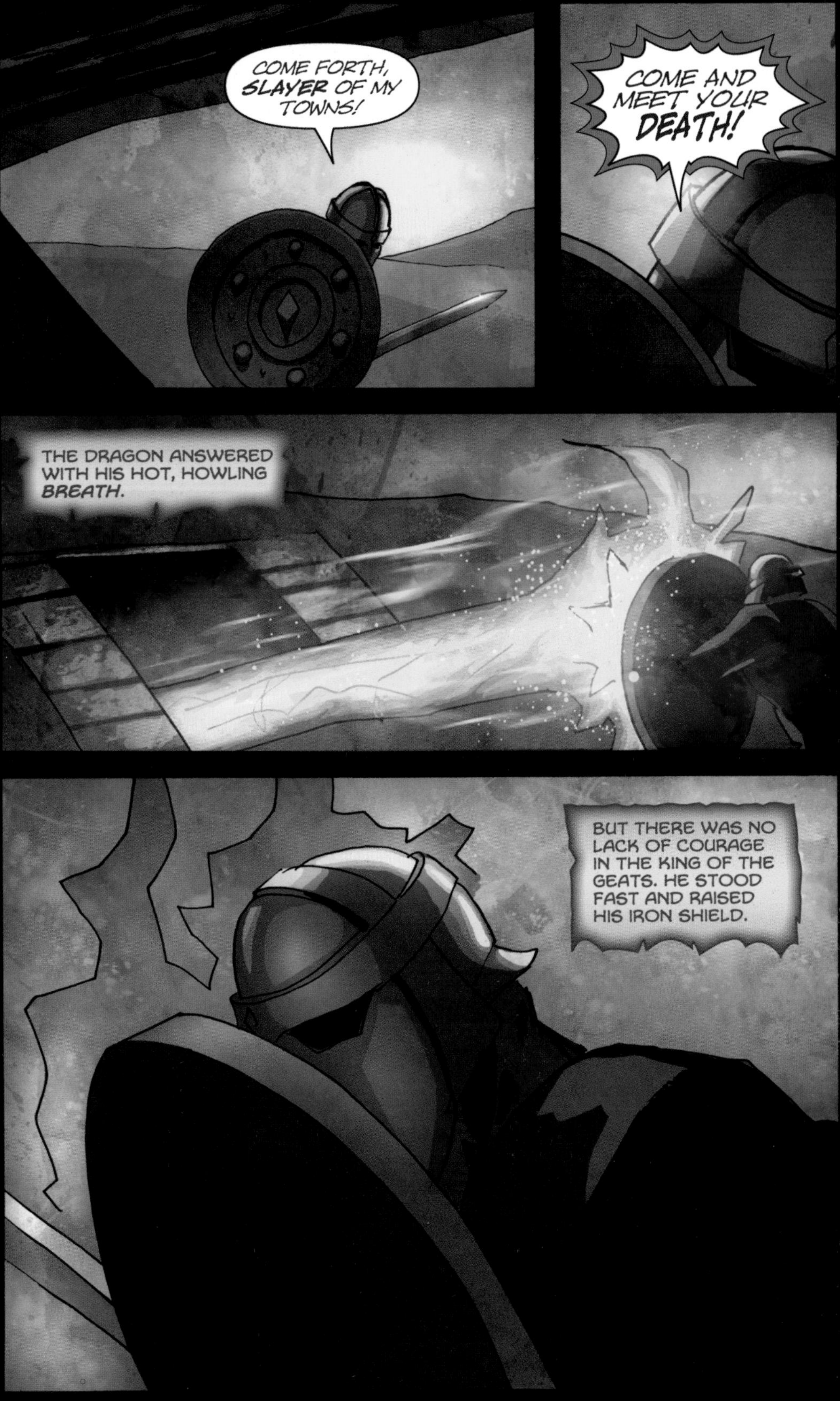

COME FORTH, **SLAYER** OF MY TOWNS!
COME AND MEET YOUR **DEATH!**
THE DRAGON ANSWERED WITH HIS HOT, HOWLING *BREATH*.
BUT THERE WAS NO LACK OF COURAGE IN THE KING OF THE GEATS. HE STOOD FAST AND RAISED HIS IRON SHIELD.

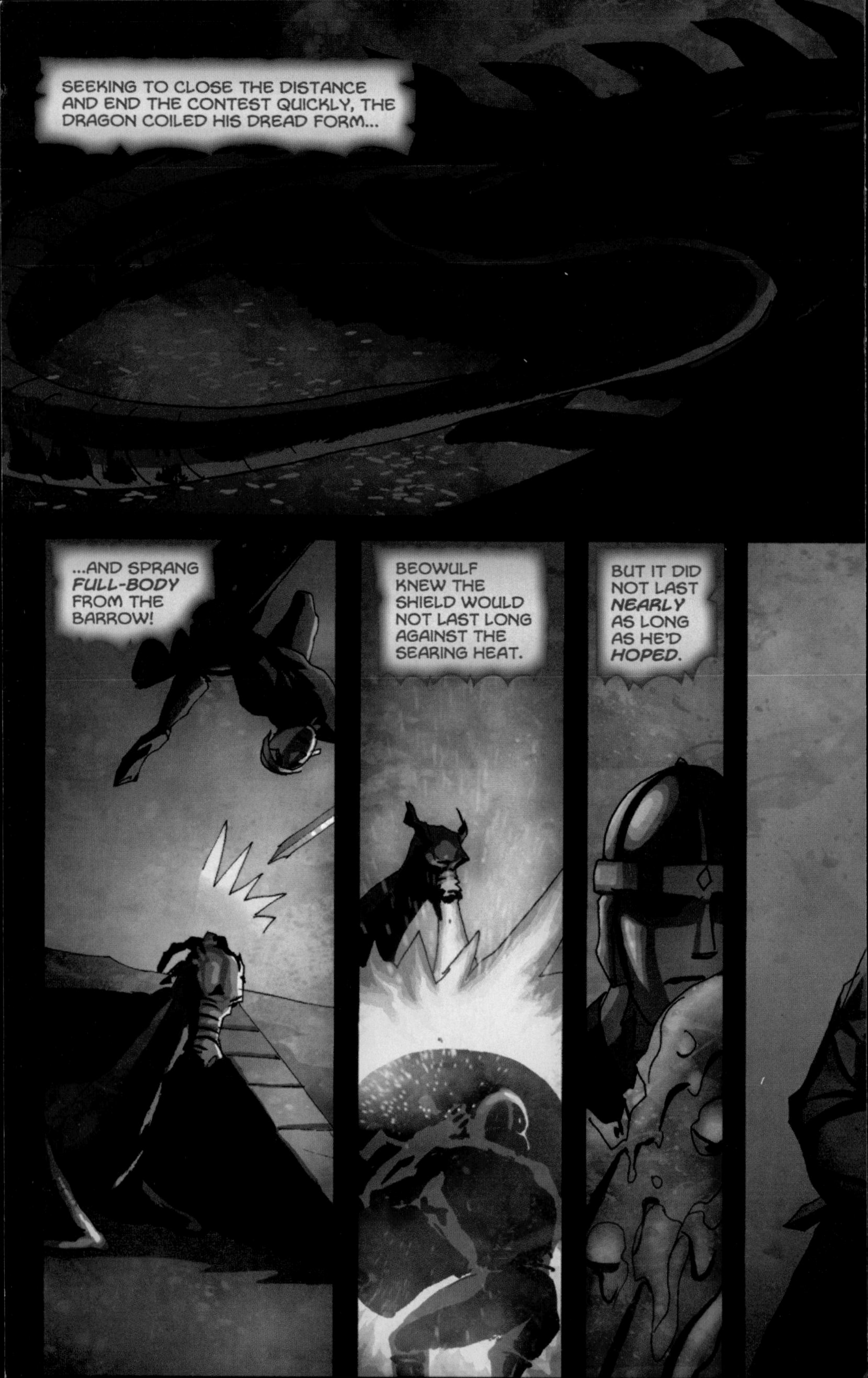
SEEKING TO CLOSE THE DISTANCE AND END THE CONTEST QUICKLY, THE DRAGON COILED HIS DREAD FORM...
...AND SPRANG *FULL-BODY* FROM THE BARROW!
BEOWULF KNEW THE SHIELD WOULD NOT LAST LONG AGAINST THE SEARING HEAT.
BUT IT DID NOT LAST *NEARLY* AS LONG AS HE'D *HOPED*.

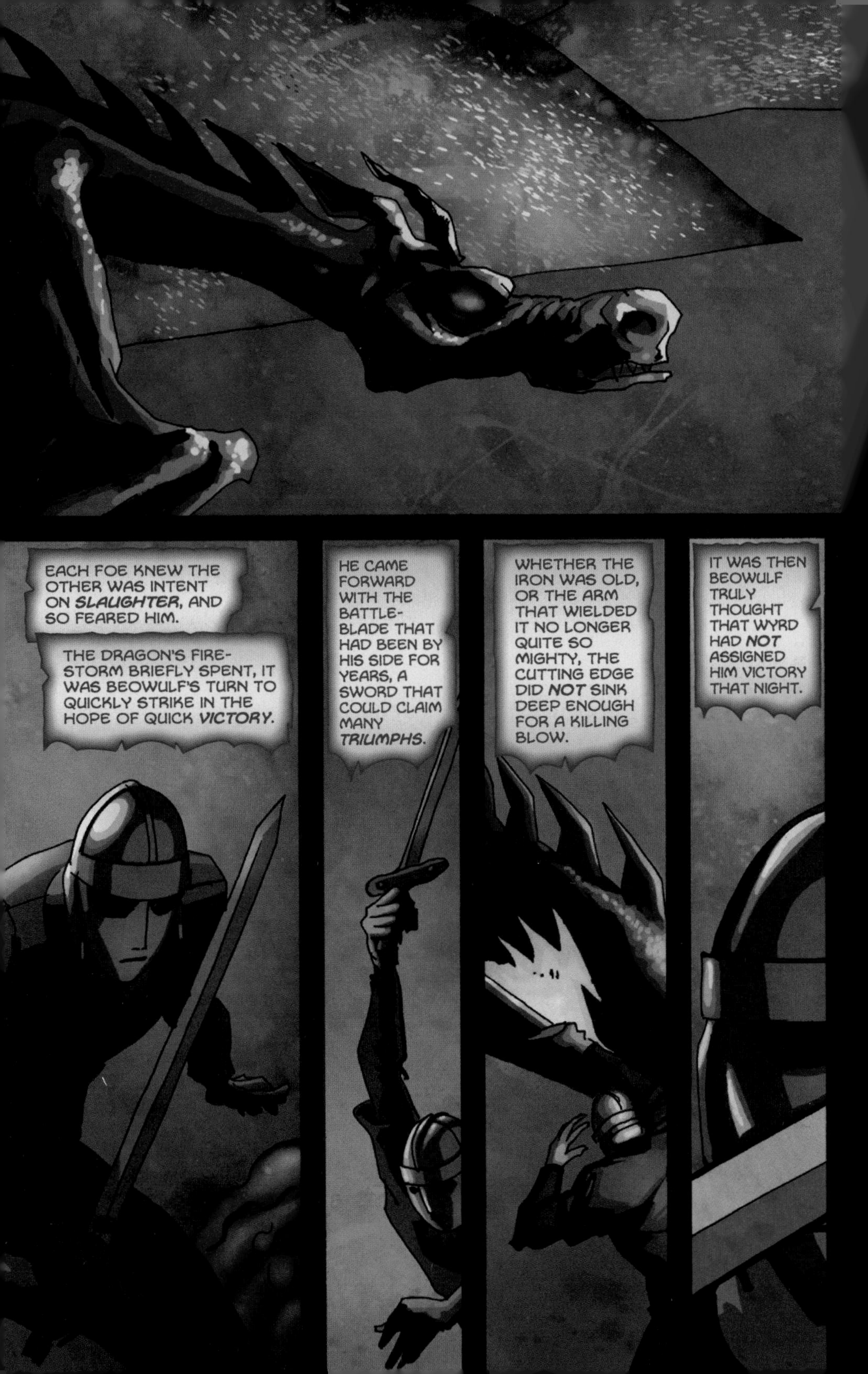
EACH FOE KNEW THE OTHER WAS INTENT ON **SLAUGHTER**, AND SO FEARED HIM.
THE DRAGON'S FIRE-STORM BRIEFLY SPENT, IT WAS BEOWULF'S TURN TO QUICKLY STRIKE IN THE HOPE OF QUICK **VICTORY**.
HE CAME FORWARD WITH THE BATTLE-BLADE THAT HAD BEEN BY HIS SIDE FOR YEARS, A SWORD THAT COULD CLAIM MANY **TRIUMPHS**.
WHETHER THE IRON WAS OLD, OR THE ARM THAT WIELDED IT NO LONGER QUITE SO MIGHTY, THE CUTTING EDGE DID **NOT** SINK DEEP ENOUGH FOR A KILLING BLOW.
IT WAS THEN BEOWULF TRULY THOUGHT THAT WYRD HAD **NOT** ASSIGNED HIM VICTORY THAT NIGHT.

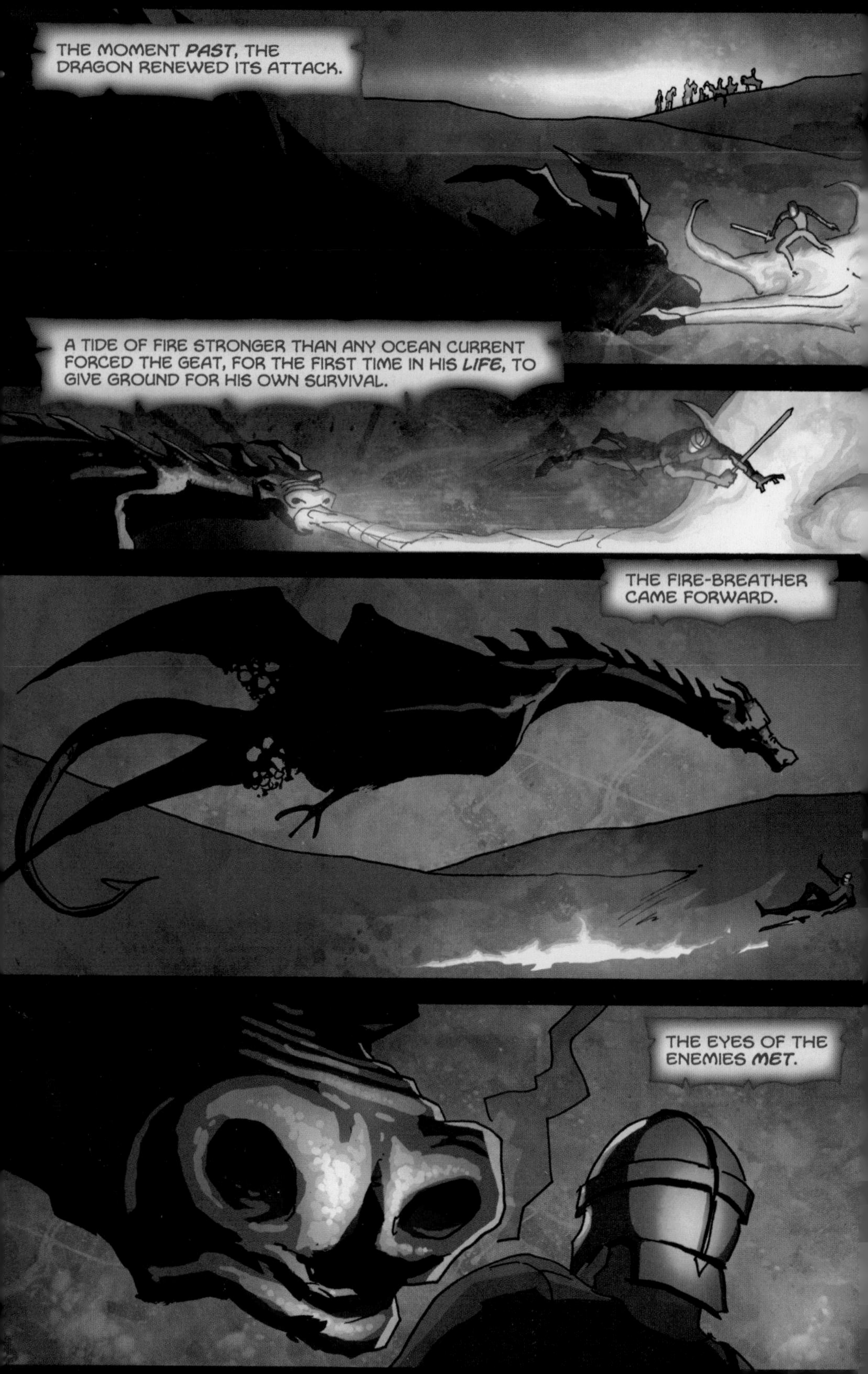
THE MOMENT PAST, THE DRAGON RENEWED ITS ATTACK.
A TIDE OF FIRE STRONGER THAN ANY OCEAN CURRENT FORCED THE GEAT, FOR THE FIRST TIME IN HIS LIFE, TO GIVE GROUND FOR HIS OWN SURVIVAL.
THE FIRE-BREATHER CAME FORWARD.
THE EYES OF THE ENEMIES MET.

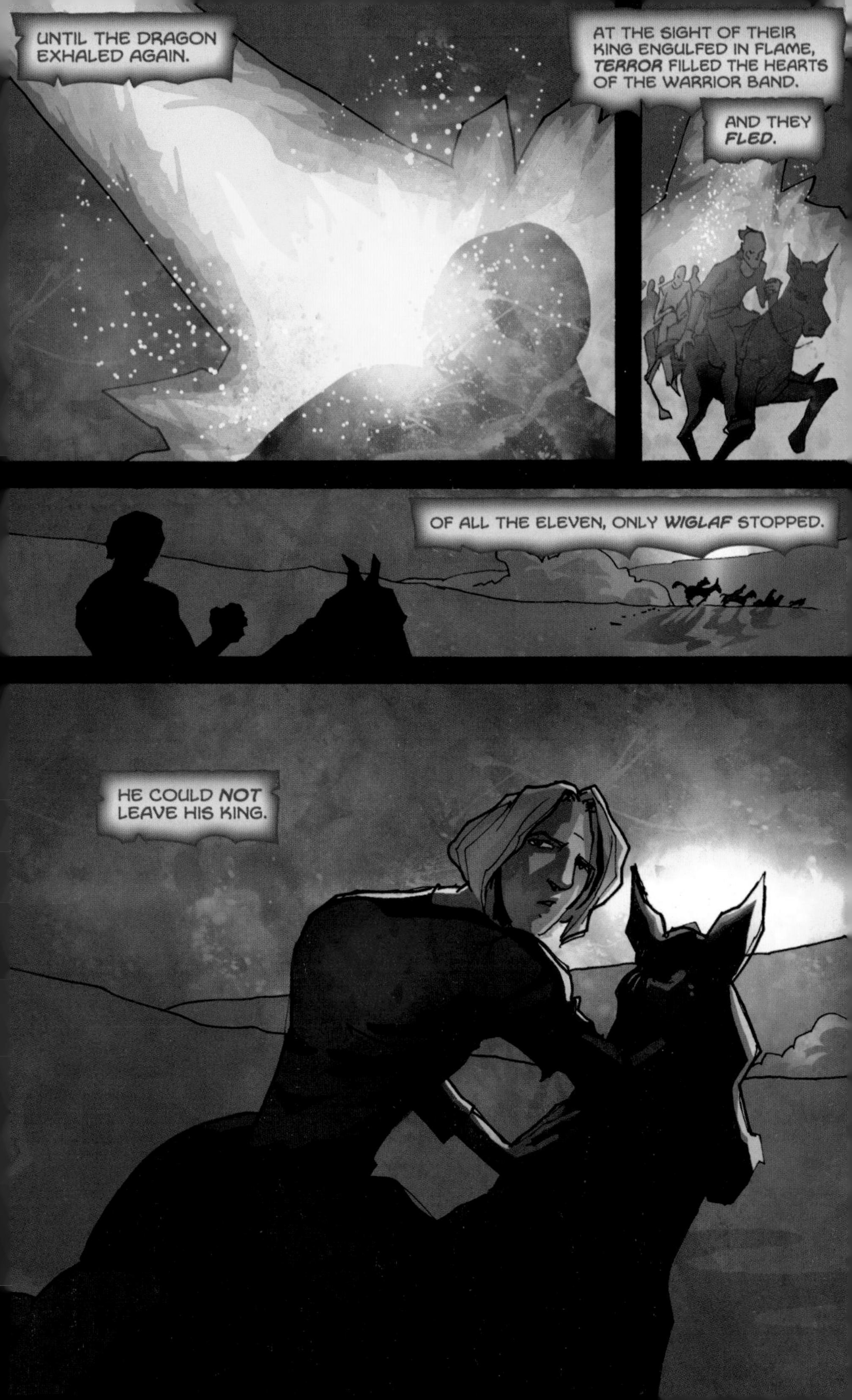
UNTIL THE DRAGON EXHALED AGAIN.
AT THE SIGHT OF THEIR KING ENGULFED IN FLAME, TERROR FILLED THE HEARTS OF THE WARRIOR BAND.
AND THEY FLED.
OF ALL THE ELEVEN, ONLY WIGLAF STOPPED.
HE COULD NOT LEAVE HIS KING.

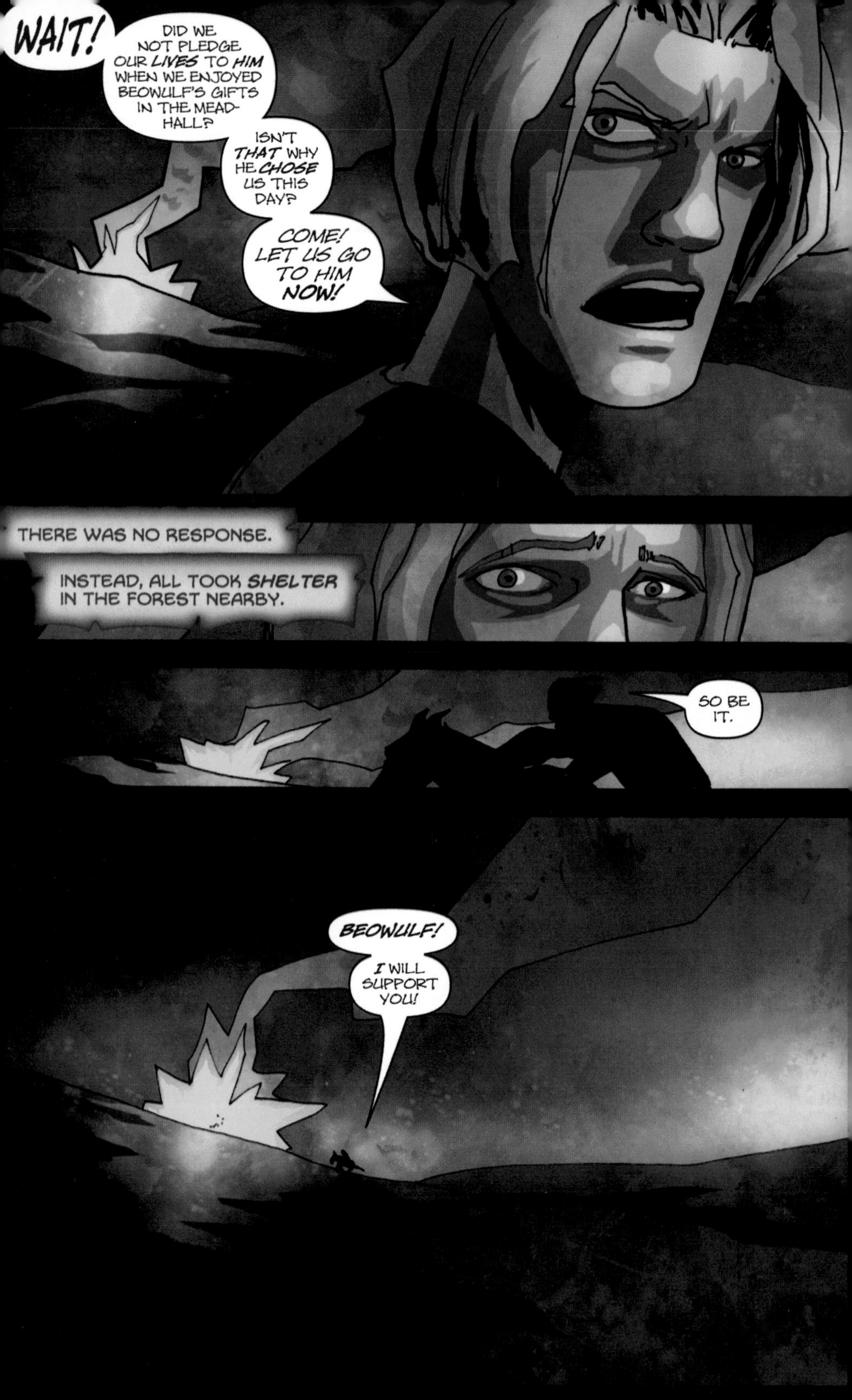
WAIT!
DID WE NOT PLEDGE OUR LIVES TO HIM WHEN WE ENJOYED BEOWULF'S GIFTS IN THE MEAD-HALL?
ISN'T THAT WHY HE CHOSE US THIS DAY?
COME! LET US GO TO HIM NOW!
THERE WAS NO RESPONSE.
INSTEAD, ALL TOOK SHELTER IN THE FOREST NEARBY.
SO BE IT.
BEOWULF!
I WILL SUPPORT YOU!

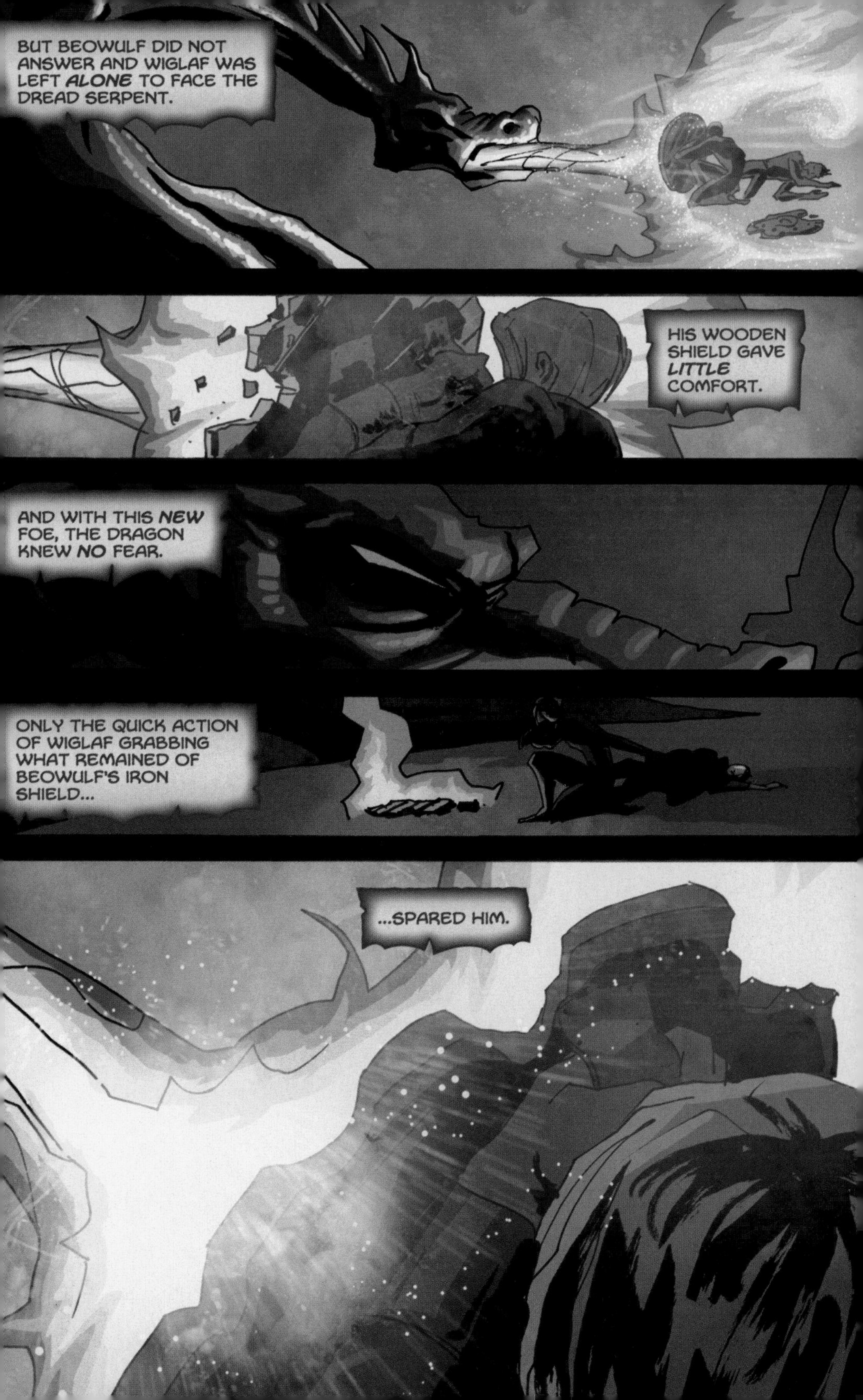
BUT BEOWULF DID NOT ANSWER AND WIGLAF WAS LEFT *ALONE* TO FACE THE DREAD SERPENT.
HIS WOODEN SHIELD GAVE *LITTLE* COMFORT.
AND WITH THIS *NEW* FOE, THE DRAGON KNEW *NO* FEAR.
ONLY THE QUICK ACTION OF WIGLAF GRABBING WHAT REMAINED OF BEOWULF'S IRON SHIELD...
...SPARED HIM.

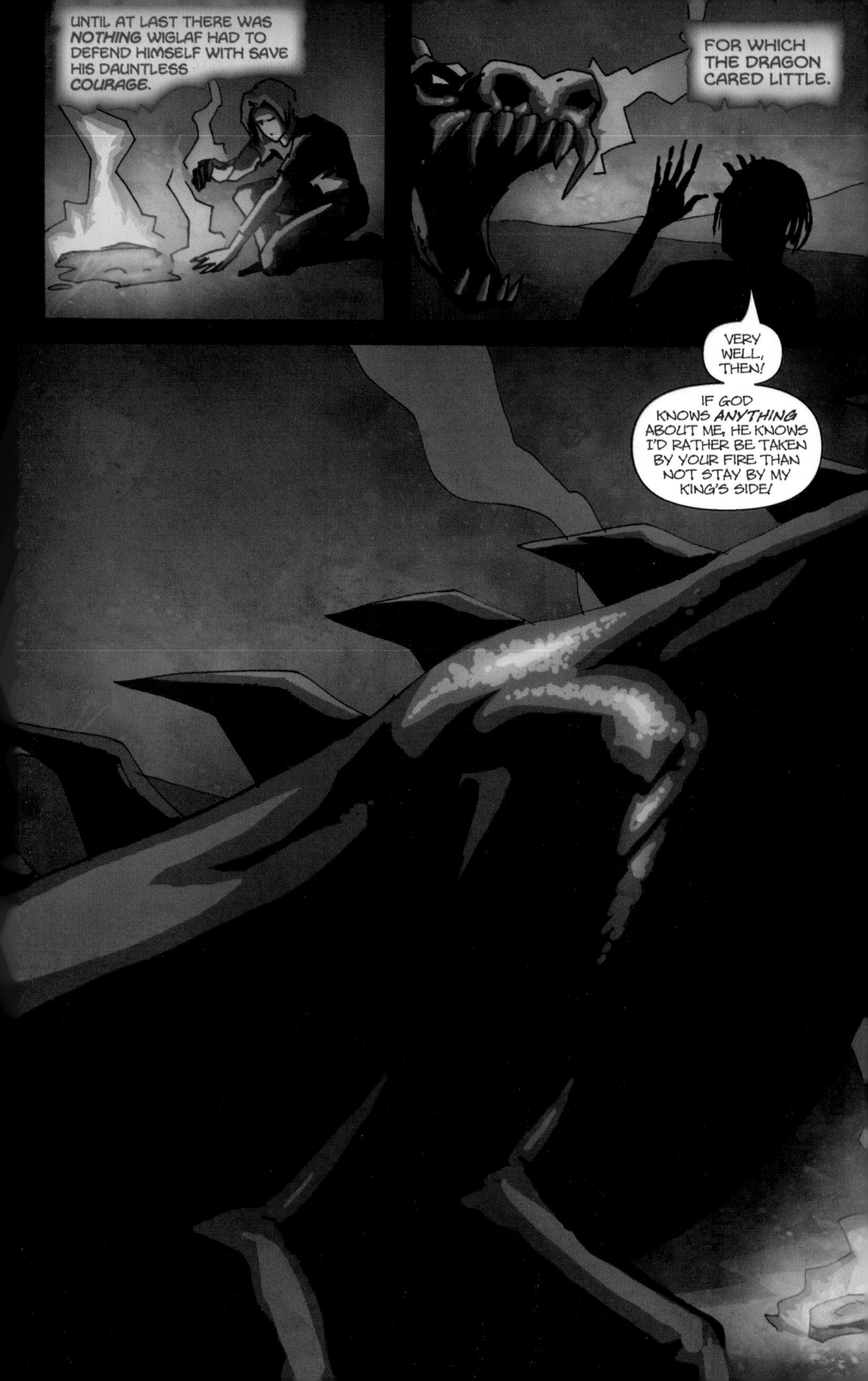
UNTIL AT LAST THERE WAS NOTHING WIGLAF HAD TO DEFEND HIMSELF WITH SAVE HIS DAUNTLESS COURAGE.
FOR WHICH THE DRAGON CARED LITTLE.
VERY WELL, THEN!
IF GOD KNOWS ANYTHING ABOUT ME, HE KNOWS I'D RATHER BE TAKEN BY YOUR FIRE THAN NOT STAY BY MY KING'S SIDE!

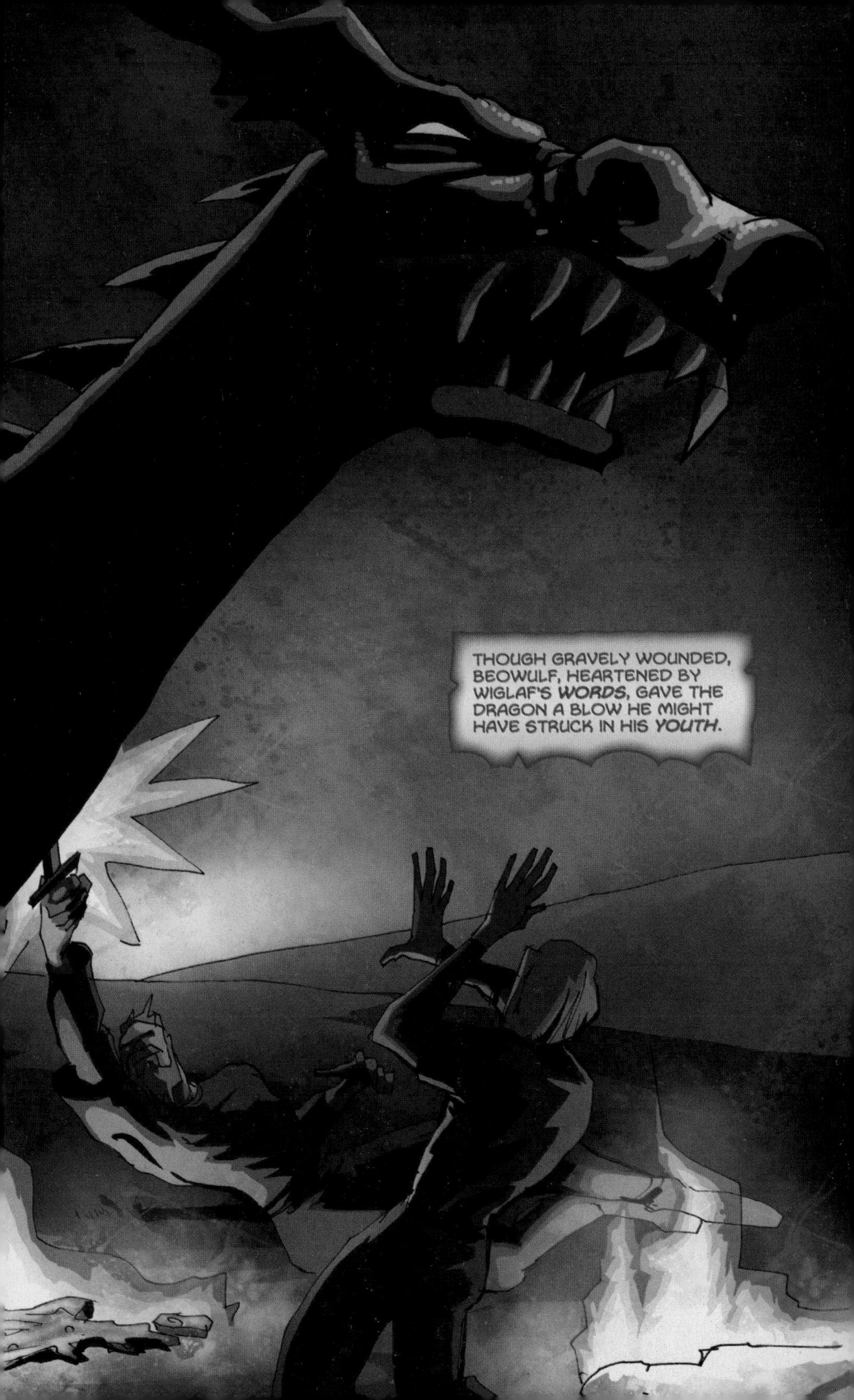
THOUGH GRAVELY WOUNDED, BEOWULF, HEARTENED BY WIGLAF'S *WORDS*, GAVE THE DRAGON A BLOW HE MIGHT HAVE STRUCK IN HIS *YOUTH*.

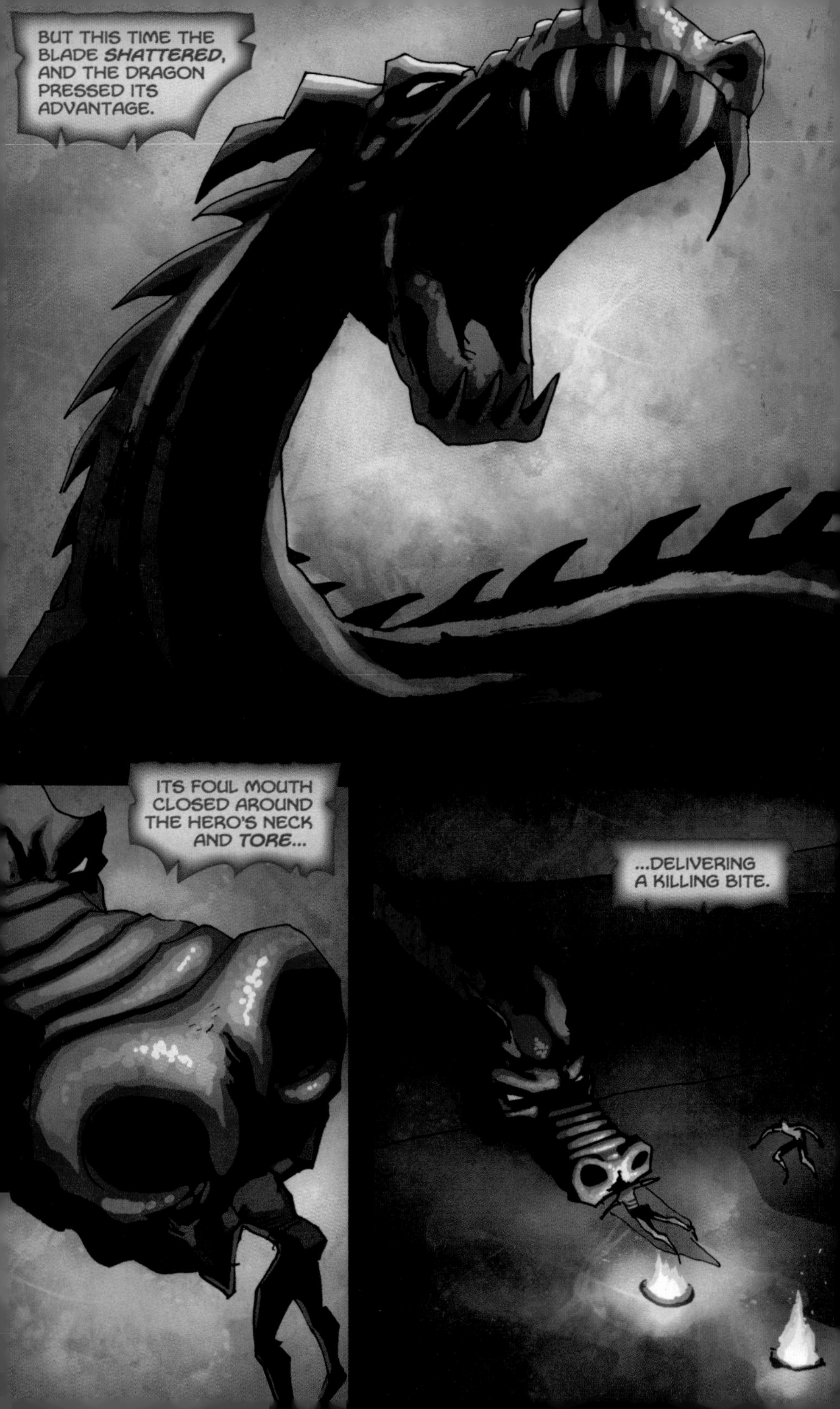
BUT THIS TIME THE BLADE SHATTERED, AND THE DRAGON PRESSED ITS ADVANTAGE.
ITS FOUL MOUTH CLOSED AROUND THE HERO'S NECK AND TORE...
...DELIVERING A KILLING BITE.

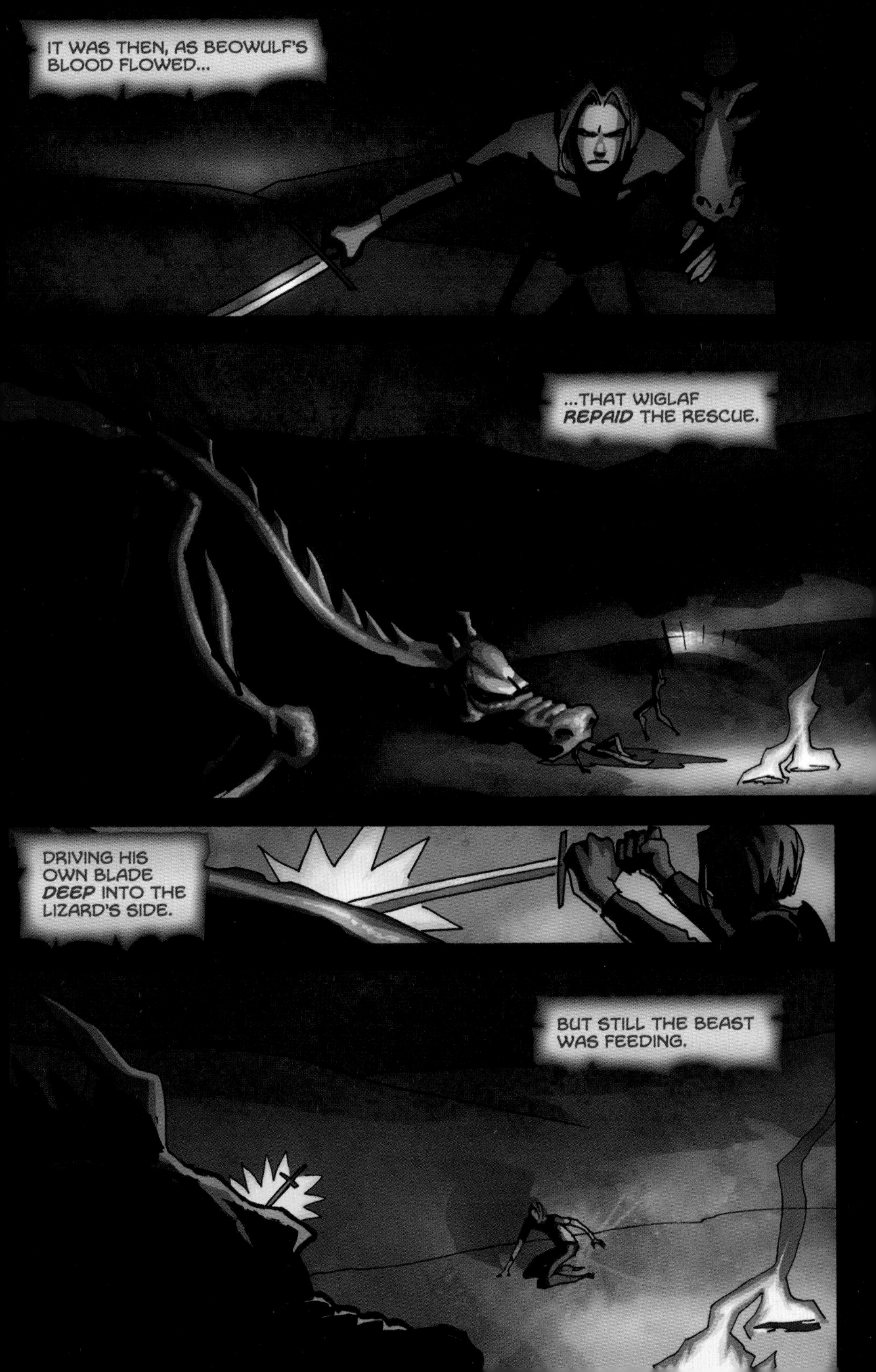
IT WAS THEN, AS BEOWULF'S BLOOD FLOWED...
...THAT WIGLAF *REPAID* THE RESCUE.
DRIVING HIS OWN BLADE *DEEP* INTO THE LIZARD'S SIDE.
BUT STILL THE BEAST WAS FEEDING.

AS HIS LIFEBLOOD *EMPTIED* FROM HIS WOUNDS, BEOWULF'S HAND FOUND THE *HILT* OF HIS SHORT-SWORD.

THE BLADE WAS MEANT FOR CLOSE COMBAT, AND NONE COULD BE CLOSER THAN *THIS*.

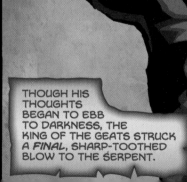

THOUGH HIS THOUGHTS BEGAN TO EBB TO DARKNESS, THE KING OF THE GEATS STRUCK A *FINAL*, SHARP-TOOTHED BLOW TO THE SERPENT.

AND FEELING THE BLADE FIRMLY INSIDE HIS FOE, *PULLED*.

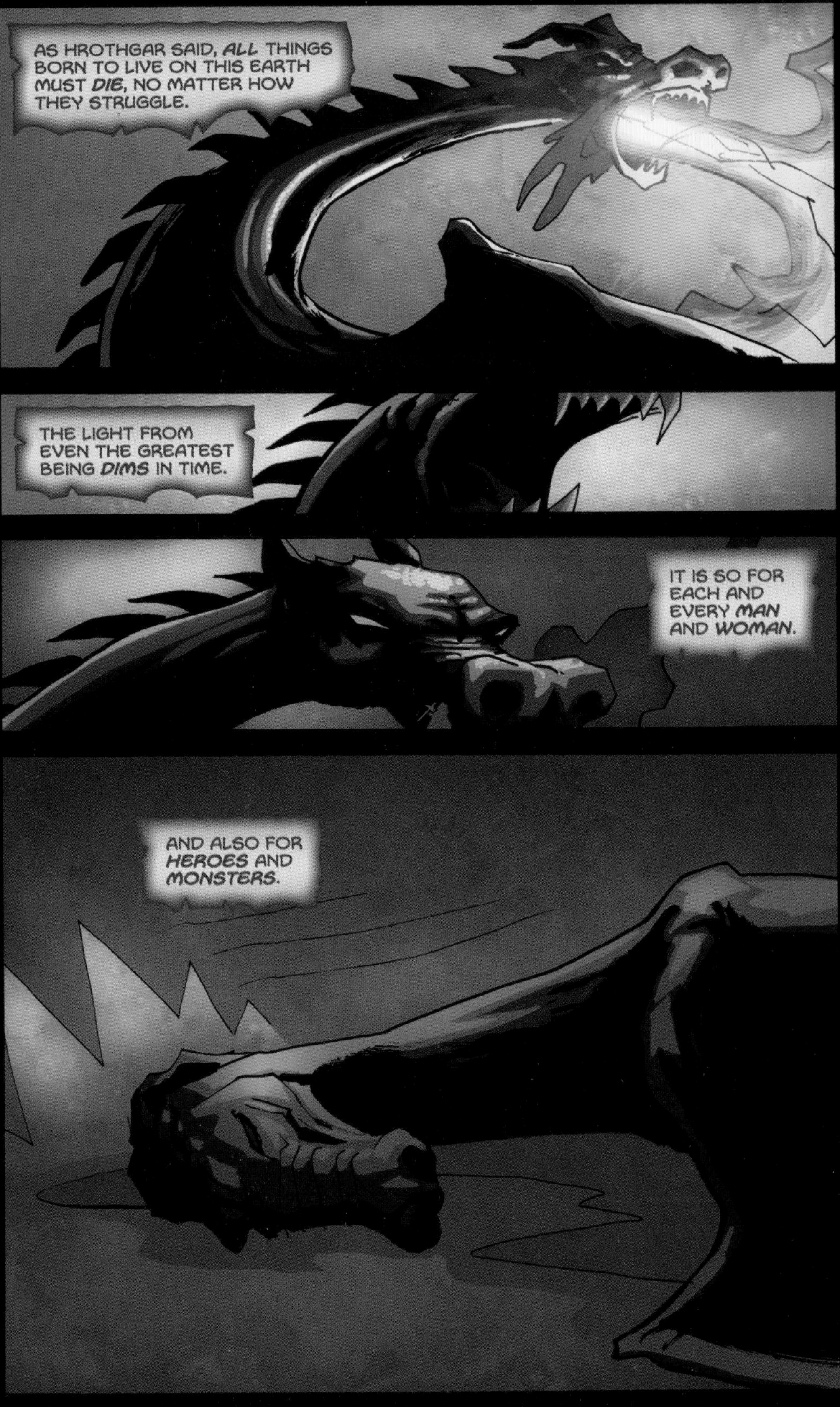
AS HROTHGAR SAID, ALL THINGS BORN TO LIVE ON THIS EARTH MUST DIE, NO MATTER HOW THEY STRUGGLE.
THE LIGHT FROM EVEN THE GREATEST BEING DIMS IN TIME.
IT IS SO FOR EACH AND EVERY MAN AND WOMAN.
AND ALSO FOR HEROES AND MONSTERS.

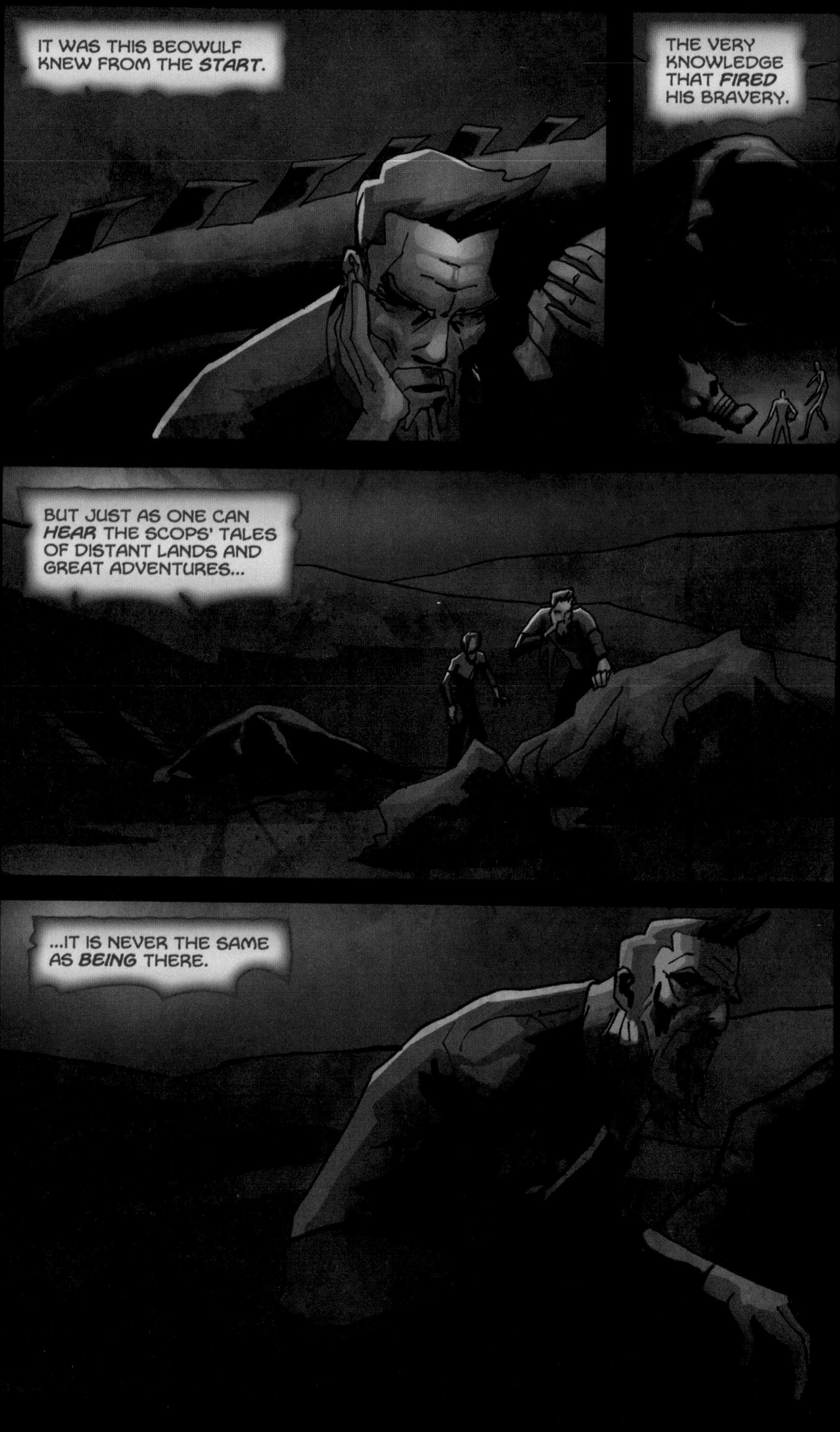
IT WAS THIS BEOWULF KNEW FROM THE START.
THE VERY KNOWLEDGE THAT FIRED HIS BRAVERY.
BUT JUST AS ONE CAN HEAR THE SCOPS' TALES OF DISTANT LANDS AND GREAT ADVENTURES...
...IT IS NEVER THE SAME AS BEING THERE.

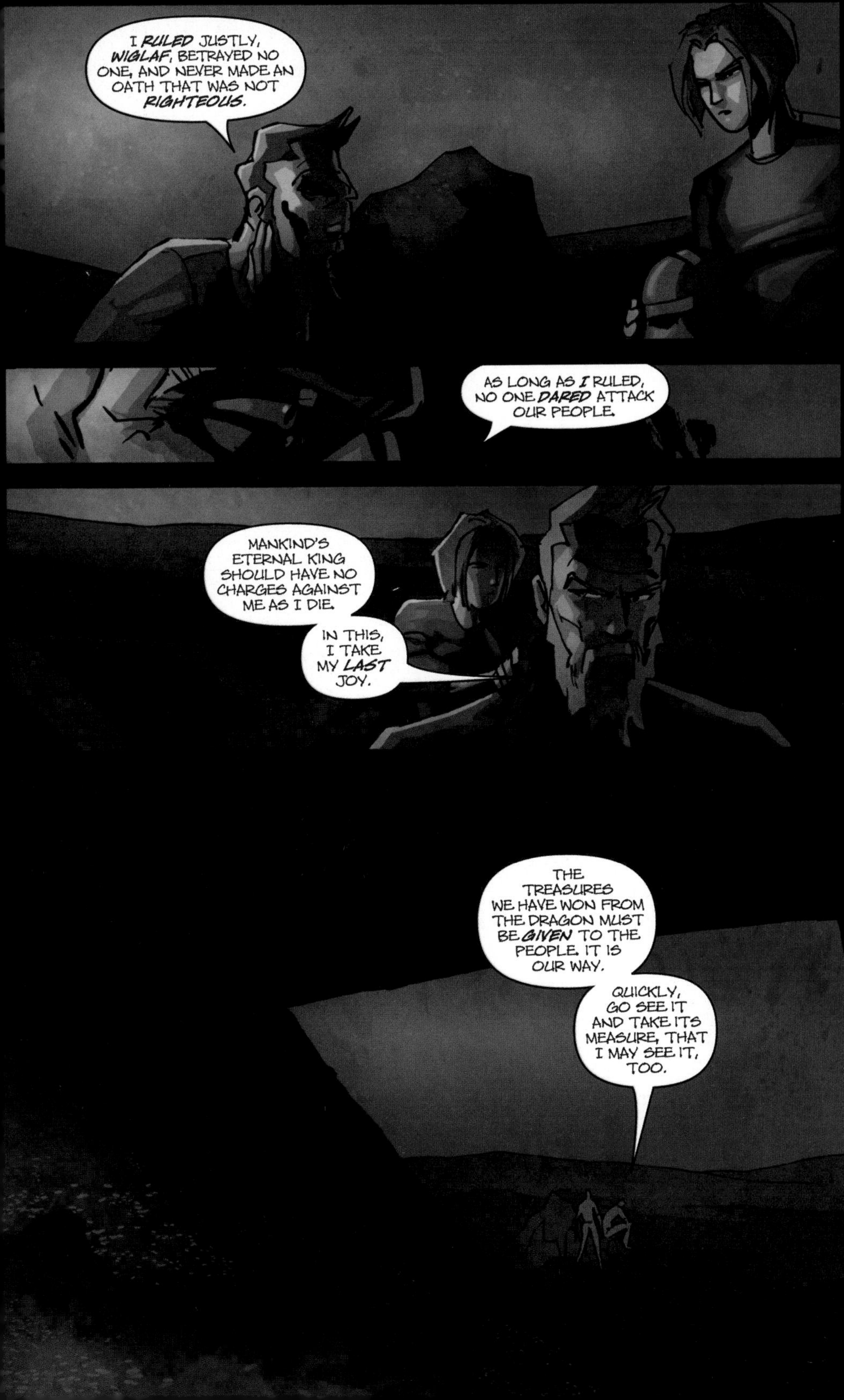
I RULED JUSTLY, WIGLAF, BETRAYED NO ONE, AND NEVER MADE AN OATH THAT WAS NOT RIGHTEOUS.
AS LONG AS I RULED, NO ONE DARED ATTACK OUR PEOPLE.
MANKIND'S ETERNAL KING SHOULD HAVE NO CHARGES AGAINST ME AS I DIE.
IN THIS, I TAKE MY LAST JOY.
THE TREASURES WE HAVE WON FROM THE DRAGON MUST BE GIVEN TO THE PEOPLE. IT IS OUR WAY.
QUICKLY, GO SEE IT AND TAKE ITS MEASURE, THAT I MAY SEE IT, TOO.

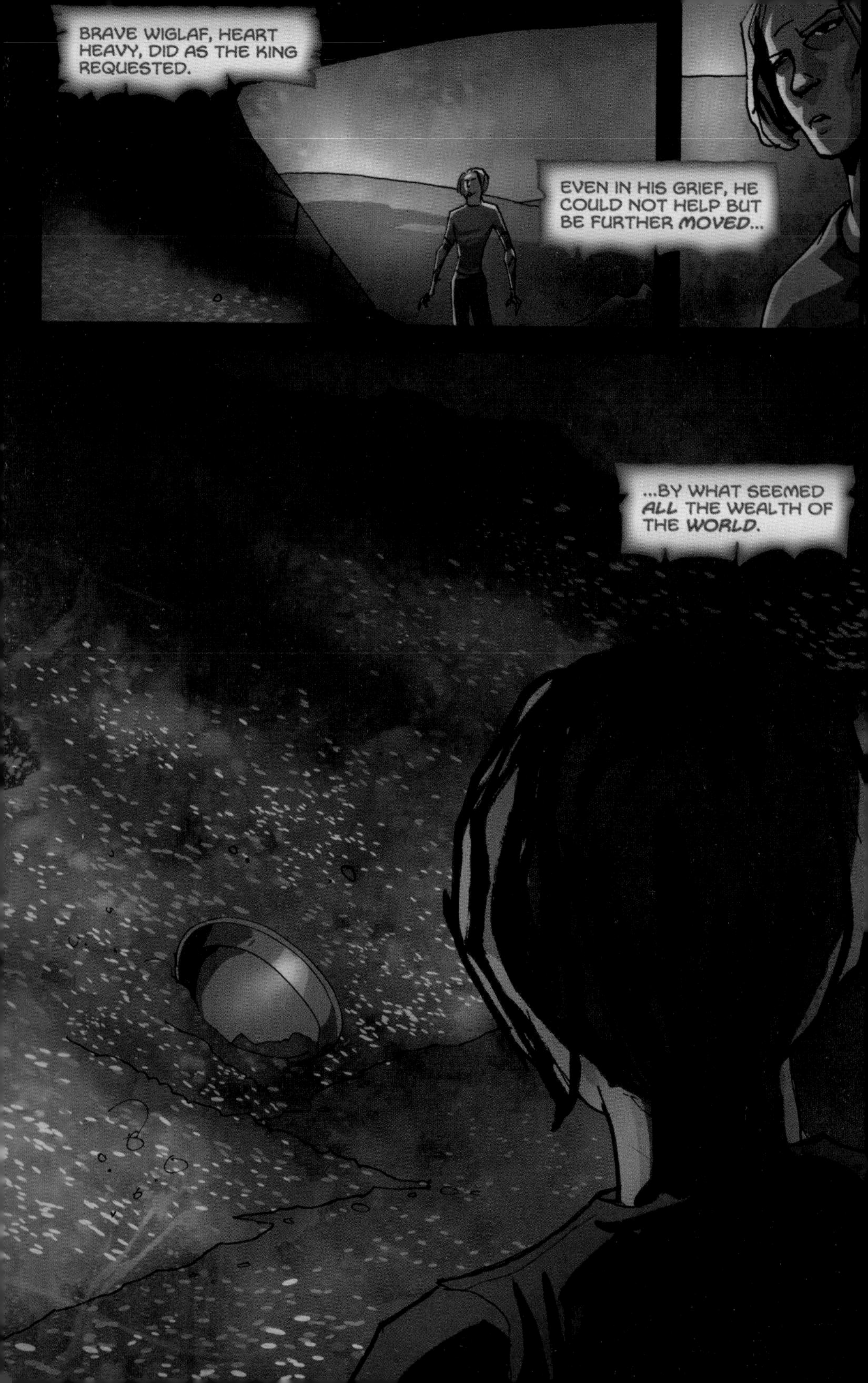
BRAVE WIGLAF, HEART HEAVY, DID AS THE KING REQUESTED.
EVEN IN HIS GRIEF, HE COULD NOT HELP BUT BE FURTHER MOVED...
...BY WHAT SEEMED ALL THE WEALTH OF THE WORLD.

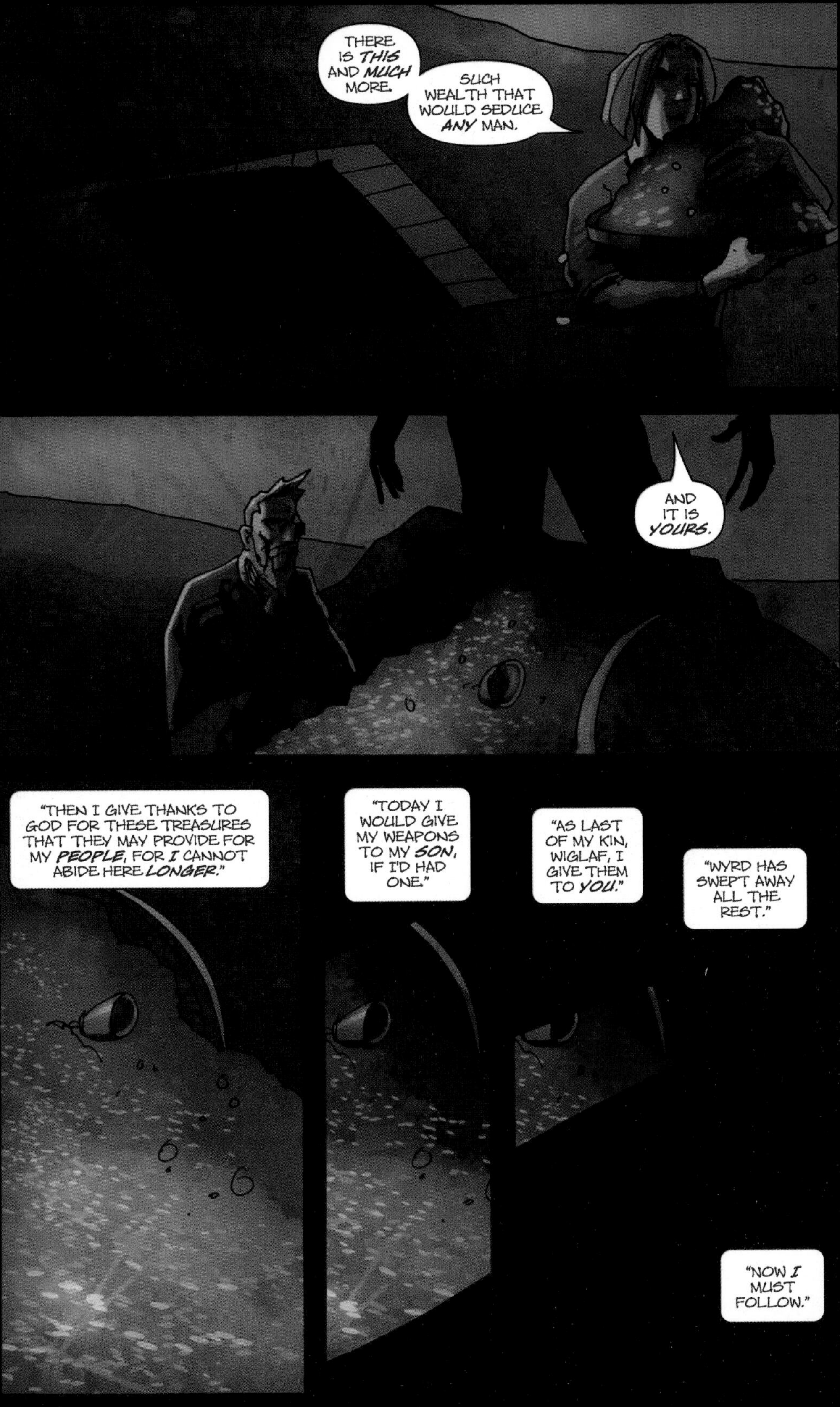
THERE IS THIS AND MUCH MORE.
SUCH WEALTH THAT WOULD SEDUCE ANY MAN.
AND IT IS YOURS.
"THEN I GIVE THANKS TO GOD FOR THESE TREASURES THAT THEY MAY PROVIDE FOR MY PEOPLE, FOR I CANNOT ABIDE HERE LONGER."
"TODAY I WOULD GIVE MY WEAPONS TO MY SON, IF I'D HAD ONE."
"AS LAST OF MY KIN, WIGLAF, I GIVE THEM TO YOU."
"WYRD HAS SWEPT AWAY ALL THE REST."
"NOW I MUST FOLLOW."

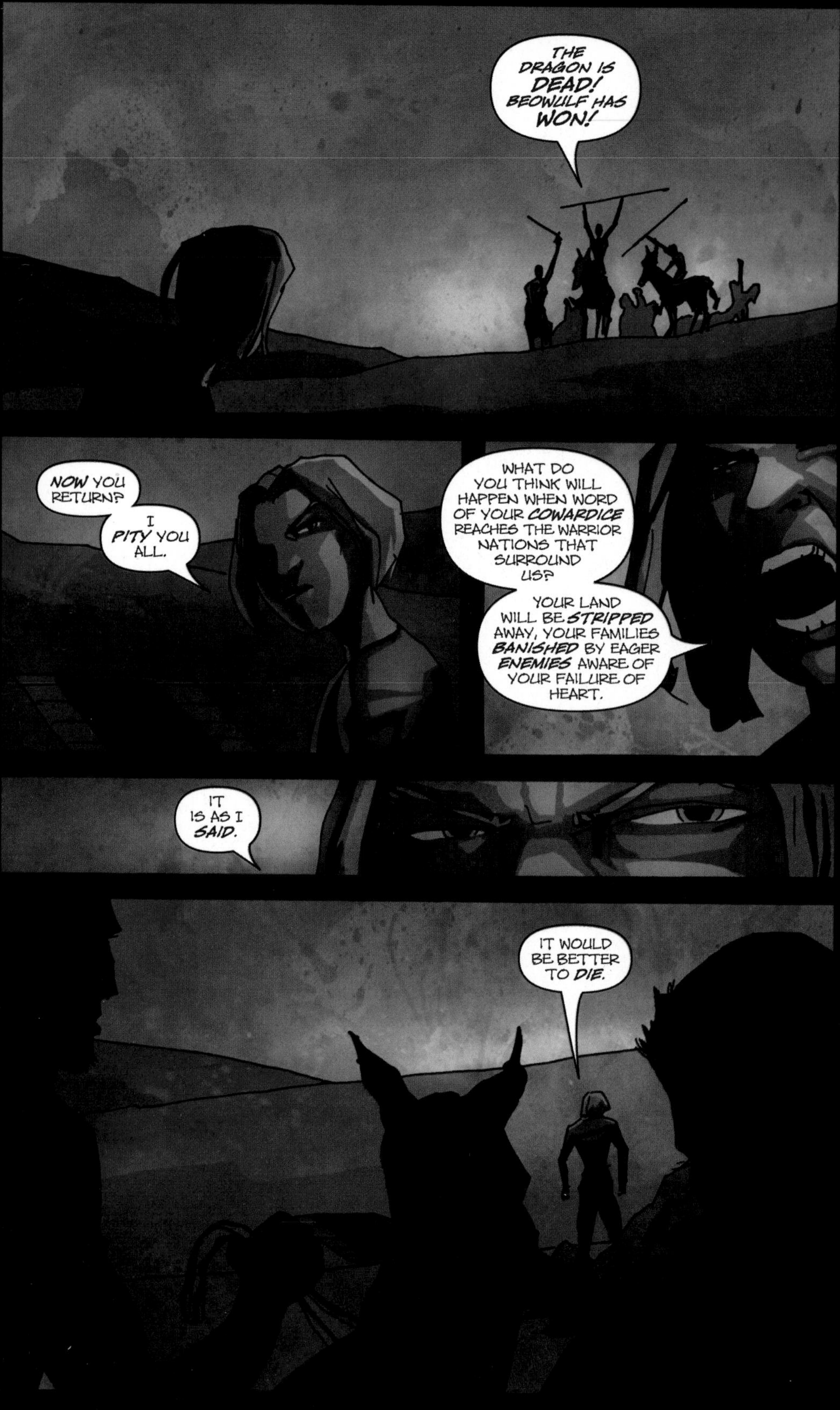
THE DRAGON IS DEAD! BEOWULF HAS WON!
NOW YOU RETURN?
I PITY YOU ALL.
WHAT DO YOU THINK WILL HAPPEN WHEN WORD OF YOUR COWARDICE REACHES THE WARRIOR NATIONS THAT SURROUND US?
YOUR LAND WILL BE STRIPPED AWAY, YOUR FAMILIES BANISHED BY EAGER ENEMIES AWARE OF YOUR FAILURE OF HEART.
IT IS AS I SAID.
IT WOULD BE BETTER TO DIE.

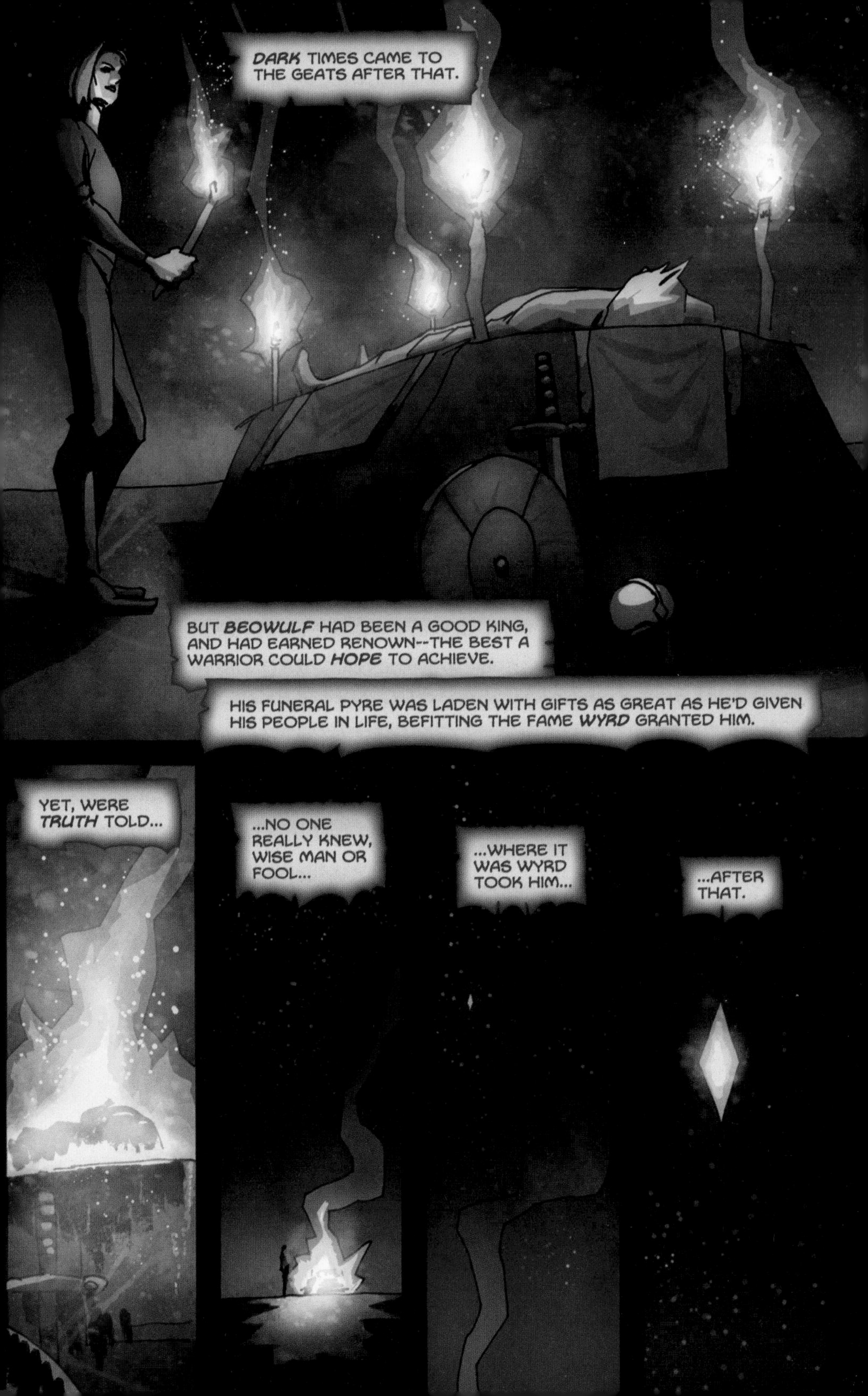
DARK TIMES CAME TO THE GEATS AFTER THAT.
BUT BEOWULF HAD BEEN A GOOD KING, AND HAD EARNED RENOWN--THE BEST A WARRIOR COULD HOPE TO ACHIEVE.
HIS FUNERAL PYRE WAS LADEN WITH GIFTS AS GREAT AS HE'D GIVEN HIS PEOPLE IN LIFE, BEFITTING THE FAME WYRD GRANTED HIM.
YET, WERE TRUTH TOLD...
...NO ONE REALLY KNEW, WISE MAN OR FOOL...
...WHERE IT WAS WYRD TOOK HIM...
...AFTER THAT.